BEL LAMINGTON

Bel Lamington, the orphan daughter of an Army colonel, is brought up in an English village and flung into the whirl of London life to earn a hard living as a secretary while attempting to navigate romance, unexpected friendships and urban life. Shy, sensitive, and innocent, she is unaware of the pitfalls that surround her. But when Bel is offered a chance to leave London and venture to a quiet fishing hotel in Scotland for a much needed holiday with an old school friend, things begin to change. There she learns that you cannot escape from your troubles by running away from them . . .

Books by D. E. Stevenson
Published in Ulverscroft Collections:

VITTORIA COTTAGE
MUSIC IN THE HILLS
WINTER AND ROUGH WEATHER
THE YOUNG CLEMENTINA
LISTENING VALLEY
FLETCHERS END
THE FOUR GRACES
SPRING MAGIC

D. E. STEVENSON

BEL LAMINGTON

Complete and Unabridged

ULVERSCROFT
Leicester

First published in Great Britain in 1961

This Ulverscroft Edition
published 2020

The moral right of the author has been asserted

A catalogue record for this book is available
from the British Library.

ISBN 978–1–4448–4436–8

Published by
Ulverscroft Limited
Anstey, Leicestershire

Set by Words & Graphics Ltd.
Anstey, Leicestershire
Printed and bound in Great Britain by
T. J. International Ltd., Padstow, Cornwall

This book is printed on acid-free paper

SPECIAL MESSAGE TO READERS

THE ULVERSCROFT FOUNDATION
(Registered UK charity number 264873)
was established in 1972 to provide funds for
research, diagnosis and treatment of eye diseases.
Examples of ꞁꞁ   ꞁ ꞁ ‑
the Ulver꞊ ꞁ ꞁꞁ Foundaꞁ ꞁ ‑

- The Children's Eye Unit at Moorfields Eye
  Hospital, London
- The Ulverscroft Children's Eye Unit at Great
  Ormond Street Hospital for Sick Children
- Funding research into eye diseases and
  treatment at the Department of Ophthalmology,
  University of Leicester
- The Ulverscroft Vision Research Group,
  Institute of Child Health
- Twin operating theatres at the Western
  Ophthalmic Hospital, London
- The Chair of Ophthalmology at the Royal
  Australian College of Ophthalmologists

You can help further the work of the Foundation
by making a donation or leaving a legacy.
Every contribution is gratefully received. If you
would like to help support the Foundation or
require further information, please contact:

THE ULVERSCROFT FOUNDATION
The Green, Bradgate Road, Anstey
Leicester LE7 7FU, England
Tel: (0116) 236 4325

website: ꞁn.org.uk

000003003768

Part One

1

It was a day in early March and, after a spell of cold wet windy weather, Spring invaded London. Bel Lamington noticed the difference the moment she awoke; the bedroom in her little flat faced east so the rising sun shone into her window. Her flat was high up amongst the roof-tops in an old house in Mellington Street. Long ago these houses had been occupied by well-to-do families, but they had gone down-hill and several of them had been bought up cheaply by a builder and converted into a rabbit-warren of small flats. There was no lift, of course, but merely an ill-lighted stone stair with doors on every landing.

Presumably people lived in these other flats but Bel had lived in her flat for eighteen months — and she knew nobody. Sometimes she met people on the stairs but they passed by as if she were invisible. It was very different from Southmere where she knew everyone and everyone knew her and where, even if you did not know a person, it was correct to say 'Good morning' as you passed.

There was something frightening in the anonymity of London, especially to an imaginative person. Sometimes as she lay awake at night Bel wondered what would happen if she were ill. Nobody would know — or care. She might fall down and break her leg and lie there for days!

Sometimes she wondered if she had done wisely to leave Southmere . . . but what else could she have done?

Bel had lived at Southmere all her life, or at least as long as she could remember. She had lived with her aunt and they had been very happy together. Then Aunt Beatrice died and the house had been sold. Fortunately there was a little money — just enough to pay for secretarial training — so Bel packed up and said goodbye to all her friends and came to London. She worked hard to make herself employable and took the first job that offered; she went as a typist to a firm in the City, the firm of Copping, Wills and Brownlee.

On this particular day in March the sun had awakened Bel earlier than usual so she had plenty of time to get up and prepare her breakfast, plenty of time to tidy the little flat before setting out for the office. It was a pleasant little flat and she was aware that she had been lucky to get it. She had brought some furniture from Southmere which made it seem more friendly: the carpet in the sitting-room and a couple of comfortable chairs and an oak book-case. The furniture in her bedroom had come from Southmere too.

Outside the window of the sitting-room there was a flat roof with a stone coping all round it. When Bel first came to London she had put a few pot-plants on this roof but this had not satisfied her craving for a garden, so she bought some window boxes and a couple of stone troughs and filled them with seedlings.

Gradually, in spite of the soot and the smoke and the depredations of pigeons, the flat roof had become a tiny garden, a piece of the country wedged in amongst the bricks and mortar of the city. Some plants refused to grow, they pined for their proper milieu as Bel herself had pined, but others consented to bloom quite cheerfully. They had to be coaxed, of course, watered and drained and repotted, their leaves sponged and their roots cosseted with bone-meal, but Bel had no other hobby and when she returned from working all day in a stuffy office it was delightful to climb out of her sitting-room window and enjoy the pleasance which she had created. The little garden was wonderfully private, it was not overlooked by the windows of the surrounding houses; she could take a deck-chair and sit there enjoying the colour and fragrance of her flowers. She could see the sky, blue and hazy above the chimneys; often she sat and watched the sky darken and the stars appear.

But the little garden was a summer joy, there was nothing much to be done with it during the winter, so Bel was glad that winter was over and Spring was here.

2

Spring was here. There was no doubt about it. The sky was blue, the sunshine was golden and there was a balmy feeling in the air. Bel Lamington felt a queer stirring in her blood as she walked down the street on her way to the office. There might be more bad weather — winds and rain — but winter was definitely past and over. Bel wished she were in the country. She always wished that, of course, but today even more than usual. Spring in the country! Fresh delicious smells and buds swelling on the trees and tiny spikes of crocuses pushing up through the soil!

Spring had invaded the office of Copping, Wills and Brownlee but here its invasion was not so welcome. The office had been bearable during the winter for it was well-warmed and well-lighted (it had been quite pleasant to arrive here and escape from the cold dark streets) but today it felt like a prison, everyone in the place was longing to get out, and this unsettled feeling interfered considerably with the routine. There were stupid mistakes in the typing of letters and tempers were short.

'I don't know what's got into everyone this morning,' said Helen Goudge crossly.

'It's Spring,' said Bel.

'Nonsense!' exclaimed Miss Goudge. She frowned as she spoke and her thick black eyebrows met in a thick black bar across her forehead.

'Spring gets into people and unsettles them,' Bel explained.

'Spring is no excuse for carelessness.'

'I wonder if I could get home early,' said Jane Harlow.

'Why?' enquired Miss Goudge. 'Why should you get home early? You'll have to stay on longer than usual unless you pay more attention to your work.'

'There's no need to bite my head off,' muttered Jane Harlow angrily. 'Everyone makes mistakes sometimes — '

'Some people make mistakes too often — '

The atmosphere was becoming sultry and Bel hated unpleasantness so she was delighted when Mr. Brownlee's bell rang and she was able to escape. She seized her notebook and made off as quickly as she could.

'There goes the private secretary — so keen!' exclaimed Miss Goudge with a nasty laugh.

Bel had been private secretary to the junior partner of the firm for three months now (previously she had been one of the typists and had shared a room with the other girls); unfortunately her appointment had caused a good deal of ill-feeling. Helen Goudge was furious; she had been with the firm for five years and thought the appointment with its increase of salary should have been hers. Why should Bel Lamington be chosen?

As a matter of fact Bel Lamington knew why she had been chosen but she kept her own counsel. It had happened just before Christmas when all the others had been anxious to get away early to do some Christmas shopping before going home. Bel had no Christmas shopping to do so she had stayed on in the office to finish some letters and tidy up. It was warm in the office and quiet and pleasant so she was in no hurry to sally out into the cold street. She had just finished work and was about to put on her coat when Mr. Brownlee came in.

'Hullo!' he said. 'I thought everyone had gone. I've got an important letter to type. I'll do it myself.'

'I'll do it, Mr. Brownlee.'

'Don't you want to get home?'

'I'm not in any hurry,' Bel told him. She smiled cheerfully and sat down at her typewriter without more ado.

It was a long letter and extremely complicated and it took some time before it was hammered into shape. Then it had to be re-typed before it could be done up and sealed. Mr. Brownlee asked her again if she were not in a hurry to get home.

'I'd rather finish it,' she said frankly. 'It's interesting. I mean it's worth while getting it right.'

Mr. Brownlee agreed. 'Look here,' he said. 'Miss Storey is leaving to be married. How would you like her job?'

'Me?' asked Bel in amazement. 'You mean — you mean — '

'Private secretary to the junior partner,' said Mr. Brownlee smiling. 'D'you think you could bear it, Miss Lamington?'

Miss Lamington thought she could.

The job was no sinecure of course, for Mr. Brownlee was a whale for work; like many junior partners, he did more than his share of the business and expected his secretary to be at hand when he wanted her services. This meant longer hours for Bel — but that did not matter; she never went to parties, there was nobody waiting

8

for her at home. It meant higher pay (which was important) and it gave her an insight into the working of the business which was very interesting indeed. Copping, Wills and Brownlee was a firm of importers and owned large warehouses at the Pool of London. Ships came from all over the world bringing cargoes of fruit and tea and coffee to be unloaded and stored in the warehouses and, later, distributed to various towns. Occasionally Bel's duties took her down to the wharf and this made a pleasant break in office routine. Another advantage, in her new job, was the fact that she was no longer under the jurisdiction of Miss Goudge and did not have to listen to the bickerings of the other typists. The ill-feeling occasioned by her promotion had been hard to bear, but that could not be helped.

3

Mr. Brownlee was particularly busy this morning but even he was suffering from the strange malaise which had affected the office staff. He stopped in the middle of dictating a letter and looked up at the slice of blue sky which was visible in the corner of his window.

'It's a lovely day, Miss Lamington,' he said.

'It's Spring,' said his secretary.

She had made the remark before but this time the reaction was different.

'Yes, it's Spring,' agreed Mr. Brownlee. 'There are crocuses coming up in the garden. I noticed them this morning before I left home. I wonder if we could rush things through a bit. It would be nice to get away early.'

'You've got that meeting at three-thirty, Mr. Brownlee.'

'Damn, so I have,' agreed Mr. Brownlee with a sigh.

Bel was sorry. She would have liked to give Mr. Brownlee the afternoon off so that he could go home and gloat over his garden — but of course she couldn't. The idea made her smile.

'What's the joke, Miss Lamington?' he asked.

Unfortunately Miss Lamington could not tell him.

By this time Miss Lamington knew a good deal about her 'boss'. She knew that he was thirty-six (which was 'quite old' in her estimation); he lived with his mother at Beckenham and travelled to the office every day — sometimes in his car but more often by train. On one occasion when Mr. Brownlee was laid up with a cold Bel had been summoned to Beckenham to deal with some urgent correspondence and had been charmed by his delightful house and big old-fashioned garden. Mrs. Brownlee was charming too, she had insisted that Miss Lamington should stay to lunch and had talked about her son without stopping. From her Bel learnt that 'Ellis' had been a fighter-pilot during the war and had been severely wounded. She was shown photographs of 'Ellis' in his uniform, photographs of 'Ellis' in his school XI, photographs of 'Ellis' digging castles on the sands.

10

Some people might have been bored but Bel was interested for it gave her a clearer picture of Ellis Brownlee, it showed her the man from a different angle. It made him more human, somehow. As a matter of fact Mr. Brownlee had scarcely changed at all. The photograph of nine-year-old Ellis digging in the sand was easily recognisable and Bel had no difficulty in picking out Ellis in the picture of the school XI. The same thin face and wide mouth and the same thick brown hair!

Bel was thinking of all this while she waited for Mr. Brownlee to continue his dictation of the letter, but Mr. Brownlee seemed to have forgotten about the letter.

'I wish I had time to go down to the wharf,' he said.

'Oh, so do I,' agreed Bel. 'It would be lovely today with the sun shining on the river — and it's so interesting, isn't it? I like seeing the ships coming in to unload. Ships from all over the world!'

'Triremes from Nineveh? They brought ivory, apes and peacocks, didn't they?'

Bel laughed and said, 'I wonder who bought their cargoes.'

'That's a very interesting point,' said Mr. Brownlee smiling.

His face was thin with high cheekbones; it was rather a stern face, but when he smiled his eyes crinkled at the corners and his mouth widened to show beautifully white teeth. His whole appearance changed completely when he smiled, even his thick brown hair seemed to

11

join in the transformation.

'I wish we could both go down to the docks,' he told her. 'Perhaps some day when there's a specially interesting trireme due to arrive we could wangle an excuse . . . and that reminds me to tell you that I've got to go to South America sometime soon. There are various business matters to settle — that trouble with our agent at Buenos Aires for instance. Mr. Copping thinks it would be a good plan for me to go there and see what's what.'

Bel nodded. 'It would be rather a nice trip.'

'Not too bad. I don't want to be away for long of course. There's too much to do here.'

'I could take my holiday while you're away.'

'No,' said Mr. Brownlee firmly. 'You can have your holiday when I come back. I want you to work for Mr. Wills while I'm away.'

'Oh, Mr. Brownlee!' exclaimed Bel in dismay.

'Why not?'

There were various reasons why not. The chief one was that Bel did not like Mr. Wills — but this reason could not be offered.

'It ought to be Miss Goudge,' said Bel. 'She's been here much longer and — and she knows Mr. Wills much better than I do.'

'Why should that matter?'

'She's much more efficient than I am,' said Bel desperately. 'I mean she's so accurate. She never makes mistakes.'

'Yes, she's a very efficient machine but she doesn't use her brains.'

'My shorthand — ' began Bel. 'Mr. Brownlee, you know my shorthand is — is — '

He laughed. 'It is, rather, isn't it?' he agreed.

'Oh yes, you can laugh! You don't mind when I get tangled up and can't read my own shorthand. I can come to you and ask you about it. Mr. Wills won't laugh. He'll be angry.'

'It doesn't happen very often, and shorthand isn't everything. You know the work. That's the important thing. Listen, Miss Lamington,' said Mr. Brownlee earnestly. 'Everything will get into a frightful muddle unless there's someone here who knows the work. I don't want to come back to chaos — see?'

Bel saw. She said doubtfully, 'There will be trouble.'

'But you'll do your best.'

'Yes, of course,' said Bel.

She was obliged to agree for she was an employee of the firm and if Mr. Brownlee wanted to lend her to Mr. Wills while he was away she had no option in the matter . . . but there would be trouble not only with Mr. Wills but also with Helen Goudge.

2

What with one thing and another it was later than usual when Bel got away from the office but it was such a lovely evening that she decided to walk part of the way home. She had discovered a route which avoided the jostling crowds and the streets full of noisy traffic; it was longer, of course, but much more pleasant. On leaving the office you turned down a narrow lane between tall houses — a paved lane with wooden posts at each end to show that it was intended for foot passengers only — the lane led into a large square where some of the houses had been bombed. In the middle of the square was a garden which at one time had been protected by railings, but these had been removed for scrap and never replaced. All that remained of the garden was a large area of scrubby grass with some bushes and plane trees in the middle. It was not a very attractive spot, but it was quiet and secluded and there was an iron seat beneath the trees. Sometimes in fine weather Bel brought sandwiches and a flask of coffee and had her lunch here. People passed to and fro but nobody bothered her or took the slightest interest in her. She ate her lunch in peace and scattered crumbs for the sparrows.

Bel made up her mind that if the fine weather continued she would have a picnic here one day soon.

She walked on through several quiet squares which had once been fashionable but were now full of boarding-houses and turned through an archway into a mews. This was a delightful part of her walk. It was like a little village and consisted of a narrow cobbled street with garage doors on each side and little flights of stairs which led to flats with small windows and gabled roofs. The odd thing was that, whereas the large houses in the squares had gone down-hill and were shabby and neglected-looking, these little houses had gone up in the world. The woodwork was brightly painted and there were tubs with little bay trees outside each door. One of the garages was open and a large raking sports car could be seen inside. Yes, nowadays it was fashionable to live in a mews. It was THE THING.

Bel walked on and turned left into a street of small shops. There was a flower shop here with the window full of golden daffodils and white narcissus and mimosa from the South of France . . . It was Spring here too, thought Bel, pausing to look at the display. She would have loved to buy a sheaf of daffodils but managed to resist their appeal. She could not resist the wallflowers. There they were, in the corner of the shop, dozens of tiny seedlings huddled together in a shallow box. 'Buy us,' they were saying. 'The daffodils will have faded in a week but we'll go on living for months.' She imagined them blooming, a mass of brown and gold, in the big trough outside her sitting-room window; she could almost smell the scent of them, sweet as honey. Just a dozen, thought Bel, or perhaps two dozen, it would be silly to skimp them.

'I'll give you the lot for three and six,' said the florist. 'You may as well take them, they won't last till tomorrow.'

Bel had not meant to pay so much. It was an extravagance. But she had to have them. She paid the three and sixpence and continued on her way with the large damp parcel clasped in her arms.

2

Compared with the usual monotonous routine today had been adventurous. First there was Spring, then came her chat with Mr. Brownlee about the triremes from Nineveh — a very interesting and unusual chat — and now, best of all, her wallflower seedlings. These events were enough to make this a red-letter day! But the day's adventures were not over for when she took her key and opened the door of her flat Bel's nostrils were assailed by the smell of tobacco smoke. Yes, there was no doubt about it, somebody was in the flat — and was smoking!

At first Bel was alarmed and envisaged a burglar . . . and then common sense came to her rescue. She realised that it was unlikely to be a burglar or anyone with nefarious intent. Such a person would not advertise his presence by smoking. But, if not a burglar, whom could it be, wondered Bel.

She hesitated for a moment and then pushed open the door of the sitting-room. Nobody was

16

there. Nobody had been there. The room was in perfect order just as she had left it that morning. There was nobody in the little kitchen; nobody in the bathroom; nobody in her bedroom. She looked in the cupboard, she looked under the bed — nobody.

The whole thing was most mysterious and Bel did not feel she could settle down until she had got to the bottom of it. She went back to the sitting-room and stood there sniffing. The smell was strongest here . . . and it was not cigarette smoke . . . it was smoke from a pipe. Then she saw a faint blue haze of smoke drifting in through the partly-open window. She advanced very quietly and peered out from behind the curtain.

A man was sitting in her garden, sitting upon Bel's deck-chair; his long legs, clad in grey flannel trousers, were stretched out comfortably and his feet were resting upon the edge of a wooden tub — large feet in dirty white tennis shoes. His shirt had once been white but was white no longer; his sleeves were rolled up above his elbows and his hands were clasped behind his head. His hair was fair, it was sleeked back from his forehead. A pipe was stuck in the corner of his mouth. The whole effect was that of a young man enjoying himself, relaxed and perfectly at ease.

Bel had been frightened, now she was angry. She threw up the window and leant out. The young man sat up and looked at her. For a moment there was silence.

'Oh, I say!' exclaimed the young man, removing the pipe from his mouth. 'Oh, I say! I

17

hope you don't mind! I mean does it belong to you?'

'Of course it belongs to me,' said Bel crossly. 'Who did you think it belonged to?'

'I thought it would be a man.'

'A man?'

'Yes, I never thought it might be a girl; not for a moment.'

'Why?'

'Oh, because — well, look at the work! I mean making it. The troughs and the window-boxes — and all that. I never thought for a moment — '

'I don't see the difference.'

'Oh, there's a lot of difference,' said the young man earnestly. 'Of course it was frightful cheek anyhow — I grant you that — but if it had been a man I could have brazened it out. As a matter of fact I had made up my mind what to say to the fellow.'

He had risen by this time and his height and largeness seemed to dwarf the little garden.

'It's so enchanting,' he said, smiling at her. 'It's so amazing to find a little secret garden in the middle of the town. You aren't cross, are you?'

'I was frightened.'

'Oh goodness! I'm sorry about that, but honestly I'm quite harmless. You've only got to say the word and I'll vanish.'

'Vanish?'

'Yes, I'll go the way I came; over the roofs.'

'You came over the roofs?' asked Bel incredulously.

'I like climbing,' he explained. 'It's one of my Things. I've done quite a lot of climbing in Switzerland. London roofs are a bit different of course but they're better than nothing.'

'They're frightfully dirty.'

'Oh yes, frightfully dirty,' he agreed. 'I keep these bags specially for climbing — that's why I look such a sweep. I'm not really a sweep,' he added smiling.

Bel had not thought he was a sweep. He was dirty, of course, but still . . .

'I paint pictures,' continued the young man. 'At least I try to paint pictures. Sometimes they come off and sometimes they don't. I've got a studio — quite a decent studio — and a small room where I sleep. It's right at the top of a house in the attic. When I want some exercise I climb about on the roofs outside my window. That's what I was doing this afternoon when I happened to see your garden. At first I couldn't believe my eyes — it was like an oasis in the desert of bricks and mortar — so of course I had to climb down to see if it was really an oasis or only a mirage. Then when I got here I couldn't resist sitting down and enjoying it. That's how it happened, you see.'

The explanation satisfied Bel and she was no longer angry. There was something very engaging about her visitor from the skies. 'Yes, I see,' she said.

'I'll go now, shall I?' he asked. 'I mean you've only got to say the word.'

'You can stay if you like but I can't talk to you. I've got a lot to do. I've got some wallflower seedlings to plant and I must get them in tonight.'

'Perhaps I could help you,' he suggested.

Bel did not want help. She had been looking forward to a quiet hour in her garden; there was nothing that gave her so much pleasure and satisfaction as planting out seedlings — making the little holes, putting in the plants and tucking them up firmly and cosily. She liked to be silly about it ('There you are,' she would say. 'That's comfy, isn't it? You'll grow into a big plant with lovely flowers') but how could she be silly with a large young man sitting and watching her? It was impossible.

The large young man had been looking at her face and Bel's face was very expressive. 'All right,' said the large young man. 'I can see you don't want anyone to help you. It's more fun doing it yourself. I'd rather do it myself if this were my garden. I'll sit here for a bit if you don't mind — I promise not to be a nuisance — I'll be so quiet you won't know I'm here.'

Bel agreed to the proposal somewhat reluctantly.

'By the way,' he said. 'My name is Mark Adam Desborough. What's yours?'

'Beatrice Elizabeth Lamington.'

'Beatrice,' he said, looking at her thoughtfully. 'Yes, it suits you. I don't know anyone else called Beatrice.'

'Oh, but nobody ever calls me that,' declared Bel. 'It was my aunt's name, you see. I've always been called Bel — because of my initials of course.'

'That's nice too,' said Mr. Desborough. He laughed and added, 'Lots of people call me by my initials but mostly behind my back.'

3

Mark Desborough had promised not to be a nuisance and he kept his word. When Bel really got down to the job of planting out the wallflower seedlings she almost forgot he was there. The task of singling out the little plants and tucking them into their places took up all her attention. They had been lamentably over-crowded, some of them had been choked to death and were useless, but fortunately when she had put these aside there were enough to fill the stone trough quite comfortably.

By this time Bel was hungry — it was long past her usual hour for supper — and it struck her that her visitor might be in need of food. She was too compassionate to send him away starving to his attic amongst the roof-tops so she suggested he might like to stay. Bread and cheese and salad was all she had to offer him but Mr. Desborough seemed quite contented with the fare. He helped her to make coffee and they sat down together at the table. It was only then that he produced his sketch-book and showed her what had kept him so quiet.

'Is that supposed to be me?' asked Bel, looking at the roughly sketched figure of an angular female kneeling upon the ground.

'It's Greenfingers. I don't say it's you

— exactly — but you inspired it.'

'It isn't like me.'

'No, of course not,' said Mark, whisking the sketch-book out of her hands. 'If you want a likeness you can have your photograph taken.'

Bel was silent. She did not understand.

'It's going to be good,' declared Mark defiantly.

'Is it?'

'Yes, it's going to be the best thing I've done. This is only the rough draft, of course. I shall do it in oils. You'll let me do it, won't you?'

'Let you do it?'

'You'll give me one or two sittings,' he explained. 'Please do. It's important. If I can get it done in time I can send it to old What's his Name's exhibition of Moderns in the Welcome Gallery. I was going to send a thing of roofs — a sort of fantasy — but this will be better. Don't say no. It's important.'

Bel could not say no. She was not quite sure whether she wanted to say no.

'It's awfully good of you,' said Mark Desborough, taking her silence for consent. 'But you understand, don't you? My painting is important to me — just as your garden is to you. I'll come tomorrow at the same time.'

3

When Mark Desborough had gone the whole thing seemed like a dream. Bel might have dismissed it as a dream if it had not been for his cup and saucer and plate which she had to wash up. Somehow she did not believe that he would come tomorrow and when she returned home at the usual hour and found him sitting in her little garden she was quite surprised. He had brought his canvas with him and all the necessary equipment in a haversack and was painting industriously. The background of roofs and sky was taking shape — for Mark was a quick worker — but the woman's figure was missing.

'Put on that green overall and kneel down, just as you did yesterday,' said Mark. 'That's all I want.'

It did not sound much — the way he put it — but Bel found it tiresome and exhausting. She had not found it tiresome when she was engaged in planting her wallflowers but it was quite a different matter to kneel there doing nothing. However Mark was so excited about the picture and so grateful for her co-operation that she could not let him down — and afterwards when the light faded and he came in and had supper with her it was very pleasant indeed.

Hitherto Bel's life had been bounded by her work in the office and pottering in her garden; Mark was the first 'outside person' she had

23

spoken to for months. He had dropped into her life from the skies and brought fresh interests and new ideas. He was a sociable friendly creature; his life had been varied and he had plenty to say for himself. He was considerate, too, and brought Bel parcels of food, saying that he was not going to 'sponge' on her for supper.

When she had known Mark for a week she felt as if she had known him for years. Her life was completely changed by his advent.

By this time the picture was finished. Mark was delighted with it and kept on saying that it was all her doing that it was such a success. Bel could not see this. She had posed for him of course but the female in Mark's picture was no more like her than the man in the moon.

'Oh well, you wait,' said Mark. 'Wait and see what other people say about it. As a matter of fact I'm having a party in my studio tomorrow night — just to show it off. You must come.'

'I don't ever go to parties.'

'Nonsense! You'll have to come. They'll want to see you.'

'Who?'

'Everybody of course.'

'I haven't got a party frock.'

'Goodness, it isn't that sort of party. It's just a few friends coming in for a drink and to look at the picture. You must wear the green overall — '

'The green overall! But it's dirty.'

'Of course it's dirty,' said Mark. 'Greenfingers got dirty working in her garden. It's right for Greenfingers to be dirty. You can't come over the roofs of course, but you can come round by the stairs. I'll fetch you about eight.'

'No,' said Bel firmly. 'I wouldn't know any of your friends and I don't like parties. Honestly, Mark, I don't want to come.'

'What a funny girl you are!' exclaimed Mark, laughing.

2

When Bel got home the following evening Mark was not in the roof-garden and somehow she felt a little disappointed. Although it was only a week since his first appearance she had got used to finding him there, waiting for her . . . but of course the picture was finished now, so there was no reason for him to come. Perhaps he would not come any more! This idea gave her a queer empty sort of feeling which was most unpleasant. As she prepared her supper and ate it and washed up the dishes, the idea loomed bigger, like a thunder cloud. Perhaps she would never see Mark again. She did not even know where he lived for he had just said vaguely that his studio was 'right at the top of a house in the attic'. It was not in this house, she knew, for there was only one flat above her own and it was occupied by an elderly man with a lame leg. She had seen him several times on the stairs, toiling up laboriously, and had felt sorry for him. It seemed a most unsuitable dwelling-place for a man with a lame leg. Mark's attic might be in the house next door or several doors away or even further.

On thinking about their last conversation Bel

had an uncomfortable feeling that she had been rather ungracious — not to say rude. Mark had asked her to his party, and said he would fetch her, and she had refused to come. She had not thanked him for the invitation but had just said she didn't like parties. Yes, it was rude, thought Bel. It was quite horrid of her. Even though she didn't like parties she might have gone for a short time and come away. But it was no good thinking about it; she had refused the invitation point blank. The whole thing was over and done with.

Bel had scarcely reached this decision when her front-door bell rang — and there was Mark. He looked different this evening, clean and tidy in pale-grey slacks and a tweed jacket.

'Come on,' he said, smiling down at her. 'They all want to see you.'

'What?' exclaimed Bel in surprise.

'It's my party. Had you forgotten?'

'But — but I said I wouldn't come — '

'They've sent me to fetch you.'

'But, Mark — '

'Hurry up,' he said impatiently. 'Put on your Greenfingers overall. You've got to come.'

3

It was quite a long way to Mark's studio; down the stairs of number 27 and along the street to number 23 and up five flights of stairs to the very top of the house. As they toiled up the last flight Bel became aware of a curious humming

26

sound — it reminded her of a swarm of bees which, long ago, had flown in a dense cloud across Aunt Beatrice's garden. The sound became louder and louder; it was no longer like bees, it was more like the parrot-house at the Zoo. When Mark threw open the door of his studio the noise was mysterious no longer, it emanated from Mark's guests. The studio was full of people talking to one another, shouting at one another to make themselves heard. The din was indescribable.

It was all the more frightful because the attic was large and bare and the ceiling was low. The place was not very well lighted; it was fogged with tobacco-smoke and the heat was intense.

A sudden silence fell as Mark and Bel appeared. Everybody's head turned to the door.

'Here's Greenfingers!' cried Mark. 'You wanted to see her — and here she is!'

The noise broke out again as loud as ever. People surged round Bel. Her hand was shaken; she was patted on the back; she was dragged to the end of the room where the easel stood with the picture upon it. Somebody put a glass into her hand containing a queer cloudy sort of liquid. She was besieged with questions about the picture.

'But it isn't like me,' said Bel. 'Yes, of course I posed for it — but it isn't like me.'

'He's got your soul,' declared a young man with a beard. 'Mark, you've got her soul there.'

'It's an evocation,' said somebody else.

There was so much noise and confusion that

Bel scarcely knew what was happening until she found herself sitting upon an old oak settle which had been pushed into a corner near the window. She had drunk some of the queer concoction from her glass — it tasted very nasty — but whether it was this that confused her and made her head buzz, or whether it was the noise and the heat and the odd behaviour of her fellow guests Bel did not know.

Mark had disappeared. She could not see him amongst the crowd. There was a thin girl sitting beside her on the settle — a girl with a long nose and dark velvety eyes. She said something to Bel.

'What did you say?' asked Bel, trying to concentrate.

The girl laughed. 'I said I supposed you were Mark's latest.'

'Latest what?'

'Victim,' said the girl, opening her eyes very wide. She leaned forward and added, 'I shouldn't have thought you were Mark's cup of tea, but perhaps you aren't as innocent as you look.'

At this moment somebody turned on the gramophone and several couples began to dance, but it was so crowded that there was scarcely room for them to move. Mark appeared suddenly and said, 'What's Enid been telling you?'

Enid rose and replied, 'Only the truth, darling. Come and dance with me.'

'I'm going to dance with Greenfingers,' said Mark.

The girl gave a hoot of laughter and moved away.

Bel found herself dancing with Mark, and then with one of Mark's friends — a small neat man in a brown lounge suit.

'Do you like this sort of thing?' he asked.

'Not awfully,' replied Bel.

'I hate it,' he said. 'I came to have a look at Desborough's pictures. I didn't know it was a party or I wouldn't have come.'

'I'm not used to parties.'

'That's obvious. You look dazed. I'm going away in a few minutes; I've got to be up early.'

Somehow it had not occurred to Bel that she could escape, but of course there was nothing to prevent her, so she found her host and said goodbye.

'Goodbye!' exclaimed Mark in surprise. 'But the party is only just beginning. Aren't you enjoying yourself?'

'I've got an awful headache,' declared Bel, quite truthfully. 'I think it's the heat — or something.'

'Poor darling! Yes, you look a bit rotten. I had better take you home.'

'Oh Mark, you can't! I mean it's your party. I can go home myself — '

'They won't miss me,' said Mark laughing. 'We needn't worry. They'll all be quite happy without me.'

It was true, of course. The party was well under way and the guests would not notice his absence, but all the same it did not seem right to Bel. She tried to explain this, but Mark took her by the arm and piloted her safely to the door.

4

It was bliss to escape from the hot overcrowded studio and the intolerable noise. They went down the stairs together and out into the quiet street. Mark was still holding Bel's arm.

'What a lovely night!' he exclaimed. 'Look at the stars! Do you know about the stars, Bel?'

'A little,' she replied. 'That's Orion, isn't it? But we mustn't dawdle. You'll have to go back, won't you?'

'Why do we have parties?' said Mark with a sigh.

Bel did not know the answer so she was silent.

They went up the stairs of number 27 and Bel opened the door of her flat. It looked peaceful and homelike; it was quiet and cool. It had never seemed more pleasant.

'Thank you, Mark,' she said, turning to him and holding out her hand. 'Thank you for having me to your party.'

'You didn't enjoy it a bit, did you?' said Mark anxiously. 'You were upset about something — I could see that. I suppose it was Enid. What was Enid saying to you?'

'Enid?'

'Yes, she was sitting beside you on the settle — a dark girl with a long nose. What did she say?'

'Oh, nothing much.'

'She's a menace,' said Mark earnestly. 'She's a predatory female. You needn't take any notice of what she says.'

'Oh, I didn't.'

'What did she say?' asked Mark, somewhat unreasonably. Bel had not intended to tell him, but she found herself saying, 'Oh, just that she wouldn't have thought I was your cup of tea.'

'Oh, she did, did she!' Mark exclaimed. 'That's what she thought! Well, she was mistaken. It's Enid who isn't my cup of tea — nor any of that crowd. Of course I like running about with them and having fun but they aren't really my sort — if you know what I mean.' He hesitated and then added softly, 'You're different, Bel.'

'Different?'

'Yes, you're my sort of person. You're a darling.'

She was too breathless to speak — and anyhow she did not know what to say. They stood for a few moments in silence. Mark was holding both her hands so she could not move.

'I must go back,' said Mark at last. 'You're tired, Bel.'

'Yes, awfully tired,' she whispered.

'Go to bed, darling.'

'Yes.'

'Sweet dreams,' said Mark. 'I'll be seeing you — ' He bent down and kissed her lightly on the forehead and turned away.

She stood at the door and watched him running down the stairs.

4

The next morning was so fine that Bel decided to take a picnic-lunch and have it in the garden near the office. She was still suffering from the effects of the heat and noise of last night's party and felt she wanted as much fresh air as she could get.

Mr. Brownlee was a little late in arriving so Bel went straight into his room and began to open his letters. Some were urgent and required his personal attention but others were merely routine and could be dealt with by Bel herself. As she sorted them out and made notes for his perusal she realised that she knew a good deal about the business and about Mr. Brownlee's methods — and, this being so, she realised that Mr. Brownlee was quite justified in wanting her to be here to help Mr. Wills while he was away. She had said she would, of course, but she had said it reluctantly. Now, quite suddenly, she saw that it was really a compliment and she should have shown more appreciation.

There was no opportunity of speaking to him that morning for he came in late and several people were waiting to see him so Bel worked away industriously and left some notes and letters on his desk. Then she took the bag containing the Thermos flask of coffee and the sandwiches and went out to have her lunch.

It was a delightful day, sunny and warm; the

garden was deserted except for flocks of sparrows. Bel sat down upon the iron seat and opened her bag. She was happy. There was a strange feeling of excitement inside her. The party had been quite frightful, but afterwards going home with Mark had been — nice. She remembered all he had said — every word — and he had kissed her. It was quite a small kiss, and of course it meant nothing, but still . . .

Aunt Beatrice would not have approved. Aunt Beatrice had been very much against anything of that sort. Easy kissing made a man think less of you. But I couldn't help it, thought Bel. I didn't know he was going to kiss me, so how could I have prevented it?

Bel had just reached this point in her reflections when she saw Mr. Brownlee walking towards her across the grass. There was a notice which said, KEEP OFF THE GRASS, but Mr. Brownlee was paying no attention to it. She wondered how he had found her. Perhaps he had followed her when she left the office; perhaps he wanted to speak to her about one of the letters which she had left on his desk for him to sign.

'Was the letter all right?' she asked anxiously.

'The letter?'

'The one to Mr. Anderson.'

'Oh — yes — quite all right,' said Mr. Brownlee vaguely.

It was obvious that he was not thinking about the letter but, if not, why had he come? She wondered whether she ought to offer him some sandwiches; it seemed rude to go on eating without offering some to him. She looked at him doubtfully. 'Have you had lunch — ' she began.

'Don't worry about me, Miss Lamington. I'm lunching with Mr. Copping at his club, but not till one-thirty. I'll just sit down here for a few minutes if you don't mind.'

Miss Lamington did not mind. She could hardly have objected for the garden did not belong to her. It was free to all.

'What a nice quiet place!' said Mr. Brownlee, looking round with interest. 'You'd never think you were in the middle of London. It's a sort of back-water.'

'Haven't you been here before?'

'I didn't know it existed.'

For a few moments there was silence. Bel continued to eat her sandwiches and drink her coffee. The sun shone brightly and the sparrows twittered in the trees.

At last Mr. Brownlee said, 'Mr. Copping wants his son to come into the firm. I'm all for it, but Wills isn't too keen. Keep this under your hat of course, Miss Lamington.'

'Of course.'

'We're having a chat about it today — at lunch. That's the object of the exercise.'

Bel nodded. She said, 'Why doesn't Mr. Wills — '

'Oh you know what he is! He likes everything to go on exactly the same — no change; but it's a good thing to have young men to carry on. Besides young Copping has every right to come into the firm. It was his great grandfather who founded the business.'

'Then Mr. Wills can't object, can he?'

34

'Not really. He can only make things rather unpleasant,' said Mr. Brownlee smiling.

Bel had an urge to say, 'That won't be anything new,' but she managed to control the impulse.

There was another silence — a companionable sort of silence — there was nothing embarrassing about it. Mr. Brownlee lighted a cigarette. At last he said, 'Do you often come and have lunch here?'

'Quite often in fine weather. I like fresh air,' explained Bel. 'As a matter of fact I was at a party last night — you could have cut the atmosphere with a knife — so I felt I wanted fresh air even more than usual.'

Mr. Brownlee looked at his secretary in surprise. There was nothing surprising in what she had said, but there was something very surprising in the way she had said it. There was a warmth in her — a sort of glow — which was quite unusual. Miss Lamington had been his secretary for nearly four months but he had never really seen her until this moment. She had been his secretary — an exceedingly good secretary — he had never had such an intelligent secretary nor one who could be relied upon so absolutely; he had never had a secretary who was so interested in her work that she would stay on quite cheerfully as long as he wanted her. Miss Storey had been extremely efficient but she was constantly asking to get off early to meet her young man. Miss Lamington never wanted to get off early. Perhaps she hadn't a young man to meet, but if so it was rather astonishing because she was very attractive.

Mr. Brownlee looked at her and, for the first time he saw her not as his secretary but as a young woman. Yes, she was very attractive indeed. He liked her well-shaped head with the brown hair brushed back from her forehead in a smooth shining wave. Her eyes were grey and widely spaced, her mouth was rather large but curved delightfully. Her skin was smooth and unblemished as the skin of a child.

'You look — different — today,' said Mr. Brownlee impulsively.

Bel smiled and replied, 'So do you, Mr. Brownlee.'

'I'm different?'

Bel nodded. He had taken off his hat and the breeze had ruffled his thick hair. He was human and vulnerable and ever so much younger.

'Can you explain it?' he asked, looking at her and smiling.

'Nobody is the same person to more than one other person,' suggested Bel.

'I know what you mean,' said Mr. Brownlee. 'And, what's even more strange, people vary according to time and place. For instance I'm one sort of person in the office and quite another sort of person when I'm at home with my mother at Rose Hill.'

Bel laughed. She said, 'Here and now you're quite a different sort of person altogether. The Mr. Brownlee I know is a law-abiding citizen.'

'What have I done?' he exclaimed in mock dismay.

36

'That notice says, KEEP OFF THE GRASS.'

'So it does,' he agreed, smiling. 'And I can't even say I didn't see it — because I did — but the grass in this curious backwater of yours is so unkempt that it scarcely merits the name and I didn't think it would mind my walking on it. That's the explanation of my unlawful conduct.'

'Poor grass!' said Bel. 'I'm sure it would much rather be growing in the country.'

Mr. Brownlee nodded.

'Sometimes I play a game with myself,' continued Bel. 'I watch people coming into the garden and bet myself twopence whether they'll walk round by the path — as law-abiding citizens should — or ignore the notice and walk on the grass. I can usually tell by their appearance which they'll do.'

'You thought I would go round by the path?'

'I was sure of it.'

'So you've lost twopence!'

She smiled. 'But fortunately only to myself.'

'Wouldn't it be more amusing to play the game with other people?'

'I daresay it would, but I don't know any other people, you see.' This was not quite true, of course, and as Bel was a very truthful person she hesitated and then added, 'At least I didn't until ten days ago.'

'That sounds rather mysterious.'

'It isn't really. You can live in London for months without getting to know a single creature. Nobody looks at you, nobody sees you; it's as if you were invisible.'

Invisible; it seemed fantastic to Mr. Brownlee for he had never been invisible. He had a number of friends. He met them in the train and exchanged greetings with them. He was a well-known figure at the Golf Club . . . but he saw that Miss Lamington really meant what she said (she was perfectly serious) and of course when he considered the matter he realised that Miss Lamington had been invisible to him — until this morning.

'But you aren't invisible any longer?' he suggested.

It was a question, really, but Bel did not answer it. She had finished her lunch by this time and was scattering the remains of her sandwiches for the birds. Mr. Brownlee watched her. He would have liked an answer to his question. Something had happened to his secretary. Something had made her visible; something had lighted a lamp inside her so that she was lit up with an inward glow.

Bel turned her head suddenly and saw that Mr. Brownlee was looking at her in an unusual sort of manner — but perhaps that was just because they were both feeling a bit different today. She remembered that she had something rather important to tell him.

'Oh, Mr. Brownlee,' she said. 'It's very nice of you to want me to stay on and help Mr. Wills when you're away.'

'You said you would.'

'I know, but I should have thanked you. I see now it was really a sort of — well, a sort of compliment.'

'It is a compliment,' he replied smiling.

'I was just wondering about Miss Snow. I mean she's his secretary of course. D'you think she'll be annoyed about it?'

'I don't see why she should be,' Mr. Brownlee said. 'Of course she'll go on doing her usual work for Mr. Wills. My idea is that you should use my room and carry on with your work — keeping the ledgers and dealing with matters which normally would be my affair. You know as well as I do that there are all sorts of matters which Mr. Wills knows nothing about. I want you to keep in touch with Nelson at Copping Wharf. I'm telling him to ring you up if there's anything he wants; he doesn't get on with Mr. Wills.'

Bel knew this already. She nodded.

'I'll write to you,' he continued. 'You'll be interested to hear how things are going.'

'Yes, of course I shall.' She hesitated and then added, 'I'm a bit worried about Miss Snow. I wouldn't like her to think — '

'She never thinks.'

'Never thinks!'

'Never,' said Mr. Brownlee seriously. 'Miss Snow is a very efficient machine. She suits Mr. Wills but she wouldn't suit me. She comes at the right time and does what she's told and goes away when the clock strikes the hour for her release. She has a face like a wooden effigy and takes not the slightest interest in the affairs of the firm. 'Faultily faultless, icily regular, splendidly null' — that's Miss Snow.'

Bel was laughing. She said, 'Oh, I think you're

39

doing her an injustice.'

'I don't think so,' declared Mr. Brownlee. He had an impartial air — the air of a wise judge — but his eyes were twinkling.

Soon after this he rose and said he must go, adding that it would not do to be late for his lunch with the Senior Partner.

'Oh, by the way,' he added. 'Mr. Copping will come in more often while I'm away. He'll deal with the foreign letters.'

2

Mr. Copping, the Senior Partner, was a delicate man, tall and gaunt with thick silver hair and very light blue eyes. He was devoted to the interests of the firm — which had been founded by his grandfather — and, although he was unable to come to the office regularly, he did a good deal of business at home. Papers were sent to him for his perusal and no major decisions were made without his consent.

One afternoon, when Bel was alone in Mr. Brownlee's room typing some letters, Mr. Copping walked in and looked round.

'Brownlee out?' he enquired.

'He's at a meeting, sir,' replied Bel. 'I'm expecting him back in about twenty minutes.'

'I'll wait,' said Mr. Copping, sitting down in Mr. Brownlee's chair. He looked at Bel and added, 'You're new, aren't you? I don't think I've seen you before.'

Bel had seen him, of course, but that was

different. She explained that she had come to the firm as a typist but was now Mr. Brownlee's secretary.

'More interesting?' he asked.

'Oh yes, much more interesting,' replied Bell emphatically.

'Seeing how the wheels go round, eh?'

'Yes.'

'D'you ever go down to the wharf?'

'Oh yes, often. I love it. Mr. Nelson showed me all over the warehouses one day — and the picture in his office of the China Clipper — '

Mr. Copping nodded. 'My grandfather built the wharf. It was quite small to begin with — didn't need so much room in those days — my father took in more ground and expanded it considerably, but that wasn't enough. I've had to put up two new warehouses . . . so it goes on.'

'Your son is coming into the firm, isn't he?'

'Oh, you know all about it, do you?' said Mr. Copping, looking at her and smiling.

'Mr. Brownlee told me. I think it's splendid. Four generations of Coppings!'

'Yes,' agreed Mr. Copping. 'Four generations of us. It covers a good deal of history: — from China Clippers sailing round the Cape to modern ships steaming through the Suez Canal. Jim will carry on the tradition. He's a good lad — a bit scatterbrained perhaps, but I daresay he'll settle down. Can't expect an old head on young shoulders. The main thing is he's keen on the old firm. Interested in it, you know, always has been. Spends hours down at the wharf

41

watching the ships come in.'

'It's good, isn't it?'

'Good?'

'I mean sometimes sons aren't interested in their father's business.'

'That's true,' Mr. Copping agreed.

'But of course it's a terribly interesting sort of business!'

'You think so?'

'Yes, I do.'

'So do I,' declared Mr. Copping with a chuckle.

Bel had been a little shy of Mr. Copping at first, but he was so friendly that she was shy no longer; besides, it was obvious that he wanted to chat while he was waiting for Mr. Brownlee's return.

'When is your son coming, Mr. Copping?' she asked.

'Well, that's the question. Brownlee thinks he should wait a bit. Brownlee thinks we should put it off until he returns from South America. I don't know, I'm sure.'

Bel did not know either. She was aware that Mr. Wills was making trouble about the matter, but that was delicate ground.

'Jim is abroad at present,' continued Mr. Copping. 'He's coming back soon and wants to start at once — learning the ropes as he calls it — and if he doesn't start at once he won't have anything to do. I don't want him running about idle. It isn't good for a young chap — 'specially a chap like Jim. He's keen as mustard. Bit of a problem, isn't it?'

'Yes,' said Bel. 'Yes, it is.'

'We called the boy James,' continued Mr. Copping in a reflective tone. 'We called him after his great grandfather, who began the whole thing. I thought it time there should be another James Copping. His mother agreed. You see, Miss — er — '

'Lamington,' Bel told him.

'Lamington? That rings a bell. I used to know a fellow called John Lamington. He was a gunner — awfully nice fellow with a pretty wife. Frightful thing happened. They were both killed in a motor smash — absolute tragedy.'

'My father and mother,' said Bel looking at him with wide eyes.

'What? Not really? My dear girl, I'm sorry. Shouldn't have mentioned it — blurted it out like that!'

He looked so distressed that Bell hastened to re-assure him. 'It's all right,' she said, somewhat incoherently. 'I mean it's so long ago — I was only three years old — I don't remember them at all. My aunt brought me up. She was a wonderful person.'

'Your aunt?'

'My father's sister, Beatrice Lamington,' Bel told him. 'She had a house in Southmere and I lived there with her all my life. Then she died, so — so I came to London.'

'I see,' said Mr. Copping, gazing at her with his very blue eyes.

Somehow Bel had a feeling that those very blue eyes saw a good deal — a great deal more than what appeared on the surface. She had

43

been inclined to think that Mr. Copping was what is known as 'a sleeping partner' of the firm; she thought so no longer.

'Go on,' said Mr. Copping encouragingly. 'You came to London and you got a job with Copping, Wills and Brownlee. How did you like it, eh? A bit lonely, wasn't it?'

'Yes, it was, rather. I enjoy the work very much — I told you that, didn't I? — but London is rather a lonely sort of place unless you've got a lot of friends.'

'What are you going to do while Brownlee is away? Having a holiday?'

'Mr. Brownlee wants me to be here,' explained Bel. 'You see I know quite a lot about how things are done.'

'Oh, you do, do you? That's very interesting,' said Mr. Copping. 'Very interesting indeed.'

When Mr. Brownlee returned from his meeting he found his senior partner and his secretary chatting together as if they had known each other all their lives. He was pleased, but rather surprised because he was somewhat in awe of his senior partner. Unfortunately the letters which ought to have been ready for him to sign were lying neglected upon the table. His secretary apologised for the delay.

'My fault, my fault,' declared Mr. Copping. 'If anyone gets the sack it'll have to be me.'

They all laughed heartily at this preposterous jest.

Bel gathered up the letters and hastened from the room, leaving the two gentlemen to have their talk in private.

The Welcome Gallery consisted of two large rooms over a curio shop in a turning off Shaftesbury Avenue. The entrance was anything but imposing for the shop was small and dirty; it sold pictures and artists' materials and various pieces of china and second-hand furniture. When Bel Lamington pushed open the door a bell rang and the proprietor — a tall old man with a bald head and enormous spectacles perched on a beaky nose — appeared from the back premises and asked her what she wanted. Coming from the bright sunlit street into the dim overcrowded shop Bel's eyes were blinded and for a moment or two she hesitated, uncertain whether she had found the right place.

'The Welcome Gallery?' she said doubtfully.

The old man gestured to a steep stair at one side of the shop and stood there amongst his treasures watching her go up.

Bel did not look back, but all the same she was aware that he was watching her with considerable interest.

The stairs emerged into a surprisingly large room, full of light. It was bare except for the pictures on the walls and some wheel-back wooden chairs. About a dozen people were there, walking round with catalogues in their hands, looking at the pictures and talking to each other. There were two men with beards and a girl with shaggy hair and bare legs and sandals. There were several other people as well but they did not look 'hopeful'. None of them looked as if they had money to spend on pictures; most of them looked as if they lacked money to spend on a square meal.

Bel seized a catalogue and sat down on a chair in the corner. Later she would have to walk round and look at the pictures, because Mark would ask her about them, but at the moment she wanted to hide. It would be so awful if any of these people recognised her — so dreadfully embarrassing. They wouldn't, of course, thought Bel. They couldn't possibly recognise her because, although she had posed for the picture, the woman wasn't like her at all. Bel could see no resemblance between the woman she saw in the mirror when she did her hair and the angular female in the picture. She had said so at the party and that queer young man with the beard had told her it was a picture of her soul. She had not bothered about it at the time because she was too dazed with the noise and the heat to take it in properly, but now that she thought about it she found the idea distinctly unpleasant.

From where she was sitting she could not see 'Greenfingers'. There were so many pictures and they leapt at you from the walls, clamouring for attention. Some of them clamoured by reason of their colour — reds and yellows and blues and greens, so bright that they hurt your eyes — others by reason of the queer angles from which they had been painted. They seemed to be toppling out of their frames.

There was a very large picture just in front of where she was sitting; it depicted a table with a coarse white cloth and two jars of flowers. Bel liked the flowers, they were lovely, but the table was tilted so acutely that it looked as if the jars were about to slide off and upset onto the floor. The moment she saw it she felt an almost uncontrollable desire to leap up and avert the impending disaster. Of course this showed that the picture was extremely well painted, but what an unrestful picture to have! She tried to imagine it hanging upon the wall of her sitting-room and decided that she couldn't bear it. No, not even if it was given to her as a present.

Beside this picture there was one of a sea-green monster with a rock in the background and some tangled seaweed. There was something rather horrible about it — horrible but interesting. Bel was sufficiently interested to look it up in the catalogue and discovered that Number 21 was 'A Woman resting'. She wondered vaguely whether some woman had posed for it — as she herself had posed for 'Greenfingers' — and if so whether the woman had been pleased.

Bel felt rather depressed by her inability to understand the pictures . . . but it was no use sitting here glooming, she had got to go round and look at them as intelligently as she could, so she rose and began her survey.

4

There was a second room, through an archway, and there were only two people in it: a young girl in well-cut tweeds and a man with grey hair.

Their backs, which was all that Bel could see, were so alike that she immediately decided they were father and daughter. She was interested in them because they were different from the other people in the gallery ('Not artistic' as Bel put it to herself) but all the same they were going round in a conscientious manner, looking carefully at each picture and comparing it with the catalogue.

'Oh Daddy!' exclaimed the girl. 'Here's one that looks quite like a human being!'

This was said in a highly surprised tone and although she had not spoken loudly the girl's voice was perfectly distinct. It was also familiar . . . and when the girl turned towards her father and smiled Bel recognised her at once. It was Louise! Yes, quite definitely Louise Armstrong! They had been at school together. It was five years since she had seen Louise but there was no mistaking the beauty of her profile, the small nose, the dark curls and the charming smile. How strange to see Louise here!

They had not been close friends at school for Louise was two years younger which made a lot of difference when you were sixteen and eighteen, but now of course it made no difference at all. We're the same age, thought Bel vaguely as she went forward to speak to Louise.

'Goodness, it's Bel!' cried Louise. 'How amazing! You haven't changed a bit!'

'Neither have you! I knew you at once.'

'It seems ages!'

'Yes — ages.'

'But you're just the same.'

When they had finished assuring each other that they had not changed and exclaiming at the coincidence of their meeting Louise turned to her father.

'It's Bel Lamington, Daddy. We were at St. Elizabeth's together. Isn't it lovely meeting her like this?'

'Delightful,' he agreed, smiling and shaking hands.

He was very like Louise, thought Bel. The same shape of nose — though somewhat larger — and the same charming smile. Bel remembered that he was a doctor and that they lived somewhere near Oxford . . . she could not remember the name of the town.

Having chatted agreeably for a few minutes their attention returned to the picture on the wall and Bel saw that it was her picture — or more correctly Mark's picture — which Louise had pronounced to be 'quite like a human being'. Bel knew it well, of course, but somehow it looked different now that it had been framed and was hanging on a wall. The girl in the green overall was kneeling upon a stone-paved floor with a trowel in one hand and a seedling in the other. Before her was a stone trough filled with soil. The girl was thin and angular with a very long neck and windswept hair, she was bending over the trough absorbed in her work.

'Number thirty-five, 'Greenfingers' by Mark Desborough,' announced Louise, reading from the catalogue.

'Oh Daddy, it's Mark's picture!'

'I like it,' declared Dr. Armstrong. 'Yes, it's

49

interesting and unusual — much better than I expected. What a relief!'

'A relief?' asked Bel.

Louise laughed. She said, 'We came here to see Mark's picture and now that we've found it we needn't look at any more pictures. We can go and have tea. That's why Daddy is relieved.'

'Not only that,' said Dr. Armstrong. 'Tea will be welcome of course, but I shall be able to tell my nephew that I think his picture is interesting and unusual.'

'Daddy is a very truthful person,' explained Louise.

'How extraordinary!' Bel exclaimed in astonishment.

'Extraordinary to be truthful?' asked Dr. Armstrong smiling.

'No, of course not. Extraordinary that Mark is your nephew.'

'Do you mean you know Mark?'

Bel nodded. 'As a matter of fact Greenfingers is me.'

'Greenfingers is you? Do you mean you posed for the picture?'

'Yes,' said Bel.

Dr. Armstrong looked at the picture more carefully and then looked at Bel. 'I see no resemblance,' he declared.

'It isn't the least bit like you!' exclaimed Louise.

Bel was delighted to hear their verdict but she felt it her duty to explain. 'No, it isn't,' she agreed. 'But Mark didn't intend it to be like me. He said if I wanted a likeness I could go and

50

have my photograph taken.'

'But you posed for the picture?' asked Dr. Armstrong.

'Yes.'

'How very strange!'

'Let's go and have tea somewhere,' suggested Louise. 'We don't have to look at any more pictures and I'm longing for a cup of tea. Bel can come too, and we can talk.'

'That would be very pleasant indeed,' agreed Dr. Armstrong.

5

There was a tea-room quite near the Welcome Gallery and here the Armstrongs and Bel found a table and settled down.

'Now, tell us all about everything,' said Louise as she took off her gloves.

'That's rather a tall order,' said Bel smiling. As a matter of fact she was so unused to talking about herself that she found it difficult to begin. Besides, she was not sure that the Armstrongs really wanted to hear 'all about everything'. Why should they?

'Do you still live in Sussex with your aunt?'

'No, Aunt Beatrice died two years ago. I live in London.'

'What do you do?' asked Dr. Armstrong.

'Business,' replied Bel. 'I've got a post as secretary to Mr. Brownlee. He's a partner in Copping, Wills and Brownlee.'

'It's a very good firm.'

'I know. I was lucky to get it. Mr. Brownlee is very nice.'

'Where do you live?' Louise enquired.

'In a flat in Mellington Street.'

'But you've got a garden,' suggested Dr. Armstrong. He was thinking of the picture of Greenfingers.

'Not a proper garden,' Bel told him. She hesitated for a moment and then continued, 'I had to have something. I mean I missed the garden — frightfully. There was a flat roof outside the window of my sitting-room so I started with a few pot plants . . . '

When Bel had finished telling them about her garden — and a little about her life — she decided she had told them enough and it was her turn to ask questions.

'Oh we still live at Ernleigh,' said Louise. 'Daddy is the doctor of course so he's kept very busy looking after his patients and I'm kept very busy looking after him. We've lots of friends but they're mostly a good deal older than I am. I mean most of the girls have jobs of one sort or another.'

'You have a job,' said Dr. Armstrong.

'Oh yes,' she nodded. 'You're a whole-time job, darling. I just meant most of the girls go away from home. It's a pity, really. I mean it would be nice if I had more friends of my own age. Of course I've got lots to do so I'm perfectly happy, but still . . . '

'Perhaps Miss Lamington could come to us for a weekend,' suggested Dr. Armstrong.

'Oh — yes — lovely idea!' exclaimed Louise.

'Bel, you must. When can you come?'

Bel hesitated. People sometimes said this sort of thing without meaning it . . . and she was not sure whether she really wanted to go away just now. Perhaps Mark would not come any more now that the picture was finished — but perhaps he would.

'It's awfully kind of you,' said Bel. 'But — but I don't quite know. I mean — '

'Let's leave it,' Dr. Armstrong suggested. 'You could ring us up, couldn't you? Ring us up if you find you can come. Any time will suit us, won't it, Lou?'

'Any time means never,' said Louise in a disappointed voice.

It was obvious that the Armstrongs really meant it . . . which was nice of them, thought Bel.

5

He won't be there, said Bel to herself as she took the latch-key out of her handbag. Of course he won't be there. The picture is finished. There's no reason for him to come.

But no sooner had she opened the door than she smelt tobacco-smoke. Bel went to the window and peeped out . . . and there he was, sitting in the deck-chair with his long legs stretched out and his feet in the usual dirty tennis shoes propped upon the edge of the green tub.

As she opened the window he looked round and smiled.

'Hullo!' he said.

'I wasn't expecting you,' declared Bel a trifle breathlessly. 'I mean the picture is finished.'

'Pictures aren't everything.'

'I thought they were — to you.'

'They mean a lot but not quite everything. Did you go and see it?'

'Yes, of course. That's why I'm late.'

'How did it look?'

'Different,' said Bel thoughtfully. 'The frame makes it look more like a real picture — if you know what I mean.'

Mark roared with laughter.

'Oh Mark, I'm sorry!' exclaimed Bel. 'I didn't mean it like that at all. I only meant that I'm used to seeing pictures framed and hanging on walls.'

'Oh well, I'll forgive you this time. What about the other pictures? Did you see Edward's?'

'Edward's?'

'Yes, Edward Yates, that fellow you met at the party.'

Bel had met a great many people at the party (and knew none of their names) so she had no idea whether she had seen Edward's picture or not. She wondered if Edward Yates was the man with the beard who had said that 'Greenfingers' was a picture of her soul . . . but somehow it seemed safer not to pursue the subject.

'Oh, there were hundreds of pictures,' said Bel vaguely. 'I hadn't time to look at them all.'

'Which did you like best?'

This was easy. 'Greenfingers, of course.'

'Really?'

'Yes, really. It was much the best. The Armstrongs thought so too.'

'The Armstrongs?'

'Your uncle, Dr. Armstrong, and Louise,' explained Bel. 'I met them quite unexpectedly. You see Louise and I were at school together so I knew her at once . . . ' and she proceeded to tell Mark all about her meeting with the Armstrongs and about having tea with them and their invitation to visit them for a weekend whenever she could manage it. This was a much safer subject than pictures and, as she had already put her foot in it so stupidly, she dilated upon it as long as she could.

'Oh yes,' said Mark. 'I used to stay with them sometimes in the summer holidays. Uncle Jack is my mother's brother. As a matter of fact my grandfather Armstrong had an enormous family so I've got any amount of uncles and aunts and cousins. I don't know how many.'

Bel was singularly devoid of relations so she could not understand Mark's attitude of indifference. 'Don't you know them?' she asked incredulously.

'I know some of them. There's Aunt Margaret — she's married and has a huge family — and there's Uncle Jack and Louise — and there's Uncle Henry. He's quite a decent sort of uncle. I go and see him sometimes. He's a bachelor with lots of money. Sometimes he remembers my birthday and sometimes not. If he happens to remember he weighs in with a cheque. I hope he'll remember it this year,' added Mark with a sigh.

'Who else?' asked Bel.

'There's Harriet Fane.'

'You mean the actress?'

'Yes, she's a sort of cousin. Her father and my mother were first cousins. Of course she's not as young as she was — but she can act. She's in that play, 'Where the Gentian Blooms' — we might go and see it sometime. Harriet Fane's real name is Armstrong but her parents blew up when she went on the stage so she called herself Fane. She has several sisters; one of them is married to a farmer in Scotland. I went and stayed with them once. They were very decent to me but it was frightfully dull — miles from anywhere — not my idea of a holiday.'

'What's your idea of a holiday?' asked Bel, smiling.

'France or Italy — somewhere warm and cheerful,' Mark replied. 'As a matter of fact Edward Yates asked me to go to Florence. He's got a small flat in an old palace and he said he could put me up — but of course I can't. It takes money to go abroad and I haven't a bean. Well, never mind that. What about supper? Let's go out and have a meal.'

'We could have it here.'

'No, let's go out.' He rose and added, 'I shall have to change of course. I can't go out like this.'

Bel agreed that he couldn't. He was wearing the clothes which he kept for scrambling about the roofs and he looked dirty and disreputable.

'I'll change,' he said. 'I'll come down the stairs and fetch you. There's no need for glad rags — I'm not proposing to take you to the Savoy — we'll go to a little place in Soho where they give you very decent food. You'll like it.'

'Yes,' said Bel. 'I'm sure I shall. It will be fun.'

'I'll fetch you,' Mark repeated. 'It will take me about half-an-hour to clean myself up. Be ready, won't you?' He swung himself on to the stone-coping and disappeared.

Bel changed and was ready at the appointed time and they went out together. It was a delightful evening — Bel enjoyed it even more than she had expected.

2

On Sunday morning Bel went to church at eight o'clock. There was a church only ten minutes' walk from Mellington Street; she often went there. It was somewhat dark and not very well attended but there was something about it which appealed to Bel, and she liked the old white-haired vicar. She walked home slowly after the service; Sunday was a peaceful day to Bel, it was the only day upon which there was no need to hurry.

As she climbed the stairs she became aware of a thumping noise — a loud banging sort of noise — and when she got to the landing she saw that it was Mark knocking on the door of her flat.

'What are you doing?' she exclaimed.

He turned and looked at her. 'Bel! Where on earth have you been? I've been knocking on your door for ten minutes. I thought you were asleep.'

'I've been to church.'

'To church!' echoed Mark in amazement. 'What a funny girl you are! Here, give me the key, I'll open the door for you.'

He opened the door and followed her into the flat.

'Look here, Bel,' he said. 'I've got a car. Peter said I could have his car for the day. Where shall we go? Where would you like to go?'

'You mean today?' asked Bel. She felt slightly dazed for she was not a 'sudden' person. She had envisaged a quiet day doing various odd jobs for which she had no time during the week.

'Yes, of course, today,' replied Mark. 'We've only got the car for today. I thought we'd go to Brighton; you'd like that, wouldn't you? It's a cheerful sort of spot. Have you got anything to make sandwiches? We could take a flask of coffee

58

and have lunch on the beach — or on the pier if you'd rather. Sorry I can't run to a proper meal in a restaurant but funds are a bit low at the moment.'

By this time Bel had managed to readjust herself. She said, 'Yes, of course. We can easily take sandwiches — but why Brighton? It will be awfully crowded, won't it? Wouldn't it be nicer to go to a quiet place in the country?'

'Brighton will be more fun,' Mark declared. 'Hurry up, Bel, we haven't much time.'

Bel was taking off her gloves. She said, 'I can't be ready till eleven. I can't, really. I haven't had breakfast — or anything.'

'All right,' said Mark smiling. 'Don't look so worried. Eleven will do splendidly. Just as well, perhaps. It'll give me time to have a look at the car. It isn't a posh car,' he added. 'But it goes like smoke. That's the main thing.'

It was the first really fine Sunday of the year so the Brighton Road was uncomfortably crowded — cars were nose to tail all the way — and presently Mark grew tired of the endless procession and suggested they should turn into a side road where they could put on some speed. They turned at a sign-post which said LESSTON HAINES, climbed a steep hill and arrived on the edge of the Downs. Mark turned off the engine and they sat for a few minutes looking about.

'You were right,' said Mark. 'This is much nicer than Brighton.'

It really was lovely; quiet and peaceful. There was a little breeze ruffling through the grass, a fresh breeze, clean and invigorating. The sun was shining and a lark was singing high up in the blue sky. They decided to leave the car and take their lunch and walk up the hill to a little wood which they could see in the distance.

Bel was a country lover; she delighted in open spaces and loved walking over the hills. Mark was not particularly fond of this form of entertainment but today he enjoyed it. Perhaps it was partly because he was thoroughly fed-up with the noise and the petrol-fumes of the main road to Brighton and the frustration of driving an unknown and somewhat temperamental old car through the traffic; perhaps it was partly because he was pleased with the society of his companion. Who knows?

They walked up the hill together and presently arrived at the wood. The wood consisted of a few old oak-trees gnarled and twisted by the wind. They were beginning to bud and it was fascinating to see the tiny fresh green leaves appearing upon the ancient twigs. Up here the wind was chilly so Bell and Mark were glad to find shelter in a little quarry in which to sit and have their meal.

'It's nice to get away from town,' said Mark thoughtfully.

'I wouldn't like to live in the country — it would be deadly dull — but this is delightful. How I wish I had a car!'

'The country isn't really dull,' Bel told him. 'I lived in the country all my life until I came to London. All sorts of things happen. You know all your neighbours so you're never lonely.'

'Lonely!' exclaimed Mark in surprise. 'There's

no chance of being lonely in town. There are far too many people knocking about. Sometimes I wish I didn't know so many people; there would be more time for work. It's simply sickening when you're painting to have people battering at your door.'

'You needn't open your door.'

'No,' he agreed. 'But then it might be somebody I wanted to see. It might be you, for instance.'

'I don't batter at your door,' said Bel, smiling.

When they had finished lunch they walked on over the hill and saw the sea in the distance; it was very blue today and there were little white waves like frills all round the rocks. Far off there were several ships steaming up the channel.

'I wonder where they've come from,' Bel said.

'What? Oh, the ships?'

'Ships are terribly interesting. Ships are really my job.'

'I thought you just typed letters in an office.'

'Mostly about ships and their cargoes,' explained Bel. 'Sometimes I have to go down to Copping Wharf and I watch the ships come in. They come from Brazil and the Argentine — all sorts of places. It's the nicest part of my work.'

'I wonder,' said Mark thoughtfully. 'Perhaps I could go down to Copping Wharf one day. It might give me an idea for a picture. I suppose anyone can go.'

Bel did not think that 'anyone' would be allowed in, but she promised to ask Mr. Nelson, who was the manager of Copping Wharf, whether Mark might come and make some sketches.

6

It was nearly five o'clock when Bel and Mark got back to the car so they decided to leave the car where it was and walk on to Lesston Haines and have tea at the Inn. Lesston Haines was a very small village; it consisted of a few cottages with flowers in their gardens and an Inn set back from the road with a drive in front and a bench at the door. The Inn had been newly painted and was very clean and neat; there were tables laid with red-and-white check tea cloths and red-and-white cups and saucers. Mark and Bel found a table near the window and ordered tea from an elderly woman in a clean white apron.

'Quite a decent little place,' said Mark looking round.

Bel agreed.

There was nobody else in the room and she could not help wondering how the proprietors managed to make enough money to live on in such an out-of-the-way place. She was too shy to ask the woman but Mark was not shy and the woman seemed pleasant and friendly. In answer to Mark's questions she told them that she was Mrs. Poulson and that she and her husband had bought the Inn recently and had it all done up. It certainly was very isolated, agreed Mrs. Poulson, but quite a number of people came to lunch or tea on a Sunday and they were hoping more would come during the summer months.

Sometimes people stayed the night — but not often. There was a bar round at the side of the house and a skittle-alley. When asked by Mark whether it was not very dull and lonely Mrs. Poulson sighed and admitted that it was.

Bel and Mark were hungry after their walk and enjoyed the buns and jam and the gingerbread which was homemade and really excellent.

After tea Mark went off to get the car and Bel waited for him sitting by the window. She waited for a long time and at last she went out and gazed down the road. It was only five minutes' walk to where they had left the car so she could not understand why he was taking so long. She had just made up her mind to go and see what had happened when she saw Mark walking towards her up the road.

'What's happened?' she exclaimed.

'1 can't get the blinking thing to start.'

'You can't get it to start?'

'No. I don't know what on earth is the matter with it.'

'Mark!'

'Nuisance, isn't it? Gosh I'm hot,' he added. 'I've been cranking it for about half-an-hour.' He threw himself down on the bench at the door and wiped his forehead.

'What are we to do!' cried Bel in consternation.

'I shall have to get hold of a mechanic,' said Mark wearily. 'There must be a garage somewhere about.'

'We'll ask Mrs. Poulson,' said Bel.

It soon became evident that Lesston Haines was one of the worst places in England to get marooned. There was no telephone in the village and the nearest garage was five miles away. Mrs. Poulson was doubtful whether it would be open on a Sunday — it might, of course, but then again it might not. Mr. Poulson was consulted and gave it as his considered opinion that George Stock's garage would be shut. George Stock, being a Methodist, was very particular about Sundays.

'But perhaps he would come,' suggested Mark. 'If I could borrow a bicycle I could — '

'He wouldn't come,' declared Mr. Poulson. 'I told you he's very particular about Sundays. He doesn't hold with all this rushing about in cars. You'd get short shrift from old George Stock if you was to knock him up on a Sunday.'

'What are we to do!' cried Bel.

'I'll come and have a look at the car myself,' suggested Mr. Poulson.

Mark and Mr. Poulson went off down the road together and Bel was left once more to her own devices. She went into the lounge and sat down. Somehow she had little faith in Mr. Poulson; she did not like him. She did not like his ferrety face and his large sticking-out ears. Mrs. Poulson was nice, but there was something rather horrid about Mr. Poulson. Bel felt cold and shivery and miserable. The inn, which had seemed so pleasant, was pleasant no longer. Bel's one hope was to get away from it — but how? That was the question.

The two men were away for a long time — or

so it seemed to Bel — but at last when she had begun to get quite desperate they returned.

'It's no good,' said Mark, coming into the lounge where Bel was sitting. 'Poulson knows quite a lot about cars and he says it's hopeless. The battery is as flat as a pancake, there must be a short in one of the leads.'

This verdict was quite unintelligible to Bel. She said, 'Mark, are you sure? Isn't there anyone in the village who knows about cars? Couldn't you try — '

'It's frightfully cold and it's beginning to rain.'

This was true, as Bel could see for herself. The wind had risen and was driving the rain against the windows. By this time it was beginning to get dark, which did not help matters.

'It's hopeless — honestly,' declared Mark. 'I'm sorry, Bel, but it's not my fault, you know.'

'But what are we to do!'

'We'll have to stay here for the night.'

'That's right,' agreed Mr. Poulson who had followed Mark into the room. 'We'll give you a nice little supper and you can stay the night. I'll send the boy over to George Stock first thing in the morning.'

'Stay the night!' cried Bel. 'Oh no, we can't do that!'

'There's nothing else for it,' said Mark.

'I can't!' cried Bel. 'I've got to be at the office at nine tomorrow morning! Besides — '

'It's all right,' Mark told her. 'No need to panic. We'll ring up the office in the morning and explain what's happened.'

'Mark, I can't! I must get home!'

'How can you?'

'I could walk, couldn't I? There must be a station somewhere. I could get a train. Or perhaps I could walk down to the main road and get a bus. I must get home somehow!' cried Bel in desperation. 'Surely there's some way — '

'Bel, darling, don't panic,' said Mark in reasoning tones. 'Anyone would think something frightful had happened if they could see your face. Nothing frightful has happened. It will be rather fun to stay here for the night. The Poulsons can give us two nice rooms — '

'That we can,' agreed Mr. Poulson rubbing his hands. 'Two nice rooms there is. Mrs. Poulson will get them ready in a minute — and the beds aired. We'll light the fire and give you a nice little supper.'

'No, I can't,' declared Bel. 'No, really. I must go home.'

'You can't go home,' said Mark somewhat impatiently. 'It would mean walking for hours in the dark. Look at the rain! It's pouring now. Do be sensible, Bel.'

Bel tried to be sensible but she was frightened. She did not want to spend the night at Lesston Haines. She wanted to go home. There was something quite unreasoning about her desire to go home.

It was at this moment that Mrs. Poulson appeared and said doubtfully, 'There's Mr. Darley, of course.'

'Mr. Darley!' exclaimed Bel, clutching at a straw. 'Who is Mr. Darley?'

'He's just come in for a bit of supper,' Mrs. Poulson replied.

'That's no good,' declared Mr. Poulson angrily. 'You could never send the young lady with Mr. Darley. Where's your wits, Annie?'

'I just thought — '

'You go and get the rooms ready and don't talk nonsense.'

'Has Mr. Darley got a car?' asked Bel.

Mrs. Poulson nodded.

'Bel, don't be silly!' exclaimed Mark. 'Just make up your mind to stay here for the night.'

'That's right,' put in Mr. Poulson.

'You can't go off in a car with a strange man,' added Mark.

'He wouldn't take you,' said Mr. Poulson.

'I could ask him,' said Bel.

'Ask him!' echoed Mark in dismay. 'You can't possibly go off by yourself with a stranger. I can't come with you because I shall have to stay here and see about the car. It's Peter's car and I can't just abandon it.'

'No, of course not,' agreed Bel. 'You must stay here and I'll go home — if that man will take me.'

'Do be sensible!' Mark exclaimed. 'Bel, listen. It will be fun to stay here and have supper together. It will, really.'

'I'd rather — go home,' said Bel with a little catch in her breath.

3

By this time Bel was so desperate that she found it quite easy to walk into the dining-room and accost a total stranger. Mr. Darley was the only

67

person in the room; he was sitting at a table in the corner having his supper — as Mrs. Poulson had said. He was quite young and good-looking, with dark hair and brown eyes; he was dressed in a lounge suit and a white shirt with a green tie. His socks also were green. His shoes were brown. Bel noticed these details as she approached him.

'Mr. Darley,' said Bel breathlessly. 'Do you think you could possibly give me a lift. Our car has broken down.'

He looked up at her and smiled. 'Where do you want to go?'

'Anywhere,' said Bel. 'I mean I want to get a train or a bus back to London. Any station would do.'

'What's the matter with London?' said Mr. Darley. 'That's where I'm going when I've had my supper.'

'Do you mean you would take me?'

'For better for worse,' said Mr. Darley cheerfully.

When Mark heard that the matter had been arranged so simply, and without the slightest difficulty, he was very much annoyed. Mr. Poulton was annoyed too, for he had hoped to let his rooms. Of course Mr. Poulton's feelings did not matter but Mark's feelings mattered a good deal. Fortunately Bel had time to soothe him down while Mr. Darley was finishing his supper; she assured Mark that she would have liked to stay but it was absolutely essential that she should be at the office at nine the following morning. Mark received the impression that Mr.

Brownlee was an absolute tartar and that Bel was terrified of him — it was an erroneous impression but that could not be helped.

'Oh well, if you're determined to go I can't stop you,' said Mark with a sigh. 'I quite see you can't risk losing your job.'

'You understand, don't you?'

'Yes,' said Mark. He sighed again and added, 'If only we had gone to Brighton, as I suggested, this would never have happened. There are hundreds of garages in Brighton.'

'I know,' agreed Bel. She had no intention of reminding Mark that it was he who had become weary of the endless procession of cars on the Brighton Road and had suggested they should turn up the side road to Lesston Haines. 'I know,' repeated Bel. 'If we had gone to Brighton I could easily have got a train back to London, couldn't I?'

'There would have been no need. Any garage could have found the short and given us a new battery in twenty minutes.'

'You aren't angry with me, are you?'

'No, of course not — but I'm awfully worried. You'll be careful, won't you, Bel?'

'Careful?' asked Bel in surprise.

'We don't know anything about the fellow,' Mark explained. 'Poulson seems to think he's a bounder.'

'Oh he isn't really!' exclaimed Bel.

'You wouldn't know if he was,' said Mark with unusual perspicacity. 'You wouldn't know until he began to bound and then it would be too late. I shan't be happy until I know you're all right.

I'll look in tomorrow at the usual time and see you.'

'Yes do,' said Bel. 'Come to supper and then you can tell me all that has happened about the car.'

Mr. Darley's car was very different from Peter's aged vehicle. It was a two-seater Sunbeam, long and low, with an adjustable hood. Its lights blazed ahead cutting through the darkness like swords. Mark who had come to the door to see the travellers start was moved to admiration. It was exactly the sort of car he would have liked to possess.

'Yes, she's not a bad little bus,' said her owner complacently. 'I've had her ticking along at a hundred but of course there's no chance of that tonight with all that beastly traffic. We'll go now if you're ready, Miss Lamington.'

Miss Lamington was ready.

4

Afterwards when Bel thought about it calmly she could not understand why she had been so desperately anxious to get away from the inn at Lesston Haines. She had told Mark that she wanted to be at the office at nine the following morning; this was true, of course, but there was more in it than that. She had actually been frightened. Why she had been frightened she did not know. It was really very strange.

The drive to London was uneventful. Mr.

Darley did not talk much and showed no signs whatever of bounderism — if there be such a word. He was intent on driving his car. If Bel had not been so taken up with her own thoughts she might have been considerably alarmed for Mr. Darley was the type of driver whose sole object is to get from one place to another in the least possible time regardless of the other traffic on the road. A vehicle in front was a vehicle to be overtaken and passed — no matter where. Mr. Darley gritted his teeth and passed it. He squeezed between buses with scarcely an inch to spare; he overshot traffic lights whenever there was the slightest opportunity. In fact he committed every offence against the good manners recommended to road-users by the Highway Code. Mr. Darley's progress was pursued by curses from his fellow motorists but the curses never seemed to catch him up and blight him — or at least they did not catch him up that Sunday evening. Bel was deposited scatheless at her door.

'That's all right,' said Mr. Darley in answer to her expressions of gratitude. 'I'm always glad to help a lady in distress. There aren't many people who could have got you here in less time.'

'Nobody could,' declared Bel enthusiastically. 'It's been marvellous. Thank you very, very much.'

'Not frightened, were you?'

'Not a bit.'

'Good,' said Mr. Darley. 'I drive pretty fast of course but I'm a very good driver. I'll take you for a spin some other day. We could have a go at

7

The next evening was wet and Mark did not come. Bel had expected him to come for he had said quite definitely that he wanted to see her and make sure she was all right. She had laid on a very special supper to please him and to make up for the way she had abandoned him at Lesston Haines, so it was disappointing when her guest did not turn up as arranged. She realised that he could not have climbed down over the roofs in their present condition, slippery with rain — it would have been dangerous — so perhaps that was the reason for his absence. Something inside her kept on hinting that if Mark had really wanted to see her he could have come by the stairs but she refused to listen to the Something.

It was fine and dry on Tuesday. Bel hurried home expecting to find Mark in her roof-garden but he was not there. He did not come on Wednesday either.

By this time Bel felt quite desperate. All sorts of horrible ideas occurred to her: perhaps he was ill; perhaps he had fallen off the roof and been taken to hospital. Something must have happened, she was sure. She decided that she could not bear the suspense a moment longer, she must go and see what was the matter with Mark.

Having made up her mind Bel did not delay. She knew where to go of course for she had been to his studio on the night of the party; it was right at the top of the house in number 23.

Bel was quite breathless when she had toiled up the five flights of stairs so she stood on the landing until she had recovered.

There was no noise today. It was very quiet indeed. She began to wonder if she should have come. She remembered Mark saying that he wished people wouldn't batter on his door. Perhaps she should go home. She could go now; there was nothing to prevent her. Mark would never know she had come.

Bel turned away and began to go down the stairs — and then she paused. Supposing Mark were ill! Supposing he was lying there ill, with nobody to look after him! This was Bel's own special nightmare so she could not brush it aside. No, thought Bel. No, I can't go home. I simply must see him and make sure he's all right.

The bell was broken, it was hanging limply from its socket, so she was obliged to knock on the door. She knocked and waited but there was no reply. She knocked again more loudly; she knocked several times, but there was no sound at all. Bel was just about to turn away when she heard footsteps from inside the flat and the door opened.

There was Mark!

'Bel!' he exclaimed. 'I didn't know it was you. I thought it was one of the gang and of course I didn't want them to see it until it was finished — but you don't matter.'

'I just came to see — '

74

'Come in, Bel. Come in.'

'I thought you must be ill.'

'Ill? Why on earth did you think that? I'm never ill.'

'I just thought — '

'Well, never mind,' he said. 'I'm glad you've come. I want you to be the first person to see it. Of course you won't like it,' he continued, seizing her by the hand and dragging her in and shutting the door with a bang. 'It's just an idea. It came to me suddenly. I don't know whether it's any good or not. It's an idea,' he repeated. 'You don't understand that, do you?'

The studio looked different today, it was bare and austere, light from the north window and the sloping skylight filled the room with light and shadow. Mark pulled the big wooden settle out of the corner and motioned her to sit down, then he lifted a canvas and put it before her on an easel.

'There,' said Mark.

For a moment or two there was silence. Bel was dazzled, almost horrified, by the splashes of brilliant colour. She did not know what to say. Then gradually as she gazed the colours seemed to take shape and she realised that the medley of greens and purples and pinks which filled the foreground were bushes — bushes of rhododendrons, perhaps. In the background there were slender grey columns stretching up into a bright blue sky.

'Oh Mark! Yes. It means something!' she exclaimed.

'Of course it means something.'

'Mark — I don't know. It's rather — rather frightening.'

Apparently she had said the right thing or at least something not too horribly wrong.

'Frightening!' he exclaimed, laughing in an excited sort of way. 'What a dear funny little mouse you are! Why does it frighten you?'

'I don't know. It's fierce and — and powerful. Tell me what it means.'

He was pleased, that was obvious. He began to tell her about his picture, about the composition of the masses and the planes of light.

Presently she said, 'It's no use, Mark. I don't understand a word you're saying. I just see what I see, but I'm quite sure it's good.'

'You're quite sure it's good?'

She nodded, 'Quite certain. It opens windows in my mind. It wouldn't do that to me if it wasn't good.'

'Bel!'

'It's magic,' said Bel seriously.

'What do you mean?'

She thought for a few moments and then said, 'You take a piece of canvas and some paint and you make something exciting. Isn't that magic?'

'You darling!' cried Mark. He sat down beside her on the settle and put his arm round her. For a moment she resisted and then she could not resist any longer. She laid her head against his shoulder. He kissed her gently on the cheek.

'Oh Mark!'

'Darling little mouse! There's nobody like you — nobody so sweet. Adorable little mouse!'

76

He kissed her again. It was a different kind of kiss this time and it alarmed her.

She disengaged herself from his embrace and stood up.

'I must go home,' she said breathlessly.

'Nonsense, you've just come. Why must you go home?'

'I've got things to do. I just came in for a minute to — to see if you were all right. You understand, don't you? I just — just came for a minute — '

Mark was silent. She looked at him in surprise and saw that he was not listening; he was gazing at his picture with half-closed eyes. He said, 'It needs something to balance that mass of purple — '

'I'll see you tomorrow of course,' said Bel.

'Tomorrow?'

'It's your birthday,' she reminded him.

'Oh yes, so it is,' said Mark. He rose and picked up his palette and began mixing paints.

'I must go now,' repeated Bel.

'Well, if you must, darling. It was sweet of you to come,' said Mark vaguely.

Bel watched him for a few minutes and then turned and went away, shutting the door very softly behind her.

It was not until she was half-way down the stairs that she suddenly remembered that there had been no mention of the adventure on Sunday. Mark had made no enquiries about Mr. Darley, nor had he asked if she had got home safely . . . but of course he was too busy thinking about his picture, and of course he could see, without asking, that she was perfectly safe and well.

Bel had not asked about the car, nor what sort of a night Mark had spent at Lesston Haines. She must remember to ask all about that tomorrow.

2

The next day was Thursday, Mark's birthday! Bel had knitted two pairs of socks for him (his socks were in a deplorable condition). She had managed to complete the socks the night before, on her return from her visit to the studio, and had done them up in a parcel with a birthday-card and left them on the top of her bookcase. She was looking forward to giving them to him; he would be pleased with them she was sure — pleased and surprised.

They had arranged to celebrate Mark's birthday by going out to dinner together but Bel had a feeling that he might have forgotten all about it. She realised that it depended upon whether or not the picture was finished . . . she was so doubtful about it that she was quite surprised when she found him waiting for her in the little roof-garden.

'Hullo!' she exclaimed, opening the window. 'Hullo, Mark! Many happy returns of the day!'

'Bel!' he cried, leaping to his feet. 'I've been waiting for ages! I thought you would never come! Marvellous news! You'll never guess! Somebody has bought the picture! Greenfingers,

I mean. Twenty-five quid! Can you beat it?'

'Oh Mark, how splendid!'

'Gosh, I'm walking on air! Greenfingers — sold! And, as if that wasn't enough, Uncle Henry has remembered my birthday. It never rains but it pours! Isn't it wonderful?'

'Wonderful!' agreed Bel.

'I feel like a millionaire,' declared Mark, laughing excitedly. 'It's a gorgeous feeling — absolutely gorgeous. I could jump over the moon.'

'We're going out, aren't we?' asked Bel. 'I mean we decided to celebrate — '

'Not tonight. I've got an awful lot to do. I just dropped in to tell you about it, that's all.'

'But you'd like supper, wouldn't you? We could have it here if you'd rather.'

'No time,' declared Mark. 'As a matter of fact I'm not a bit hungry — too excited. I've been terribly busy all day — writing letters and making plans. I'm off to Florence on Tuesday.'

'Off to Florence?'

'Yes, I told you, didn't I? Edward Yates has a flat in Florence. Marvellous!' cried Mark. 'Think of it, Bel! Think of the sunshine and the flowers and the blue, blue sky! Goodbye to dirty old London!'

'How long will you be away?'

'Oh, I don't know — haven't thought about it. Edward said I could stay as long as I liked. You can bet your boots I'll stay as long as I can — which means as long as the money holds out. I could paint a few pot-boilers which would help. Of course I shall do some serious painting as well. Edward has a studio in his flat. I've cabled to Edward, but it's sure to be all right. I could see from what he said that he really wanted me to go. I'm not worrying about that.'

'What about your studio?'

'All fixed,' said Mark laughing. 'I told you I'd been busy, didn't I? There's a chap here who's only too willing to take it off my hands. He's moving in on Tuesday . . . '

Mark went on talking excitedly and Bel listened. He was leaving London; he was giving up his studio. She would never see him again.

She realised with a sinking heart that she meant nothing to him — absolutely nothing. He had no regrets; he did not even pretend to regret that he was leaving for an indefinite period — perhaps for ever. If he had said one word — if he had evinced the slightest sign of regret at the prospect of parting from her she would not have minded . . . or at least she would not have minded so much. He was not thinking of her at all. That was obvious. He was all eagerness to go, and to go as soon as possible, and to stay away as long as he could. He was going away. She would never see him again. It was all over.

By this time Bel had climbed out of the window and they were both in the little roof-garden. She turned and leant upon the wall. She did not want to show him her face. It was the sort of face that expressed its owner's feelings much too openly. If Bel were happy, if she were sad, if she received a sudden shock it was written in her face for all the world to see. She had often wished for a 'poker face' but never more than now. A wooden face, thought Bel, miserably. One of those inexpressive faces which do not blush nor pale nor suddenly become a mask of tragedy!

Fortunately she could control her voice more easily so she was able to say the right things.

'Marvellous,' agreed Bel. 'No wonder you're excited. It will be lovely for you, Mark.'

He went on talking about his plans. He would break his journey in Paris; he had a friend there who could put him up. He might spend a couple of nights in Paris — or perhaps longer. Paris would be rather fun.

Bel could scarcely bear it. She wished with all her heart that he would stop talking and go away. Would he never go away, she wondered.

At last, she said, 'I expect you've got a lot to do, haven't you?'

'Yes,' he agreed. 'Yes, I must go. Look here, Bel, what about tomorrow night? We could do a play or something.'

'I can't,' she told him.

'Well then, what about Saturday night? That would be better, really. We could go to — '

'I can't,' repeated Bel.

'You can't?' asked Mark in amazement. 'Why can't you?'

'I'm going away for the weekend.'

'You're going away?'

'Yes.'

'Where are you going?'

'To the Armstrongs,' replied Bel. The idea had come to her suddenly. They had said they could have her 'any time.'

'Oh, the Armstrongs? That doesn't matter,' said Mark cheerfully. 'You can put them off. They won't mind.'

'I don't want to put them off.'

'But I'm going on Tuesday!'

'I know. You said so.'

'Well, don't you understand? I'm booked to leave on Tuesday morning, so this is our only chance for a final bust. We'll go to a play together and have supper afterwards. It will be fun.'

'I can't.'

'Bel, don't be silly. We can easily ring up the Armstrongs and explain. You can go to them any time, can't you?'

'I want to go. It will be lovely to have a weekend in the country.'

Mark was silent for a moment and then he said, 'Really Bel, you're most extraordinary! I thought we were pals. I thought you would give me a hand with my packing — and all that. There's no earthly need for you to dash off to the wilds of Gloucestershire *now* — just when I'm going away.'

He was so surprised and reproachful, so blatantly selfish, that Bel was forced to laugh. It was not a very cheerful laugh but somehow it raised her morale.

'What are you laughing at?' Mark wanted to know.

'You,' replied Bel with spirit.

'Me?'

'Yes, you seem to think you can always have everything your own way.'

'What on earth has come over you!'

'Nothing has come over me.'

'Then why are you so queer? Why won't you come out with me tomorrow night?'

'Because I'm going to the Armstrongs.'

Bel felt a qualm as she said it. Supposing they couldn't have her? They had said 'any time' but had they really meant it? Something unforeseen might have happened! But if the Armstrongs couldn't have her she must go somewhere else. She must take a room in a hotel. It would cost money which she could ill afford but that couldn't be helped. She couldn't stay here — not possibly — she simply couldn't bear it. She couldn't go out with Mark for 'a final bust'; she certainly wasn't going to help him with his packing.

3

It was not until Mark had gone — angry and resentful — that the misery rose and swamped her. He had gone. She would never see him again. Bel had not realised how much he meant to her; how much she had depended upon him; how much she had looked forward to his visits. She realised it now. He had walked right into her life and stolen her heart. A lonely heart is easily stolen.

Pride had helped her to disguise her feelings but now that there was no more need for pretence she sat down in the armchair by the window and hid her face in her hands. Tears

83

trickled between her fingers, tears of grief and shame.

What a fool she had been! She had listened to him and believed all he said. All the things he had said went round and round in her mind — all the things he had said! He had said, 'You're my sort of person. You're a darling'. He had called her an 'adorable little mouse'. He had whispered, 'there's nobody like you — nobody so sweet'. But it all meant nothing (probably he said the same sort of things to every girl he met; most likely he had said the same sort of things to Enid).

What a fool she had been! She had let him put his arm round her shoulders; she had let him kiss her — not once but several times! Oh, what a fool! thought Bel, her face burning with shame at the recollection.

Presently she heard the clock strike — the big clock on the church-tower. She counted the strokes — nine of them! Nine o'clock! She had no idea it was so late! If she were going to ring up Louise there was no time to be lost . . . and of course she must ring up Louise tonight. She must do it immediately.

There were other things to be done if she were going away tomorrow. She must press her grey-flannel suit and wash a couple of nylon blouses. It was ridiculous to sit here and moan!

Bel managed to calm herself; she sponged her face in cold water; she took her purse and ran downstairs to the telephone-box which stood in the hall.

It took some time to put the call through but

84

at last she managed to get the number she wanted.

Louise answered the phone. Her pretty light voice came over the wire quite clearly. 'This is Dr. Armstrong's house.'

'Louise,' said Bel breathlessly. 'Louise, this is Bel — Bel Lamington. You said I was to ring you up if I could come.'

'Yes, of course. When can you come?'

'Tomorrow — if that's any good. I could come after I've finished work at the office.'

'Bel! How lovely!'

'Are you sure it's all right?'

'It's perfect. There's a train at 6.20. Could you manage that?'

'Yes,' said Bel. 'Yes, I could. Are you sure it's all right?'

'Of course I'm sure. It will be lovely to have you. How long can you stay?'

'Just until Monday.'

'Oh, nonsense! You must stay at least a week.'

'I can't — really. I shall have to be back at the office on Monday morning.'

'Tell your boss you must have a holiday.'

Bel laughed — she could not help it. She imagined herself saying to Mr. Brownlee that she 'must have a holiday'. Of course Louise did not understand. Louise was safe. Louise did not know what it was like to lie awake at night — hour after hour — and think about what might happen if she lost her job for some reason or other — if she were ill, for instance.

'Bel, you must,' declared Louise. 'You can't go back to London on Monday. It's ridiculous.'

85

'I might get an extra day,' said Bel doubtfully. 'I'll ask Mr. Brownlee and see what he thinks about it.'

'Yes, do. Stay as long as you can. There's a dance at the Golf Club so be sure to bring a party frock.'

'I haven't got one.'

'You can wear one of mine.'

'But Louise — '

'Don't be silly,' said Louise's laughing voice. 'Of course you must come to the dance and of course you can wear my frock. If it doesn't fit we can alter it — see?'

There was no time to say more — the pips sounded and the connection was cut — but it did not matter. All that was necessary had been said.

As Bel climbed the stairs she decided that it would be a very good plan to ask Mr. Brownlee for an extra day. If she could have Monday off and return on Tuesday Mark would have gone. He had gone already as far as Bel was concerned — she faced that thought — so it would be better if she did not see him again.

Part Two

8

The Armstrongs' house was in the middle of the town; the door with the doctor's plate upon it opened on to the main street but there was a pleasant garden behind the house which sloped down to a slow-moving stream. Bel's room looked out into the garden and when she had unpacked and changed she leaned out of the window and saw the trees and listened to the singing of the birds. How lovely it was! How fresh and green! Already Bel felt more peaceful and less tangled up in her mind.

Presently Louise came and joined her.

'This is perfect,' said Louise. 'We're going to have fun together, we're going to talk and talk.'

There certainly was a great deal to talk about. There was school for instance. Bel remembered Louise standing up at the School Concert and reciting 'The Wreck of the Hesperus'.

'Oh no!' cried Louise, giggling. 'What a horrible thing to remember! Such a stupid poem, isn't it? I wonder why they made us learn such rubbish. There are lots of lovely poems we could have learnt.'

'Do you remember it?'

'Of course I do! That's what's so silly. It's such a waste remembering things like that. It does you no good and clutters up your brain. I can remember feeling frightfully embarrassed when I came to the bit about the skipper's daughter:

'Her bosom white as the hawthorn buds that ope in the month of May'. It's a private sort of word, isn't it? And how did they know what the wretched girl's bosom was like? She ought to have worn more clothes.'

Bel laughed quite heartily. It was impossible to be miserable when Louise was anywhere about.

Like all doctors' houses it was busy. The telephone rang constantly. The doctor went on his rounds and in the afternoons and evenings he saw patients in his surgery. Louise ran the house, answered the telephone and made notes of her father's appointments. It was surprising to find that Louise was so capable for Bel had always thought her a butterfly — she had seemed a butterfly at school — but Bel had a theory that people don't change, they merely develop. Who would think that the lovely fragile blossom upon an apple-tree would develop into apples? It was almost incredible when you thought about it — but so it was. The germ of the apple was there from the very beginning . . . and the same with Louise who had been fragile fairy-like blossom and was now sound fruit, sweet and juicy.

Bel soon discovered that Louise not only ran the house (and did so efficiently with a couple of dailies) but also managed the doctor. Louise decided things and usually got her own way. For instance it was Louise who decided that the doctor must have a new suit.

'Good gracious, no!' exclaimed Dr. Armstrong.

'Yes, honestly, darling,' said Louise. 'It's awfully important for you to look nice; it gives the patients a fillip if a nice smart doctor walks into their bedrooms. They feel better at once. I'll get some patterns from Walker.'

'I could get a ready-made. It would save a lot of trouble.'

'But it wouldn't look so nice, darling. I'll fix it,' she added. 'It won't be any bother at all. Leave it to me.'

That was at breakfast on Saturday morning and when the two girls went out together to do the necessary shopping they called in at the tailor's and chose a pattern and ordered the doctor's new suit.

Lunch was at one o'clock — and how delightful it was to sit down to a well-appointed table and eat food that one had not cooked oneself! Bel had almost forgotten the pleasure of graceful living. She revelled in it, she felt like a different person. She was enjoying herself so much that she was quite surprised when Louise reminded her about the dance.

'The dance?' she asked.

'Yes, I told you about it,' said her hostess. 'It's on Monday night at the Golf Club, so you'll be here for it all right. I've got a pink frock which I think will suit you splendidly. We're pretty much the same size.'

'Miss Lamington is thinner than you,' said Dr. Armstrong.

'Oh, we can take it in a bit,' replied Louise. She added, 'Don't forget you've got to come, Daddy.'

'If I can — ' he began doubtfully.

'Of course you can,' Louise told him. 'Joan promised me faithfully not to have her baby on Monday night.'

The doctor smiled, but not very cheerfully. 'I wish Joan's baby was safely here,' he said.

'Poor darling, he worries so frightfully,' explained Louise when he had gone. 'And of course Joan is rather a special friend, I like her awfully much and so does Daddy. They've been married for years and years and this is their first baby, so I hope to goodness nothing will go wrong.'

'What could go wrong?' enquired Bel, who was abysmally ignorant of such matters.

'Oh, lots of things,' replied the doctor's daughter. 'You never know with babies. Sometimes they arrive upside down or back to front — all sorts of things can happen. Of course I've known about babies all my life — ever since I was quite little. Daddy says I was an *enfant terrible* — most embarrassing!' She giggled attractively and continued, 'There was one awful day when Miss Everton came to tea. She was one of Daddy's patients, a spinster of 'uncertain age' and enormously fat. I asked her in a piercing treble if she was going to have twins! I didn't mean any harm — I just wanted to know — but it caused a frightful rumpus and Daddy lost his patient.'

'You don't mean she died!' exclaimed Bel in horrified tones.

'Worse,' declared Louise, laughing wickedly. 'She went to Dr. Slope.'

2

It was such a lovely afternoon that they decided to have tea in the garden.

'Daddy will be here soon,' said Louise. 'We'll wait for him. Meantime I ought to plant out some seedlings.'

'I'll do it,' suggested Bel.

'Goodness, no! You're supposed to be having a holiday.'

'I'd like to do it, Louise.'

'You must sit down and rest. Here's a new copy of *The Illustrated London News*.'

They were arguing about it when the telephone bell rang.

'Oh, bother!' Louise exclaimed. 'It's been worse than usual today — just when I wanted a little peace to talk to you. It's probably old Mr. Corner having hysteria or something — he's more trouble than all the other patients put together — but I shall have to answer it. You never know . . . '

The telephone call proved unimportant; none of the doctor's patients was bleeding to death nor writhing in pain, and as the doctor had returned from his rounds by this time he helped his daughter to make tea. They came out of the house together bringing the tea-things and discovered their visitor on her knees, planting out antirrhinum seedlings. She was so engrossed in this delightful occupation that she was unaware of their approach.

'Oh, how naughty of her!' exclaimed Louise. 'I told her not to — '

'Leave her alone,' said Dr. Armstrong, laying a restraining hand on his daughter's shoulder.

'But Daddy, you said she ought to rest!'

'She's happy. When people are happy you should leave them alone.' He hesitated and then added, 'That's how Mark saw her. His picture is clever — even more clever than I thought.'

'It isn't a bit like her. You said so yourself.'

'Not like her — no, but all the same — '

'You mean it's her Thing.'

'Yes, obviously it's her Thing — as you call it,' said the doctor with a smile.

'Well, what would you call it?' Louise enquired.

She did not wait for a reply (which was just as well because the doctor had no idea how to translate the word into correct English) but went forward with the teapot in her hand. As a matter of fact she was doubtful what to do. Obviously her father was right — Bel was completely happy in her self appointed task — but tea was ready and unless Bel could be induced to come and drink it while it was fresh and hot the brew would become undrinkable. Stewed tea was nasty — and unwholesome.

Fortunately the problem solved itself for at this very moment Bel looked up.

'Tea!' cried Louise, waving the teapot.

'I'll just finish — '

'No, come now.'

The job was only half done, but after some persuasion Bel consented to leave it on condition that she should be allowed to complete it later. The compromise satisfied everyone concerned and the meal was consumed to the accompaniment of pleasant conversation.

Afterwards, when Louise had gone indoors to wash up the dishes, Bel returned to her labour of love and Dr. Armstrong sat in a deck-chair and read the paper. As usual the paper was full of horrors, which distressed the good doctor considerably, and presently he put it down and strolled over to talk to his guest.

'You like doing that,' said Dr. Armstrong.

'I love it,' she replied. 'I'm not really a town-person, you see. I love gardens and trees and all sorts of country things. London is very tiring.'

'Couldn't you find some other job — somewhere else?'

She sat back on her heels and looked up at him. 'It's a good job,' she said. 'I couldn't give it up unless I could be sure of finding another. It would be — dangerous.'

Dr. Armstrong was startled when he saw her face. He remembered that she was only two years older than his daughter but she looked worn and sad — and afraid. He knew fear when he saw it. Sometimes he saw it in the eyes of his patients.

'You haven't been sleeping well,' he suggested.

'Not — very well.'

'You need a holiday.'

'I'm all right,' she told him. 'Just a little tired and — and rather silly. Lots of girls have to work for their living, don't they? I mean they have to depend upon themselves. Perhaps I was too sheltered when I was young. Aunt Beatrice was like a rock. We weren't very well-off but everything was all right as long as she was there.'

'You need a holiday,' he repeated. 'If I were your doctor I should insist upon it. That feeling of insecurity is a physical thing. It's because you're tired, Bel. You don't mind me calling you Bel, do you?'

'I like it,' she said, smiling up at him. 'It's awfully kind of you to — to talk to me like this. I expect you're right. I expect I ought to get away for a bit, but it's impossible just now. Mr. Brownlee is going to South America and he wants me to stay at the office until he comes back.'

'You'll get a holiday later?'

'Oh yes, of course. I shall get a fortnight.'

'Where will you go?'

She hesitated for a moment and then said, 'I don't go away.'

'You don't go away?'

'I can't afford it,' said Bel in a low voice. 'It costs such a lot of money. I just stay — in my flat. It isn't too bad. I go to Kew Gardens and — and things like that. Sometimes I take a bus and spend the day in the country.'

Dr. Armstrong was silent. He leant against a tree and busied himself filling his pipe.

'It isn't too bad — really,' repeated Bel.

'What about coming with us to Scotland?' suggested Dr. Armstrong.

'Coming with you!'

He nodded. 'Yes, we're going to Drumburly when I take my holiday. You could come with us, couldn't you?'

'Oh no!'

'Why not? It's an excellent plan. You're so good for Lou.'

'Good for her? I think she's good for me.'

'You're good for each other,' he told her. 'That's how it should be. That's why I want you to come. It's a bit dull for Lou at Drumburly. She needs a friend — someone to talk to. If you would come with us it would relieve my mind a lot. I could go out and fish. I could spend the whole day on the river without feeling guilty.' He smiled and added, 'Fishermen are selfish people, you know.'

'Oh, Dr. Armstrong, but I couldn't!'

'Why not?'

'I couldn't afford it,' she declared. 'I'd love it, of course, but — but I couldn't — really.'

'I'm offering you a holiday job.'

'Oh no!'

'Yes, come with us as a companion for Lou.'

Bel was almost in tears. She said, 'Oh no, it's far too kind.'

'It isn't kind at all. Please come, Bel.'

She hesitated for a few moments and then she said in a low voice, 'It's terribly kind — and anyhow I wouldn't want to be paid. I mean if you really want me — if it could be arranged — if you're quite sure about it — I could manage if you would pay my expenses.'

'Oh well, we'll see,' said Dr. Armstrong. 'We'll talk to Lou about it. We'll see what Lou thinks.'

Dr. Armstrong was sure that his daughter would be delighted at the idea of taking Bel with them to Drumburly, and he was not disappointed. It would be 'simply perfect' Louise declared. They discussed it after dinner, sitting in the drawing-room with the windows wide open and the soft mild air drifting in from the garden bearing the scent of flowers.

Dr. Armstrong did not say much, but watched and listened with a good deal of interest. Like most doctors he had studied psychology and it seemed to him that it would be difficult to find two girls so utterly different in their outlook upon life. That was why they were so good for each other, he thought. Louise was used to having her own way and, apart from his professional duties which were sacred to him, he was perfectly willing that she should 'arrange' his life. There was not a grain of selfishness in his beloved Lou; her arrangements were made for the benefit of others and were usually wise. Bel was different — utterly different, thought Dr. Armstrong. Life had dealt her some hard blows; she accepted the blows and made the best of it. She did not expect Fate to be kind.

Louise was so enchanted with the plan that she refused to see any difficulties which could not be surmounted with the greatest of ease. In ten minutes she had decided quite definitely that Bel was coming to Drumburly and was making arrangements about all the delightful things they would do together when they got there.

To Bel the whole thing was vague and dreamlike. The difficulties seemed insuperable. To begin with there was the problem of fitting in the dates. Dr. Armstrong was obliged to take his holiday when he could get a locum to attend to his practice, and Bel could not get away from the office until Mr. Brownlee returned from South America, — perhaps not even then! She would have to stay until everything was in running order and he could dispense with her services conveniently. She explained this to Louise.

'I'm sure he'll be back,' declared Louise, and went on talking about Drumburly.

Bel let her talk — as a matter of fact it would have been difficult to stop her — and there was no harm in listening as long as she did not allow herself to believe a word Louise was saying. It's a dream, thought Bel. It's a fairy-tale. Fairy-tales don't happen.

The Armstrongs went up to Drumburly every year — or nearly every year — explained Louise. It was a small town in the Scottish Borders with a very comfortable hotel. Dr. Armstrong's cousin was married to a farmer who owned the fishing rights of the river and allowed him to fish as much as he pleased. The Johnstones' farm was called Mureth and was about five miles from Drumburly.

'Aunt Mamie is a darling,' declared Louise. 'Of course she isn't really my aunt — she's Daddy's cousin — but she feels like an aunt — and Uncle Jock feels like an uncle. You'll love them, Bel. They're so kind — the kindest people in the world. They always try to persuade us to go and stay at Mureth House but it's better, really, to stay at the hotel. It's better for Daddy. He feels quite free. You never feel quite free if you're staying with people — even if they're relations, do you? And of course the hotel is frightfully comfortable and Mrs. Simpson is a pet. She doesn't mind Daddy coming in late for meals and soaked to the skin. She just takes away all his clothes and dries them. Isn't it kind?'

'Yes, awfully kind.'

'We can go to Mureth whenever we like,' Louise continued. 'Aunt Mamie is always pleased to see us. Then there's Tassieknowe. That's another farm higher up the river. It belongs to the Johnstones too. Aunt Mamie's nephew, James, lives there — and Rhoda, of course. Rhoda is perfectly beautiful, she's got the most gorgeous golden hair. She's just like an angel, isn't she Daddy?'

Dr. Armstrong smiled and agreed. He said, 'I think you've told Bel enough about it. She's looking a bit dazed.'

'But I must tell her about it,' objected Louise. 'She wants to know all about it before she comes. Don't you, Bel?'

'If I can come — '

'Of course you must come!' cried Louise. 'It will be so lovely to have you with us. We can walk over the hills together. We can have picnics. Daddy doesn't like me walking over the hills by myself but he won't mind if we're together — and he can go off and fish every day and all day long without bothering about me at all. That's what he likes doing better than anything

100

and it's *so* good for him. You *will* come, won't you, Bel?'

'Yes, if I can.'

'I'm sure you'd enjoy it.'

'I'm sure I should,' Bel agreed. 'It sounds absolutely wonderful — but I can't promise. It all depends on Mr. Brownlee.'

'Bother Mr. Brownlee!' exclaimed Louise.

9

Sunday morning was beautifully fine and sunny. The two girls rose early and went to church. This had been decided the night before but not without a certain amount of argument.

'I like going to the early service,' Louise had said. 'But my dailies don't come on Sundays so it's a bit of a rush. You must stay in bed and I'll bring up your breakfast when I get home. It may be a bit late but you won't mind, will you?'

'I'd like to come with you,' said Bel.

'Why not stay in bed? Daddy said you were to rest as much as possible.'

Bel smiled; she said, 'Your Daddy is a wonderful man but all the same I'd like to go to church.'

'Really?'

'Yes, really. I go every Sunday unless the weather is absolutely frightful.' She hesitated and then added, 'It sounds rather cowardly but I can't risk getting ill.'

Getting ill was Bel's most dreaded nightmare. Lying alone and helpless with nobody to look after her, nobody to care whether she lived or died . . . and then, if she didn't get better quickly, to lose her job!

'Yes, it's horrid to be ill,' Louise was saying. 'When I had appendicitis it was frightful. It came on suddenly in the middle of the night like a clap of thunder. I shouted for Daddy and he bundled me up in a blanket and took me straight to the hospital — then and there. You've no idea how horrible it was,' declared Louise. 'But when the horrible part was over and I began to feel better it was rather nice. People are so kind, aren't they? I was simply swamped with flowers and magazines. I suppose you've got lots of kind neighbours.'

Bel did not answer that. It was not really a question. She merely repeated her statement that she would like to go to church the following morning and asked Louise to waken her in plenty of time.

The little church was only ten minutes' walk from Coombe House. It was a small church, but old and very lovely with fluted columns supporting the huge oak beams of the roof. The morning sunshine streaming through the stained-glass windows made a jewelled pattern on the floor. Not many people were present and the service was quiet and simple; there was peace here and sincerity and a feeling of intimacy which Bel found very moving.

The two girls came out and for a few minutes they walked along together in silence.

'What a lot people miss,' said Louise at last. 'I mean people who don't go to church. It makes me feel like a little girl with a clean pinafore. Of course the pinafore gets dirty much too soon but it feels nice while it's clean.'

Bel smiled; she said, 'I don't think your pinafore is ever very dirty.'

'Oh yes, it is,' declared Louise. 'Sometimes I'm quite bad and wicked. It's a horrible feeling and it makes me miserable. I wonder why it should be. I mean,' said Louise, trying to explain. 'I mean if I *want* to be good and nice why can't I? What prevents me? That's what I'd like to know.'

Bel nodded. 'Yes, but I think everybody feels like that sometimes. Even the saints had their ups and downs. We're told that, aren't we? Oh Louise, I wish you had known Aunt Beatrice; she was so good — and her goodness made her happy. I think she was the happiest person I've ever known.'

'You still miss her?'

'Yes, I still miss her frightfully. It's two years since she died but I haven't got used to doing without her. I still keep on wanting to tell her things.'

'I know the feeling,' said Louise. 'I miss Mummy like that. It comes and goes. Sometimes I forget about it — and then the tide rises and I'm almost drowned. It happens quite suddenly — I never know when it's going to happen.' She put her hand through Bel's arm and gave it a little squeeze. 'Let's be sisters,' she said.

'Sisters?'

'Yes. Am I being silly? I just meant we could tell each other things.'

Bel did not think it silly. She thought it would be pleasant and comforting to have a sister like Louise . . . and it would be quite easy to tell her things.

'Darling Bel, begin by telling me what's the matter,' suggested Louise. 'There is something, I'm sure. That day when we met you at the picture gallery you were on top of the world. There was a sort of glow about you.'

Bel hesitated for a moment. 'Yes,' she said. 'Yes, there was something that made me feel happy, but it was just a mistake. I thought someone was — was fond of me, but he wasn't. That's all, really. There was nothing in it at all.'

'Oh Bel!'

'I was idiotic,' Bel said rather desperately. 'I can't imagine how I could have been such an absolute fool. That's the worst of it. That's what makes me so ashamed.'

'I suppose it was Mark.'

Bel was silent.

'I thought it might be him,' said Louise regretfully. 'I just thought . . . but you needn't be ashamed.'

'I am,' Bel told her.

'No, darling, honestly,' said Louise firmly. 'You mustn't feel like that. Mark is terribly attractive. Every girl he meets falls in love with Mark. They can't help it. It's just one of those things. Of course he's selfish — if you can call it selfish. He doesn't really mean to be selfish but he never thinks of anybody except himself. He just goes his own way and it's his nature to be charming — but of course you couldn't know that, could you?'

'No,' said Bel doubtfully. 'But all the same — '

'I'm so thankful I was inoculated when I was a child,' said Louise with a sigh.

'Inoculated?'

'Yes, inoculated,' said Louise seriously. 'You know how children are inoculated against scarlet fever and diphtheria and things like that — Daddy inoculates hundreds of children against all sorts of diseases — well, I was inoculated against Mark in exactly the same way. You see Mark used to come and stay with us in the Summer Holidays. That inoculated me against him.'

Bel laughed.

'It did, really,' declared Louise. 'I'm immune. I couldn't fall in love with Mark even if I wanted to. He's charming to me and I can see he's terribly attractive but he leaves me cold.'

'Perhaps there's somebody else — '

'No, there isn't. I've never been the slightest bit in love with anybody. It's because Daddy is so marvellous. There's nobody to compare with him.'

2

Dr. Armstrong stood upon the steps of his house watching the two girls approach. They were walking rather slowly, arm in arm; he thought they made a charming picture. He had been out all night at a difficult confinement and despite all his efforts the baby had died. Nobody could have saved it — he knew that — but all the same he felt sad and discouraged.

The sight of his daughter and her friend returning from church together lightened his spirits a little; he was able to watch them quite comfortably for they were so engrossed in their conversation that they did not see him. What were they talking about, he wondered. What did girls talk about? These two had talked without ceasing since Bel's arrival on Friday night.

It was good for Lou to have a friend and Bel was exactly right. He had sized her up in the first ten minutes when they had met so opportunely at the Welcome Gallery — he was used to sizing people up and was rarely disillusioned — Bel Lamington was made of the right stuff.

Dr. Armstrong hoped the Drumburly plan would come off, but he was neither as optimistic as Lou nor as pessimistic as Bel. He realised that if Bel could not come his beloved Lou would be wretchedly disappointed. Perhaps it would have been better if he had not suggested the plan or had left it for a little until he saw whether it would be possible for Bel to come. However it was no use thinking of that now. One must just hope that Mr. Brownlee would return from his South American trip in plenty of time.

The girls had arrived at the bottom of the steps, they looked up and saw the doctor.

'Oh Daddy!' exclaimed Louise. 'You've been out all night! I heard you go out. Oh Daddy, how tired you are, darling! You had better have a bath and get into bed.'

'I don't think — '

'Yes, do,' said Louise firmly. 'I'll bring up your breakfast in twenty minutes. You'll have it in bed.'

'But Lou — '

'Go now, like a lamb. Bel will help me.'

'Of course!' exclaimed Bel.

'Twenty minutes,' repeated Louise, throwing

her hat and gloves on to the hall table. 'Your breakfast will be ready in twenty minutes.'

'Well, perhaps I will go to bed,' said Dr. Armstrong with a sigh. 'I'm a bit tired. But I won't bother about breakfast — and you must be sure to wake me if I'm wanted at the hospital.'

He began to walk upstairs slowly, like an old man, and then he paused and looked back. 'Joan is all right,' he said. 'You can go and see her tomorrow.'

Bel followed her new sister into the kitchen and found her preparing a tray. 'Tell me what to do,' she said.

'Bacon and eggs,' said Louise in a queer choked voice. 'Oh dear, it's the baby of course! Oh poor Joan! You'll find the bacon in the fridge. She was looking forward to the baby so frightfully much. He likes his eggs poached. I do them in a silly little pan — '

'How do you know it's the baby?' asked Bel in surprise.

'Because,' said Louise, 'because I know. I mean he said Joan was all right, didn't he? And he wouldn't look like that if everything was all right. I know him so well, you see. Oh dear, it does seem hard — and queer — ' declared Louise, dashing away her tears and diving into the cupboard for the silly little pan in which to poach the eggs. 'I mean there's Mrs. Swinton with more children than she knows what to do with and more babies arriving every minute — '

'Toast?' asked Bel.

'Yes, two pieces. Here's the bread-knife. I wonder why everything happens on a Sunday morning when Mrs. Haggard isn't here. We'll give him his breakfast first and then have ours. You don't mind, do you? If we aren't quick he'll go to sleep.'

Bel wished she were not so useless — one felt such a fool in a strange kitchen, not knowing where anything was kept — she sliced the bread and put two pieces under the grill. 'Tea or coffee?' she asked.

When Louise had taken up the doctor's tray she returned to the kitchen and found Bel busy with preparations for their own breakfast.

'How clever of you!' she said. 'I'm sorry I was so long but I wanted to make sure he would eat it all right. It is the baby, of course. I knew it was. But Joan is being very good about it and I can go and see her tomorrow afternoon.'

'You can take her some flowers,' suggested Bel.

'Yes, of course — but what good is that? Quite useless,' said Louise miserably. 'And I can say I'm sorry — but what good is that? It's beyond all the usual kind of easy sympathy.'

They sat down to have their breakfast and for a little while there was silence.

3

Monday was the last day of Bel's short visit — she had been given leave until Tuesday — so the two girls drove over to Shepherdsford in Louise's little car. It was a beautiful day of warm sun and cool breezes, with white puffy clouds moving slowly across the blue sky. The trees were now in leaf — those first fresh green leaves which are so much more beautiful than the heavy foliage of late summer — and there was a faint haze of green over the fields where the corn was springing up.

It was so beautiful that Bel could hardly bear it. Tomorrow, at this time, she would be in London surrounded by huge stone buildings; instead of the scents of hawthorn blossom and new mown hay there would be the smell of petrol-fumes. She would have exchanged the lovely peace of the country for the bustle and noise of the town.

'I shall miss you frightfully,' Louise said suddenly.

'Oh Louise, don't!' exclaimed Bel in a choked voice. 'I can scarcely bear it. You've been so good to me — and it's all so lovely — '

'You must come back. Come any weekend you like . . . and we'll look forward to Drumburly, won't we? And we can write to each other. Don't forget we're sisters.'

'I'm not likely to forget it,' said Bel.

Shepherdsford was a village some miles from Ernleigh, it nestled at the foot of a wooded hill. There was a good golf-course here and when Dr. Armstrong managed to get away from his practice he came over for a round of golf. Louise pointed out the golf-course as they went down the hill and over the bridge to an Inn near the river where they intended to have lunch.

The Owl Inn was very old but recently it had been done up and renovated so it presented a very pleasant appearance. It was clean and comfortable with a fine array of bottles and shining glasses on the shelves. Louise often came here with her father so she was warmly welcomed by the inn-keeper and his wife. Mrs. Palmer had been a cook before she was married and for this reason The Owl was able to provide an excellent meal.

While they were eating Mr. Palmer came in and chatted to the girls, asking after the doctor and discussing the local news. He told them that The Owl was doing well now; it was gradually getting known all over the district for its excellent fare — all due to Mrs. Palmer of course. Recently he had been asked to provide meals for bus-parties but Mrs. Palmer thought he ought to refuse. She thought it would change the whole atmosphere of the place and they would lose their regular customers.

'Oh, she's right!' exclaimed Louise.

'She's usually right,' agreed Mr. Palmer with a smile.

After lunch the two girls went out and walked along a path by the river. There was a ford here, which had given Shepherdsford its name. Long before the bridge had been built shepherds from the Cotswold Hills had used this ford when they brought their bales of wool to market. In those days the Inn had been known as The Wool Pack; the shepherds had rested here and had a meal — and probably a glass of ale — before they crossed the ford.

'The Wool Pack!' said Bel thoughtfully. 'I wonder why they changed it to The Owl. It isn't nearly so nice, is it?'

'Perhaps it changed itself,' Louise suggested. 'The two names are rather alike, but The Owl is shorter. I must ask Mr. Palmer about it some day.'

It was now time to return, for Louise was going to see her friend at the hospital. She was to be there at four o'clock.

This was the night of the dance at the Ernleigh Golf Club but after some discussion they had decided not to go. Louise was not in her usual spirits today, she was feeling too sad about Joan's baby, and Bel was quite pleased to remain at home. Bel's nature was shy and retiring so she had not been looking forward to the dance and she was able to assure her hostess quite truthfully that she would infinitely rather spend her last evening quietly at Coombe House.

'Well, if you're sure — ' said Louise doubtfully. 'It seems a shame that you should be done out of the party, but if you really don't want to go we'll just have a quiet evening at home. Daddy has to go to a meeting so he won't be here. There will just be you and me.'

'That will be lovely,' declared Bel. 'Much nicer than going to the dance.'

'You must have the pink frock,' said Louise firmly. 'Yes, really, Bel. Please take it. I want you to have it. We've altered it to fit you and it suits you much better than it ever suited me.'

Bel did not want to take it (she did not see when she would ever have the opportunity of wearing it) but she saw that Louise would be

112

hurt if she refused the present so she accepted it with suitable gratitude.

4

It had been a beautiful day but the evening turned cold and wet so Louise lighted the fire in the drawing-room and they settled down comfortably to talk. Louise was making a rug and Bel offered to help her so they sat together on the sofa and got on with the work.

'I'm so glad we didn't go to the dance,' said Louise. 'Dances are fun when you're feeling in the mood but I'm not feeling in the mood tonight. This is so nice and cosy, isn't it?'

Bel agreed.

'I've done most of the talking,' continued Louise. 'All the time you've been here I've talked and talked. It's your turn tonight. Tell me what you do in the office. I've no idea what sort of things you do in an office.'

'I find it very interesting,' Bel told her. 'Of course you know I work for Mr. Brownlee. He tells me all that's going on so I've learnt a good deal about the business of the firm. I'm very lucky in that way. Miss Snow, who is secretary to Mr. Wills, just types letters and does personal business for him. He doesn't talk to her or tell her what's happening.'

'Not so interesting!'

'Not interesting at all,' agreed Bel. 'I'm awfully glad I'm Mr. Brownlee's secretary. Before that I was in the typists' room — I didn't like it at all.'

'What was wrong with it?'

'Lots of things,' said Bel smiling ruefully. 'Lots of things were wrong with it, but principally Miss Goudge. She's been there for years so she's the boss and she's very disagreeable. She's always finding fault and they all quarrel and snap at each other. The typewriters clatter all the time and make a horrid noise. I used to have a headache every night when I worked there — partly because of the noise and partly because Miss Goudge wouldn't have the windows open.'

'What is the office like?' asked Louise. 'I mean what does it look like when you go in at the door?'

Bel smiled. She said, 'Well, you go in through a revolving door. There's a big hall with seats in it where people can wait. At one side of the hall there's a window with ENQUIRIES written over the top of it. Miss Goudge sits there so that she can see all the people coming in. If they want to speak to her she opens the window and asks them what they want.'

'But you said she was boss of the typists' room.'

'Yes, it is the typists' room,' explained Bel. 'Miss Goudge keeps one eye on the typists and the other eye on the hall. The window is being opened and shut all the time. Everyone who comes to the office has to run the gauntlet of Miss Goudge. Letters are delivered to her by the postman — and telegrams and all sorts of messages. She knows all that's going on, I can tell you.'

'She sounds horrible.'

'She is,' agreed Bel. 'I always try to be at the office early, before she gets there, so that I can slink past the window and take refuge in Mr. Brownlee's room.'

'You haven't told me what you do. What's the first thing you do when you arrive?'

'That depends,' Bel told her. 'If the letters have come I open them and make notes — '

'You open his letters!'

'Only the business ones. He doesn't get many personal letters at the office.'

'What else do you do?'

'I type letters,' said Bel. 'And I keep the ledgers. They're enormous brown books which are stacked on a shelf in Mr. Brownlee's room. I have to make entries in the ledgers and balance them once a week. Thursday is the day for the ledgers. Then of course I keep a note of Mr. Brownlee's engagements — all the meetings he has to attend — and sometimes I go down to Copping Wharf with a message for Mr. Nelson. That's fun,' declared Bel smiling. 'It makes a change from office-routine, and Mr. Nelson is a dear. He's been with the firm for thirty years and knows everything about it. Usually when I go to the wharf he invites me into his room and we have coffee together. I like to get him to talk about the firm, about its history and traditions and about all the ships that come from all over the world.'

'Tell me about the ships.'

Bel told her about the ships.

One day when Bel had gone to the wharf with a message for Mr. Nelson a ship had just come

115

in from Greece and was being unloaded. Crates and boxes of all shapes and sizes were being brought up out of the hold by cranes which swung them on to the wharf and piled them neatly on to trolleys. The trolleys were driven away into the various warehouses and the goods were stacked. Mr. Nelson was busy so Bel had to wait until he had time to speak to her but that was all to the good. She stood and watched the process of unloading for at least half-an-hour. It was a fine sunny day, the sunshine twinkled on the ripples in the river and the seagulls swooped overhead uttering their weird cries.

'It was fascinating,' said Bel. 'It all went like clockwork. It was all so neat. Afterwards when Mr. Nelson was ready to speak to me he told me that long ago it was all done by hand — hundreds of lascars running up and down the gangways with the crates and boxes balanced on their heads. He showed me a picture of one of the first ships that ever came to Copping Wharf to unload its cargo.'

'He must be an interesting man.'

'Oh yes — and very clever. He can speak five languages! That's tremendously useful when foreign ships come in. I wish I could,' added Bel with a sigh.

'You don't have to meet the foreign ships.'

'No, but we get letters in all sorts of foreign languages. Mr. Brownlee deals with most of them himself. I wish to goodness I had learnt Spanish at school.'

'We hadn't time,' said Louise.

'I'd have had lots of time if I hadn't learnt to

play the piano — the hours I spent practising scales! Absolutely wasted! I never was any good at music but I had to practise just the same. If I had learnt Spanish instead it would have been very useful indeed.'

Louise laughed and said, 'But nobody knew you were going to be Mr. Brownlee's secretary, did they?'

'No, but all the same — '

'Don't you see what I mean?' asked Louise. 'It would be no good teaching girls Spanish unless you knew what they were going to do. For instance Spanish would be absolutely useless to me.'

'Nobody can know the future,' Bel agreed. She added thoughtfully 'I'm not sure it would be a good thing.'

There was a little silence after that; they both worked industriously at the rug.

Bel was envisaging her future. Her work at Copping, Wills and Brownlee was interesting, but when she thought of it going on and on for years it looked rather bleak. She would get older and older until at last she was too old for the job. Then she would retire with a small pension from the firm. Yes, rather bleak, thought Bel with a big sigh.

Soon after that Dr. Armstrong came home from his meeting and it was time for bed.

10

Bel's visit to Coombe House had been delightful and everything had been so different from her usual life that she had felt like a different creature. She had settled down comfortably into the Armstrongs' ménage so that she felt as if she had been with them for weeks. It was miserable to have to say goodbye and return to her flat in London. Bel missed the companionship of Louise; she missed the cheerful conversation; she missed the comforts of the well-run household and the beautiful garden. Her own little garden failed to charm her, she saw it with lack-lustre eyes.

Dr. Armstrong had given Bel some roots of aubrietia; she planted them carefully, of course, but even this task failed to raise her spirits. Poor little plants, thought Bel, as she tucked them into the corners of the big stone trough. Poor little things! It was a shame to bring you here. You would grow much more happily in the garden of Coombe House!

Bel had been away only for a few days but her flat looked dirty and neglected. Dust lay upon the table and the chimneypiece and upon every flat surface. Where did all the dust come from, wondered Bel, as she set about cleaning the place and putting things in order.

It was when she was dusting the book-case that she came across the brown-paper parcel which she had intended to give Mark for his birthday. She had forgotten all about it until this moment.

Bel stood there with the parcel in her hands, remembering how carefully she had chosen the wool for Mark's socks and all the hours she had spent knitting them — and all the thoughts which had made the task pleasant. Then suddenly she turned and thrust the wretched parcel into the bottom drawer of her bureau and shut it out of sight.

It was not quite so easy to shut away all thoughts of Mark but she decided to try.

Mr. Brownlee was extremely pleased to see his secretary again; he appreciated her all the more because Miss Harlow, who had officiated for her during her absence, had been a very poor substitute. Miss Harlow was not interested in the work and was so distrait that Mr. Brownlee had come to the regretful conclusion that the girl was not quite all there. It was true that her shorthand was a good deal better than Miss Lamington's but that did not make up for other things.

'Hallo, Miss Lamington!' exclaimed Mr. Brownlee with heartwarming enthusiasm. 'Did you have a good time? Thank goodness you're back! That girl is incapable of filing a letter or looking up an address; she can't even get a right number on the telephone. I feel as if you had been away for weeks. It's been awful.'

'Oh, I'm so sorry,' said Bel with rather less than her usual strict regard for truth.

Compared with Mr. Brownlee's greeting Miss

Goudge's was somewhat chilly but that did not matter in the least.

The date for Mr. Brownlee's trip to South America had now been settled. There was a great deal to do for he was anxious to leave everything in good order so that the business would flow on smoothly. It had been arranged that Mr. Copping would come to the office more frequently and keep an eye on things during his absence, but shortly before his departure Mr. Copping had a severe heart attack and was laid up in bed. This meant that Mr. Wills would be in complete charge — a state of affairs which seemed so unsatisfactory to the junior partner that if he could have cancelled his trip he would have done so, but by this time it was too late.

Mr. Brownlee endeavoured to comfort himself by the well-known saying that nobody is indispensable — but he found it difficult to believe. He felt himself to be indispensable; there were all sorts of things to be done which he alone could do. There were the foreign letters, for instance. The firm of Copping, Wills and Brownlee had a great many contacts with Spanish-speaking countries and also with German and Dutch. Ellis Brownlee was a good linguist and was able to deal with these letters himself. Mr. Copping had intended to take over this duty — but now, of course, he could not do so. There was nobody else in the office who had the ability to deal with them satisfactorily.

'There ought to be somebody,' said Mr. Brownlee to his secretary. 'It's a mistake to have nobody in the office who can deal with them. It didn't seem to matter when Mr. Copping was coming here regularly. I think I shall have to get a clerk with a good knowledge of languages when I get back.'

'But what are we to do while you're away?' asked Bel in dismay.

'You'll have to send them down to the wharf, that's all,' replied Mr. Brownlee. 'Nelson will cope.'

Another important matter to be settled was the appointment of the new agent at Leith. Mr. Brownlee interviewed several applicants for the post and decided upon a young man called Robert Anderson.

'He's the sort of chap we want,' explained Mr. Brownlee to his secretary. 'He hasn't had a great deal of experience but he's full of initiative and tremendously keen. He isn't free till September but it's better to hang on and get the right man for the job. Wills wanted an older man but I've managed to talk him over so you can write to Anderson confirming his appointment.'

Bel had always known that her 'boss' did more than his share of the business but even so she was surprised at the number of matters which had to be delegated.

Mr. Brownlee had intended to spend three weeks in South America and then fly home, but so many people were anxious to see him that it was difficult to fit in all his appointments and soon it became evident that his visit would have to be extended. When Bel realised this she was appalled. How was the firm of Copping, Wills and Brownlee to carry on indefinitely without the junior partner? Her own private plans were disorganised too. She would have to put off her holiday; she would not be free to go to Drumburly with the Armstrongs. This was a great pity of course but she was not really very disappointed for the plan had never seemed more substantial than a dream.

What with one thing and another Bel was kept so busy that she had little time to think of her own affairs. The days passed and gradually Mark faded out of her mind. She thought of him less — sometimes she forgot about him entirely — and the receipt of a highly-coloured picture-postcard from Florence with the news that he was having a marvellous time failed to upset her in the least.

I'm cured, thought Bel in surprise. It really was rather strange that she had been cured so quickly. Of course her visit to the Armstrongs had helped. Louise had consoled her. Louise had taken the sting out of the wound by giving Bel a very shrewd estimate of Mark's character: gay and charming and utterly and absolutely selfish. 'But you couldn't know that, could you?' Louise had said.

This was true of course. Bel had imagined Mark as a sort of fairy prince. She had taken him at his face value and believed every word he said.

She remembered Louise saying quite seriously that she had been inoculated against Mark when she was a child. Bel had laughed — it seemed ridiculous nonsense — but now she saw that there was a good deal of sober sense in the assertion (just as there was sense in the other things Louise had said about her cousin). Bel had a feeling that she, too, had been inoculated against Mark. It had been painful and unpleasant — as inoculations sometimes are — but she was now immune. If she were to meet Mark tomorrow she could greet him without the slightest pang and, no matter how gay and delightful and charming he was, he would not affect her at all.

Experientia docet stultos, thought Bel, as she put the highly-coloured postcard on her chimney-piece. Yes, she had been a fool but she had learnt a valuable lesson, she would guard her heart more carefully in future, and especially carefully from young men with charming manners — like Mark.

11

The office felt very strange when Mr. Brownlee had gone. Bel missed him even more than she had expected; she missed his smile which had welcomed her every morning and she missed his cheerful conversation; most of all she missed the feeling of confidence which he inspired. He was so absolutely dependable. The chilliness of Miss Goudge had not mattered when Mr. Brownlee was there but now it mattered a great deal.

Fortunately there was no trouble with Miss Snow. In fact Bel came to like her in a tepid sort of way. Nobody could have become really fond of Miss Snow — she was too cold — but compared with Miss Goudge she was admirable. She sailed along doing her duty, and doing it well. There was no meanness about her, no petty jealousy. She had exceedingly high principles. Mr. Brownlee had been a little unjust about Miss Snow, thought Bel. She might be 'Faultily faultless' and 'icily regular' but she was not 'splendidly null'. And of course Mr. Wills was a difficult man to work for. He did not want a human sort of secretary; he wanted a secretary who would do what she was told — no more and no less — so Miss Snow gave him exactly what he wanted. Perhaps if she had had a more human sort of employer to work for she, herself, might have been more human.

Now and then Bel and Miss Snow worked

together, but not very often for their work was different. Bel did most of her work in Mr. Brownlee's room and was summoned by Mr. Wills when he required her services.

One morning when Mr. Brownlee had been away for about a week Bel was summoned by Mr. Wills and given a letter to type. It was to Mr. William Masterman offering him the appointment of agent to Messrs. Copping, Wills and Brownlee at Leith.

For a moment Bel hesitated and then she said, 'But what about Mr. Anderson?'

'Anderson?' exclaimed Mr. Wills. 'What d'you mean? There was some talk of Anderson but Masterman is older and has had a great deal more experience, besides he can take up the post at once. The other man isn't free till September.'

'But I thought it was agreed, Mr. Wills.'

'Agreed!' exclaimed Mr. Wills irritably. 'It was discussed of course but I've changed my mind about it. I suppose I can change my mind without reference to you, can't I?'

'Mr. Anderson's appointment has been confirmed.'

'Confirmed? How d'you know?'

Bel had every reason to know for she had written the letter to Mr. Anderson confirming his appointment. She explained this as tactfully as she could but Mr. Wills was angry — he was also incredulous. Bel was obliged to fetch a copy of the letter from the file and show it to him before he would believe her.

He snatched it out of her hand and read it. 'Did Brownlee sign this?' he demanded.

'Yes, of course, Mr. Wills,' she replied.

The affair was most uncomfortable and Bel was distressed about it. Perhaps it was foolish to be distressed, for it certainly was not her fault. Mr. Wills had been annoyed with her and thought her interfering — but what could she have done? Should she have held her peace and allowed the appointment to be offered to Mr. Masterman? No, of course not, thought Bel. That would have been idiotic and it would have caused a lot of trouble . . . and, incidentally, wasn't it just to prevent this sort of muddle and confusion that Mr. Brownlee had wanted her to be here? The whole thing showed up Mr. Wills in a very unpleasant light; he had been vacillating, suspicious and unfair.

How different from Mr. Brownlee, thought Bel.

2

After her unpleasant interview with Mr. Wills Bel returned to Mr. Brownlee's room and got on with her work but she had not been there for many minutes when there was a knock on the door. It was a peremptory knock and at first she thought it must be Mr. Wills, pursuing her in anger. Her heart beat uncomfortably fast. Then she realised that it could not be he. Mr. Wills wouldn't knock — he would throw open the door and walk in. Having decided this Bel was about to reply but before she could do so the door was opened and a face appeared round the

126

edge. It was a young bony face topped with a thatch of unruly straw-coloured hair.

'Oh, I say, are you busy?' asked the intruder. 'I'm sorry I knocked so loud. I didn't mean to, you know. It was a mistake. I meant to knock quite softly.'

'Are you looking for someone?' asked Bel.

'You,' replied the intruder.

'Me?'

'Yes — at least I suppose you're Miss Lamington. That frightful female said you were in Mr. Brownlee's room.'

'You had better come in and shut the door,' said Bel briskly.

The intruder instantly did as he was told and was now revealed as a young man, exceedingly tall and gawky. His legs and arms were so long and loosely knit that he reminded Bel of a puppet. He was wearing grey flannel trousers and a tweed jacket and it was obvious from the appearance of these garments that their owner had grown considerably since he had bought them.

'I say,' he said smiling in a friendly manner, 'I hope I'm not bothering you.'

His smile reminded Bel of someone; she could not think of whom. 'You had better tell me what you want,' she suggested. 'I don't know who you are, or anything.'

'Oh, I say, how stupid of me!' he exclaimed. 'Of course I should have told you straight off, but that frightful female scared me out of my wits. I'm James Copping.'

'James Copping?'

He nodded.

Bel knew now. She had placed him . . . and now that she looked at him properly she realised who it was that had smiled in that same friendly way.

'James Copping,' he repeated. 'Jim to you, of course.'

'Mr. James to me.'

'Oh no! I mean — '

'Oh yes,' said Bel, firmly. 'Mr. James is the correct way to address the son of the senior partner of the firm.'

'It sounds so stuffy,' said Mr. James regretfully. He hesitated for a moment and then smiled, 'But that's just for the office, isn't it? I mean when we're having lunch — '

'Lunch?'

'I thought we could have lunch together.'

'But it isn't nearly time for lunch!'

'Oh, I know,' he agreed. 'But it will be, later.' He looked round and added, 'The room seems a bit queer without Mr. Brownlee in it. Sort of empty — if you know what I mean.'

Bel knew exactly what he meant, but she was busy. 'Mr. James,' she said in desperation. 'I've got a most awful lot to do this morning. Look at this pile of letters!'

'Have they got to be typed?'

'Yes.'

'I could help,' he suggested. 'There are two typewriters, aren't there? I can type quite decently, you know.'

By this time Bel had realised that Mr. James was at a loose end and had dropped in to the office on the chance of finding employment. She

128

remembered her conversation with Mr. Copping; he had said that Jim was abroad but would soon be returning from his travels and would have nothing to do until it was time for him to take up his position in the firm. He had said he didn't want the boy to be 'running about idle'. He had said that it was especially bad for a boy like Jim, who was 'keen as mustard', to have nothing to do. She remembered also that Mr. Copping was ill in bed and that Mrs. Copping was extremely worried about him.

All this went through her mind in a few moments. It was not her job to play nursemaid to this enormous child but she felt sorry for him and she liked him. There was something very nice about him, she decided. Suddenly she was visited by a splendid idea — it was an inspiration! She could employ him usefully and get rid of him at the same time.

'I know what you can do,' she told him. 'If you really want to help you can take these letters to Mr. Nelson at Copping Wharf and ask him to translate them for us. He can do them while you wait.' She took the bundle of letters out of the drawer and handed them to him.

Mr. James looked at them. 'They're Spanish,' he said.

'Yes,' she agreed. 'Just take them to Mr. Nelson. You can do that, can't you?'

'Yes, of course I can — but why?'

'Why?' asked Bel in surprise. 'What do you mean, Mr. James?'

'Why Mr. Nelson? It would save time if I did them, wouldn't it?'

'Do you mean you know Spanish?'

'Spanish is easy,' replied Mr. James modestly. 'I like languages, you know. They're rather fun. I'm reasonably good at German and I'm learning Dutch. That should be useful, don't you think? I mean the firm has a lot of trade with the Netherlands.'

'How clever of you!'

'Oh, lord, no! Not a bit,' declared Mr. James blushing to the roots of his straw-coloured hair. 'Not a bit clever. It's just a knack, really. Nothing in it at all. I'll get on with the job, shall I?'

Bel did not know what to say (she was dumb) but her visitor did not wait for a reply. He took her consent for granted and, sitting down at the other table, he proceeded to get on with the job in a businesslike manner.

There was silence except for the tapping of the two typewriters.

Soon after one o'clock Bel had finished her morning's work, and was ready to go out to lunch. Mr. James had finished too and produced a sheaf of neatly-typed translations of the letters for Miss Lamington's approval.

'Will they do?' he asked anxiously.

'Oh yes. They're simply splendid — couldn't be better. Thank you very much, Mr. James.'

'That's grand,' he declared. 'I've liked doing it. As a matter of fact it's my first job for the old firm. I must tell the Guv'nor about it. We'll go and have lunch now, shall we?'

'No,' said Bel firmly. 'It's very kind of you, but — '

'Oh I say! Why not? You've got to have lunch somewhere, haven't you? I thought we could have it together. There are all sorts of things I want to know and we can talk while we're pecking. Do say you will!'

'We had better not,' said Bel thoughtfully. 'It might cause trouble.'

Mr. James was no fool. He said, 'Trouble? Oh, you mean that frightful female! But she'd never know. We needn't go out together. We could meet at the end of the street and — '

'No, it wouldn't be the right thing.'

'But the Guv'nor said . . . '

'What did he say?'

'Oh well,' replied Mr. James, grinning from ear to ear. 'If you really want to know his exact words, he said, 'If you go to the office Miss Lamington's the one. She'll take you by your lily-white hand and lead you over the water'. It's a song or something,' explained Mr. James. 'I don't know the song but I know jolly well what he meant.'

Bel did not know the song either, it was before her day, but Mr. Copping's meaning was perfectly clear.

'That's what he said,' repeated Mr. James.

Bel laughed. 'But he didn't say lunch.'

'I'm saying lunch,' declared Mr. James stubbornly. 'As a matter of fact we could go to a decent place because I've just had a birthday.'

'A birthday?'

'Mun,' he explained tapping his pocket significantly.

'No,' said Bel, 'no, I'm afraid not.'

131

'Oh I say! There are all sorts of things I want to ask you.'

He looked so crestfallen that Bel relented; she hesitated for a moment and then smiled. She said, 'I usually have lunch at a small restaurant just round the corner, it's called 'Smart's', and of course if you decided to have lunch there I couldn't prevent you, could I?'

Mr. James grinned. 'But I'll pay,' he said.

3

When Bel went in to Smart's Restaurant James Copping was there, waiting for her, sitting at a table in the corner. He looked pleased with himself and so he was for he had got what he wanted. Bel was to find that in spite of his diffident manner Mr. James always knew exactly what he wanted and usually got it.

He rose politely as Bel approached and when they were seated handed her the menu. 'Have anything you like. I'm paying, remember,' he said seriously.

Bel was amused. He was such a queer mixture. He was so very young — but so very large. He had such good manners — but he was so very awkward. At first she had thought him rather stupid, but on the contrary he was quick and intelligent. If Mr. James could be steered clear of pitfalls and could settle down he would be a great acquisition to the firm of Copping, Wills and Brownlee. His languages alone would be extremely useful, but he had character as well.

Unfortunately the fact that his character was strong and determined would make the pitfalls all the more dangerous, thought Bel. She could imagine Mr. Wills resigning himself to a weak sloppy individual, but the entry into the firm of a strong determined young Copping would not suit his book at all.

Bel leant forward and said earnestly, 'Mr. James, you'll have to be careful. The office is a funny sort of place. There's a lot of — of jealousy. I've had to contend with it myself so I know a good deal about it.'

He nodded. 'Yes,' he said. 'It won't be too easy. I can see that. Old Wills doesn't want me of course. He's a stinker, isn't he?'

Bel felt like saying she couldn't agree more, which was an idiom that Mr. James would probably have used himself.

'Well, I don't care,' continued Mr. James, thrusting out his chin. 'My father wants me in the firm and he's the boss, so old Wills can go to blazes.'

Bel wondered if she should beseech him to be tactful, but she had an uncomfortable feeling that it would be useless. Mr. James couldn't be tactful however hard he tried.

'You know, Miss Lamington,' he continued earnestly. 'I've always wanted to go into the firm — ever since I was a kid. I used to go down to the Pool and watch the ships. I still do, quite often. It's fascinating when you think of all those ships bringing cargoes from all over the world.'

''Ivory, apes and peacocks',' murmured Bel.

'Yes!' he exclaimed nodding enthusiastically.

'Yes, that's the idea! You understand. It's not like an ordinary business. My great friend is reading law; he's going into his father's office — but a lawyer's office wouldn't appeal to me at all. My mother wants me to go to Cambridge but luckily the Guv'nor doesn't agree. He sees my point. It would just be a waste of time because I haven't got that sort of brain. I want to go straight into the business and learn the whole thing from A to Z — learn to pull my weight.' He paused and looked at her doubtfully. 'D'you think I could?'

'Of course you could. You're coming to the firm when Mr. Brownlee comes home. It's all arranged, isn't it?'

'Yes of course, but — '

'But what?' asked Bel.

'Listen, Miss Lamington,' said Mr. James — quite unnecessarily of course for Miss Lamington was giving him all her attention. 'Listen Miss Lamington; I didn't really mean to tell you this but I'm going to. The Guv'nor is ill — you know that. He was pretty bad, really — he gave us an awful fright — but he's getting better, thank goodness. All the same he won't ever be fit enough to do much in the office. That's why I want to hurry up and learn to pull my weight. See?'

She nodded. 'There ought to be a Copping in the firm.'

'Exactly. That's what I mean. Gosh, I wish I was older! 1 wish I was there now, pulling my weight.'

'You will,' she told him.

134

'It's going to take me a long time to learn,' he said with a sigh. 'That's why I want to start now — straight off — without waiting for Mr. Brownlee to come back. That's why I've told you all this. You'll help me, won't you?'

Bel would have done almost anything for him by this time — anything in her power. 'But I don't see how I can help you,' she said regretfully. 'Honestly, I don't see — '

'Just let me come in and potter,' he explained, 'I want to get the hang of it, if you know what I mean. Let me translate the letters. Tell me all you can. Take me by my lily-white hand — like the Guv'nor said.'

Bel smiled. 'Well, I don't see how Mr. Wills could object to you coming in and translating the letters.'

'Good!' said Mr. James nodding. 'That's fixed. It'll be the thin edge of the wedge.'

Bel had a feeling that it *would* be the thin end of the wedge and the thicker part of the wedge would soon follow.

It was now high time for Bel to return to the office. She allowed her escort to pay for her lunch — he would have been distressed if she made any objection — and collected her bag and gloves.

'Would you like to go to the Zoo on Sunday afternoon?' asked Mr. James a trifle diffidently. 'If you don't like the Zoo we'll go somewhere else. Anywhere you like. Just say the word.'

Bel laughed. 'How do you know I haven't got a date?'

'You haven't, have you? You aren't engaged or

135

anything. You aren't wearing a ring.'

'Why not take someone of your own age?'

'Oh I say, you aren't as old as all that!'

'I'm twenty-four,' said Bel frankly. 'At least I'm going to be twenty-four on Thursday — so you see!'

'That's nothing,' he declared. 'Besides, girls are so silly; I'd ever so much rather take you. If you tell me where you live, I'll call for you at three o'clock. Will that be all right?'

'You had better ask your father,' said Bel.

'Ask him if I can take you?'

'Yes. See what he thinks about it.'

'Oh well — ' said Mr. James doubtfully. 'Oh well — but if he's in favour of it you'll come.'

Bel nodded. Somehow she felt sure that Mr. Copping would not be in favour of it.

Contrary to Bel's expectations Mr. Copping raised no objections to the proposed expedition — he had known Miss Lamington's parents — so the visit to the Zoo took place as arranged. As they walked round together and looked at the animals Bel's feeling that she was playing the part of nursemaid was intensified. Her charge was a great deal larger than herself, but that seemed to make no difference to the feeling — none whatever, thought Bel, as she watched indulgently while he fed the monkeys with nuts and threw buns at the bears. He was enjoying himself immensely; that was obvious. Perhaps it was this capacity for enjoyment which made him seem so young.

Today Mr. James was immaculately attired in a lounge suit of fine brown tweed with a faint red line in it. He invited Bel to admire it — which she did.

'It's new,' he told her. 'The Guv'nor said I was to go to his tailor; he said I looked like a scarecrow. Of course I shall only wear it on Sundays.'

'You must wear it when you come to the office,' said Bel. 'Yes, really,' she added, forestalling his exclamation of protest. 'You simply must.'

'But look here — '

'It makes you look older,' said Bel craftily.

'Oh, well — ' he said. ('Oh well — ' was a favourite expression. Mr. James used it frequently and in all sorts of different ways but usually to show regretful resignation to the inevitable).

'Oh well,' repeated Mr. James more cheerfully. 'If this suit really makes me look older I'd better wear it every day.'

'Yes,' said Bel firmly.

By this time they had walked miles — or so it seemed to Bel. She suggested they should have tea.

Mr. James agreed enthusiastically. 'But not here,' he said. 'I know an awfully good place for tea. We don't want to go to a posh place where they give you a few silly little cakes. We want a place where we can get proper food. The Zoo always seems to make me hungry.'

12

It was Monday morning, the day after the expedition to the Zoological Gardens. Bel was expecting a message from Mr. Nelson at Copping Wharf so when the telephone-bell rang and she took up the receiver she was surprised to hear a feminine voice on the line.

'Is that Miss Lamington?' the feminine voice enquired. 'Oh, this is Frances Brownlee. You remember me, don't you? You came to lunch one day when Ellis was laid up with a cold.'

'Oh, yes. Of course I remember.'

'I wonder if you could possibly come this afternoon?'

Bel's instinct was to say no, for of course her job precluded social engagements, but there had been a trace of anxiety in the voice which made her hesitate.

'I do hope you can,' continued Mrs. Brownlee. 'I'm in rather a mess. Of course Ellis explained it to me before he went away — about claiming back Income Tax and all that — but there's a thing called Schedule A and I don't understand it at all. Ellis said if I got in a mess I was to ring you up and you'd come and sort things out.'

'Oh — yes — ' said Bel doubtfully. She was wondering what she ought to do. On the one hand there was her work in the office; on the other hand there was Mr. Brownlee's mother.

'Ellis said you would,' said Mr. Brownlee's

138

mother beseechingly.

'Yes, of course I'll come,' declared Bel, taking a sudden decision — for was she not Mr. Brownlee's secretary? Was she not bound to obey his commands? Fortunately she knew a good deal about Schedule A having been instructed in this somewhat puzzling matter by Mr. Brownlee himself when various repairs had been carried out upon the office-building. This made it all the more her duty to sort out his mother's troubles. 'Yes, I'll come this afternoon,' added Bel. 'I don't know what time exactly, but I'll come.'

Having decided this and listened to Mrs. Brownlee's protestations of gratitude and delight Bel made up her mind that she must see Mr. Wills and explain the matter to him; but Mr. Wills was taking the morning off (probably for golf which was his passion). The only thing to be done was to leave a message with Miss Goudge.

There should have been no difficulty about this, Miss Goudge was the right person with whom to leave a message, but since the departure of Mr. Brownlee the atmosphere in the office had become more and more unpleasant, and Miss Goudge, never very agreeable, had become very disagreeable indeed. She was especially disagreeable to Bel Lamington for she was easy game.

Like all bullies Miss Goudge enjoyed easy game; she took pleasure in being rude to people who did not answer back. Bel knew perfectly well that she ought to stand up to Miss Goudge and insist upon being treated in the proper way but this she could not do. She was much too sensitive, much too easily hurt to be able to hold her own.

Miss Goudge listened to Bel's story with a disdainful air — she was extraordinarily like the camel which Bel had seen yesterday at the Zoo —

'Mrs. Brownlee?' asked Miss Goudge. 'I didn't know he was married.'

'He isn't married. It's his mother.'

'Why should she want to see *you*.'

Bel had explained the reason already but she explained it again. 'To help her with some business matters, that's all. You'll tell Mr. Wills when he comes in, won't you?'

'I wish you would do your own dirty work!' declared Miss Goudge.

There were various replies which Bel might have made to this piece of insolence but her desire was for peace — peace at any price — so she said nothing.

Bel was just turning away when another idea came into her mind, so she paused.

'Well, what's the matter now?' asked Miss Goudge impatiently.

'I just wondered if there were any letters for me.'

'You asked me that before.'

'I know. I just wondered — '

'I suppose the boy-friend has forgotten to write?'

This was a bit much — even for Bel. She said, 'Really, Miss Goudge; I think you might answer politely.'

'Oh, is that what you think? Well, I may tell

you that I'm tired of answering silly questions. You know perfectly well that I distribute all the letters that come to this office. I distribute them every morning when the post comes in. I don't sit on them or lose them or throw them into the fire.' And with that Miss Goudge began to rattle the keys of her typewriter and jerk the carriage with resounding clangs — treatment which certainly could not have done the instrument much good.

2

Mrs. Brownlee was in her garden when Bel arrived; she greeted her visitor with enthusiasm.

'This *is* kind of you,' she declared. 'I'm really very stupid about business matters. Of course Ellis does all that sort of thing when he's here, so when he's away I'm quite helpless. Would you have time to walk round the garden? Then we'll have tea together and I'll show you those horrid papers.'

Bel could never resist a garden so they walked round together admiring the roses, which were coming into bloom. There was another bed full of Sweet William and, against the holly hedge, was a splendid array of Russell's Lupins. It was a very pretty garden, not quite so beautiful as the garden at Coombe House but for all that exceedingly pleasant.

'Ellis likes the roses best,' said Ellis's mother. 'It's such a pity he isn't here to see them coming out but he'll be home in time for the second flowering. I do miss him terribly,' she added with a sigh.

'He's badly missed at the office.'

'In what way?'

'In every way,' replied Bel ruefully. 'It isn't only the work — though that's bad enough — but the whole atmosphere is different. Mr. Wills is . . . ' She hesitated.

'Let's sit down,' suggested Mrs. Brownlee. 'I'm perfectly safe, you know, so you can tell me all about it.'

It was a great relief to be able to talk about the unsatisfactory state of affairs to someone who was 'perfectly safe'. Mrs. Brownlee listened and nodded and encouraged her visitor with exactly the right sort of questions. If she were 'stupid about business matters' she certainly was not stupid about human beings and their peculiarities.

Bel told Mrs. Brownlee about the appointment of the new agent at Leith and the way in which Mr. Wills had behaved to her, blaming her for what was not her fault and distrusting her word when she had explained the matter to him.

'Most unjust,' declared Mrs. Brownlee. 'It's dreadful for a man in his position to be unjust. Ellis always says you can be as strict as you like but you must never be unjust.'

Bel hid a smile. She could not help the smile for she had noticed that no matter what the subject happened to be — roses or business affairs or the delinquencies of Mr. Wills — Mrs. Brownlee never failed to mention her son. Ellis said this or Ellis did that and Ellis was invariably right. As a matter of fact Bel was inclined to agree with her but it was amusing all the same.

'Of course that explains the unhappy atmosphere in the office,' continued Mrs. Brownlee. 'If Mr. Wills finds fault unjustly it's bound to make people cross. They can't be cross to him so they take it out on each other. That's human nature.'

'I suppose it is,' said Bel thoughtfully.

Mrs. Brownlee was so interested and so sympathetic that Bel found herself telling her listener much more than she had intended; indeed by the time she had finished talking there was very little that Mrs. Brownlee did not know. She had heard about Mr. James and his gift of tongues and all about yesterday's expedition to the Zoo. This part of Bel's story was amusing; they were glad of a little 'light relief' from the gloomy tale of woe.

'He must be a pet,' declared Mrs. Brownlee. 'Of course I know his parents — they're charming — but I haven't seen Jim since he was a little boy.'

'He's a big boy now,' said Bel, laughing. 'You'd be surprised! He's just like a great big awkward child . . . ' and she told Mrs. Brownlee about her lunch with Mr. James at Smart's Restaurant and how he had handed her the menu and said, 'Have anything you like; I'm paying, remember.'

'Delightful!' exclaimed Mrs. Brownlee laughing heartily. 'Absolutely delightful! I simply must meet your Mr. James. Perhaps you could bring him to see me one day. It wouldn't be so amusing for him as the Zoo, but I could provide a good tea with 'proper food'. When Ellis was that age he used to like bacon and eggs for tea — or fried fish — so I expect that sort of meal would appeal to Jim, wouldn't it? — and that reminds me it's more than time we had tea ourselves. I've kept you here talking for ages.'

It was true that they had had a long conversation — much longer than they had intended — and when they had finished tea and straightened out Mrs. Brownlee's business troubles it was so late that Bel was persuaded to stay for supper.

There was more conversation at supper. Mrs. Brownlee had had several letters from Ellis and some snaps which had been taken on the boat; one was of Ellis standing on the deck with two very pretty young girls; another was of Ellis in a garden with a small boy and a dog.

'He knows I like to have photographs of him,' Mrs. Brownlee explained. 'I suppose you've had letters from him, Miss Lamington.'

'No,' said Bel. 'He said he would write but I expect he's been too busy. Mr. Wills got a letter the other day but it was just about business of course.'

'Ellis is a nice name, isn't it?' said Mrs. Brownlee. 'It was my name before I was married: Frances Ellis. That's why we called him Ellis.'

'It's very unusual,' said Bel.

Bel did not get home until after ten o'clock but, far from being tired, she felt rejuvenated. She felt she had made a friend. She did not feel so alone. It was horrid to feel that you were alone and everyone was against you. It gave her confidence to know that Mrs. Brownlee was 'on her side'. In fact it was so encouraging that she decided she really must take a firmer line with Miss Goudge and stand no more impertinence. Bel hated taking a firm line with anyone, but sometimes it was essential.

Bel had shared her worries with Mrs. Brownlee and the mere fact of sharing them and unburdening her mind had brought the worries into proper perspective and lightened her heart.

It will be all right when Mr. Brownlee comes back, thought Bel as she made ready for bed.

Mrs. Brownlee's faith in her son was infectious.

13

When Bel awoke on Thursday morning she had a feeling that something unpleasant was about to happen. For a few moments, as she hovered on the borderland of sleep, she could not think what the unpleasant happening could be — and then she remembered that it was her birthday.

At one time birthdays had been delightful; there were parcels to open and her favourite pudding for lunch and, of course, a cake with candles. There was usually a special treat: a picnic or a visit to the picture house, possibly an expedition to the sea. Now there was nothing — nothing to mark the day from any other day in the year — no presents, no cake, not even a birthday card and, worst of all, no Aunt Beatrice to hug her fondly and wish her many happy returns of the day.

Bel was in the doldrums; there was not a ray of light in the sky. Today the Armstrongs were going to Drumburly. Bel had not been very disappointed when she found she would not be able to go with them, but now, quite unreasonably, she felt very disappointed indeed. She found herself thinking about it — how lovely it would have been! How lovely to get away from the office! Her work, which had been so interesting and rewarding, had now become a penance. Everybody was disagreeable; everybody was against her; the only way she had been able to endure it was the knowledge that sooner or later Mr. Brownlee would return and put things right. Now, alas, Mr. Brownlee's return had been postponed again; he had found he must visit New York for an important conference. In addition to these major troubles various smaller annoyances conspired to depress Bel on this, her birthday morning. Her suspender broke; her refrigerator was out of order and had leaked all over the kitchen floor; her birthday-mail consisted of two bills which were a good deal higher than she had expected.

The weather was extremely unpleasant, and when Bel emerged into the street the skies above the roof tops were leaden; thunder growled in the distance and a few moments later rain began to pour down upon the crowds of miserable wretches on their way to business.

Happy birthday! thought Bel, with unwonted cynicism as she climbed onto the bus and pushed her way between dripping umbrellas and sodden mackintoshes to find a vacant seat.

Although Bel was late in arriving it appeared that Miss Goudge had also been delayed, at any rate she was not in her usual place, so Bel was spared the sight of her camel-like countenance glaring disdainfully through the grille. This was something to be thankful for, thought Bel, as she shed her dripping mackintosh and changed her soaking shoes and hastened to Mr. Brownlee's room.

It was the day for accounts so Bel took out the large brown ledgers, piled them upon her table and started work.

Soon after eleven there was a knock on the door. It was a very gentle knock — the merest tap — but as Bel was not typing she heard it quite distinctly. She felt pretty certain it was Mr. James — and it was. He came in and shut the door and advanced towards her across the room.

'Happy birthday to you!' he chanted and, grinning somewhat sheepishly, produced from behind his back a large bouquet done up in white paper.

'Oh!' exclaimed Bel. There are various ways of uttering this exclamation. Bel's 'Oh!' expressed astonishment, gratitude and pleasure — but chiefly astonishment.

'D'you like flowers?' he asked, laying his offering upon the table.

'Oh, how kind!' cried Bel. 'Of course I love flowers, but — '

'Most women do,' declared Mr. James with the air of a man-of-the-world.

'You shouldn't have brought me flowers!'

'Why not? It's your birthday, isn't it?'

'How did you know?'

'You told me.'

'I told you! I'm sure I didn't.'

'You did — really. How else could I have known?'

The logic of this was irrefutable. She must have told him, she supposed. But when had she told him? And why? Bel could not remember a thing about it.

'How very, very kind of you,' said Bel. Actually there was a lump in her throat and a pricking behind her eyes. It was silly to feel upset because somebody had remembered her birthday and taken the trouble to bring her flowers. What a dear he was, thought Bel. What a great big enormous lovable child!

'You had better open the parcel,' he suggested. 'They're sweetpeas. I thought they were rather pretty. The man said they were quite fresh from the country.'

They were indeed beautifully fresh — pink and white and lavender — like a flight of fairies in stiff silken dresses.

'How beautiful!' Bel exclaimed in delight.

'I'm glad you like them. They've got a nice smell, haven't they?'

'Perfectly lovely!'

'I'm glad you like them,' repeated Mr. James with a self-satisfied air.

2

'Now for business,' said Mr. James. 'The Guv'nor wants some papers out of his safe. I've got to get them for him. Here are the keys. You'll help me, won't you?'

'Help you?'

He nodded. 'To burgle the Guv'nor's safe.'

Bel hesitated. 'Perhaps you should ask Mr. Wills.'

'No,' said Mr. James firmly. He held up the bunch of keys and added, 'Come on, Miss Lamington, you've got to help me.'

Mr. Copping's room was sacred ground. Nobody used it except Mr. Copping himself and while he was away nobody ever entered it except the cleaners. Bel had not been in the room before so she looked round with a good deal of interest. It was a large room with a thick Turkey carpet; the furniture was large and solid, the enormous desk was mahogany and so was the big wooden chair with its carved back and arms. Two huge brown leather easy chairs stood before the fire. There was an air of permanence about the room. It had been exactly like this for a hundred years — or so Bel imagined — and would remain in exactly the same condition for another hundred years. It gave her the sort of feeling of being in church.

There were several oil paintings in heavy gilt frames hanging upon the panelled walls — portraits of dead-and-gone members of the firm. The portrait over the chimney-piece was obviously that of old Mr. James Copping, who had built the wharf and founded the firm — all the more obviously because it bore a very strong resemblance to his great grandson; the same bony features, the same straw-coloured hair! Someday his great grandson would use this room and sit in that carved wooden chair and write his letters at that enormous mahogany desk . . .

'I say, Miss Lamington,' said Mr. James in a low voice. 'It makes you think, doesn't it? I've been in here before of course, but I'm seeing it differently today. Seems queer to be here without the Guv'nor — not right, somehow.'

'It's right for you, Mr. James.'

'Yes,' he said doubtfully. 'Yes, I suppose so. I know what you mean. But I've got a long way to go.' He looked up at the portrait of the first James Copping and added, 'I wonder what the old boy thinks of me.'

'He's pleased.'

'Pleased?'

'Pleased to see his great grandson — another James Copping. He's pleased that you're coming into the firm.'

Mr. James was still looking up at the portrait. He said, 'I'll do my best.'

Bel had a feeling that this was a promise — but not to her, of course.

There was silence for a minute or two and then Mr. James came back to earth.

'We'd better get on with the burgling, Miss Lamington,' he said.

The safe was in the corner of the room behind a book-case and was opened easily enough with the keys. The door swung back and revealed a recess with shelves packed with bundles of papers tied with tape, deed boxes, jewel cases and large manilla envelopes all covered thick in dust.

'Lordy!' said Mr. James in awe.

The sight was definitely awe-inspiring, it was also somewhat alarming. Bel had taken no part in the 'burgling', she had merely stood by and provided a little moral support, but now she began to wonder whether active co-operation would be required of her, for if Mr. James was proposing to search in that cupboard for papers he would need an assistant with cleaning materials — at the very least an assistant with a damp duster, thought Bel.

'Do you know what you want and where to find it?' she enquired.

Mr. James sneezed violently several times. 'Dust,' he explained. 'I get hay-fever, you know. Yes, the Guv'nor told me. It's a big yellow envelope with an elastic band. It's got *Copping Wills and Brownlee Contracts* written on it in red ink. It's on the top shelf on the right hand side.'

With these detailed instructions Mr. James had no difficulty in finding the envelope. He bestowed it carefully in the inside pocket of his jacket and closed the door. The door closed with a 'whooff' of dust-laden air.

'Just — take a look at it,' said Mr. James between paroxysms of sneezes. 'Just make sure — atishoo — that I've shut it — atishoo — properly.'

Bel made sure by turning the big brass handle and shaking it with all her might. 'Perfectly safe,' she said. 'But you know, Mr. James, it really ought to be cleaned out.'

'Well, that's not our pigeon, thank goodness,' he replied.

There was a bundle of foreign letters to be translated; Bel had kept them for Mr. James. He accomplished this task in the same capable manner as before.

'The Guv'nor was awfully pleased when I told him about translating the letters,' said Mr. James. 'He was tickled pink. Gave me a fiver! What d'you think of that? Pretty good pay for a couple of hours' work! I spent some of it on your sweetpeas.'

Bel's sweetpeas, which she had arranged in a jam jar, were already filling the room with their fragrance. She looked at them with renewed delight and renewed her expressions of gratitude to their donor.

'It's nothing,' he declared in a dégagé manner. 'Nothing at all. I'm glad you like them. You'll take them home with you, I suppose?'

'Yes, of course I shall.'

'I wish we could have lunch together but I'd better go straight home. The Guv'nor wants these papers. Oh, he said I was to ask you if there was any news about Mr. Brownlee coming back.'

'Not yet,' said Bel sadly. 'He's going to a conference at New York so we don't know when he will be coming.' She hesitated and then added, 'I saw his mother on Monday. She was asking about you.'

'Oh yes! I remember her!' exclaimed Mr. James. 'She lives at Beckenham, doesn't she? Must be a bit dull for her living there all by herself. Perhaps I ought to look her up. What do you think?'

'I think it would be kind of you.'

'I like old ladies,' he said.

Somehow it had never occurred to Bel to class Mrs. Brownlee as an old lady. She was not young, of course, and she was definitely a lady, but the term 'old lady' conjured up the vision of a decrepit gentlewoman with silver hair and wrinkles, walking with the help of an ebony stick. Bel tried to explain that Mrs. Brownlee was not in the least like that. On the contrary she was lively and active and good-looking and very much 'all there'.

'She must be pretty old all the same,' declared Mr. James. 'I mean look at Mr. Brownlee; he's no chicken.'

14

A week passed. Mr. James had come in several times to translate letters and on one occasion he and Bel had lunched together at Smart's. This time, after some argument, they had each paid for their own meal on the principle of 'a Dutch Treat'. Bel was adamant about this. As she had said before, she could not prevent Mr. James from lunching at Smart's if he wished to do so, but she refused to allow him to spend his money upon her entertainment. It would not be right. All the same she enjoyed the company of her 'great big enormous child' and evidently he enjoyed hers. It was a very satisfactory sort of friendship.

On the following Thursday Bel was summoned by Mr. Wills and went to his room taking with her some letters for him to sign. She had not seen him for two days, which was very unsatisfactory in Bel's opinion. There were various matters which could not be settled without his authority. The most important was a message from Mr. Nelson at Copping Wharf about some urgent necessary repairs. Mr. Nelson had explained the matter on the phone and Bel, having taken notes of the estimates, was now prepared to pass on the information to Mr. Wills.

She put the notes before him and began her explanations . . . and then she realised that Mr. Wills was not listening.

'Ahem . . . Miss Lamington,' he said. 'I have decided to make some changes in the office staff.'

'Oh — yes — ' began Bel doubtfully. As a matter of fact her mind was so full of other affairs that she scarcely took in what he was saying.

'Yes,' said Mr. Wills. 'Yes, several changes — long overdue. The fact is, the office is understaffed and the work is not being properly handled. With Mr. Brownlee absent in America and Mr. Copping *hors de combat* there is far too much to do. I'm unable to get away from the office for sufficient fresh air and exercise. I'm feeling the strain, Miss Lamington.'

'I'm sorry,' began Bel. 'If I could — '

'There is only one thing to be done; I must get an efficient secretary; a thoroughly experienced man with a knowledge of Spanish.'

'Mr. James has been translating the letters for us,' said Bel quickly. 'He likes doing it,' she added.

'I don't feel that is satisfactory, Miss Lamington. No, not satisfactory at all. I have given the matter a great deal of thought. I shall keep Miss Snow as my own personal secretary, she suits me very well, but I have decided to dispense with your services and replace you with a thoroughly competent man.'

'Replace me!' cried Bel in dismay.

'Yes.'

'But Mr. Brownlee asked me — '

'Mr. Brownlee is in America — as you are aware.'

'I know — but he said — '

'In Mr. Brownlee's absence I am in full charge of the affairs of the firm. It is a heavy responsibility — very heavy indeed.'

'Yes of course, but — but I hope — ' began Bel breathlessly. 'I mean if you would just — just tell me what I've done wrong. If you have any complaints about — about my work — '

Until now Mr. Wills had been quite calm but now he was beginning to lose his temper. 'Complaints!' he exclaimed. 'Yes, Miss Goudge has complained of you. She says you're impertinent and insubordinate.'

'Oh, it isn't true!' cried Bel.

'I can't say I've found you impertinent,' said Mr. Wills grudgingly, 'but I find you extremely interfering.'

'Interfering?'

'Very interfering indeed. In the matter of the appointment at Leith, for instance. I am convinced that Anderson is not the right man — not the right man at all.'

'But the appointment had been made! I couldn't let you — '

'It was entirely through your interference that the wrong man was appointed.'

'The appointment had been made! Honestly, Mr. Wills, it isn't fair to — '

'That's quite enough, Miss Lamington!' exclaimed Mr. Wills, raising his voice and beginning to get very red in the face. 'I have no time to bandy words with you. I suppose you'll admit that I have the right to dismiss any members of the office staff if I find them incompetent?'

'Incompetent? Mr. Wills! In what way — '

'Two weeks' salary,' he said, producing a bulging envelope and laying it on the table. 'Two weeks — in lieu of notice.'

Bel looked at him in dismay. 'Do you mean I'm to go — now?'

'Yes.' He was breathing heavily. His brow was beaded with perspiration.

'But, Mr. Wills!' cried Bel. 'There's a lot of work. There are various matters — there's the matter of the estimates. Mr. Nelson rang up this morning — '

'You are being replaced.'

'But — but if you've got somebody else I must hand over.'

'No!'

'Wouldn't it be better — '

'No!' he shouted, thumping on the table with his fist. 'No, it wouldn't be better. I won't have you in the office for another day. Is that clear?'

Bel gazed at him in amazement.

'I won't have you in the office for another day!' repeated Mr. Wills, working himself up to boiling point. 'Not for another hour!'

'Why?' she whispered. 'What have I done?'

'You know perfectly well. Your conduct is most — most reprehensible — most irregular. You had no right at all to encourage young Copping and entertain him in your room.'

'Mr. Wills, I told you! He came to translate the letters!'

'He came to see you! He was with you for hours! Extraordinary behaviour! Scandalous — absolutely scandalous!'

'Mr. Wills! What do you mean?'

'Entertaining him in your room! Accepting flowers from him! Meeting him in a clandestine manner!'

'Clandestine? But I only — '

'You needn't deny it. You were seen with him.'

'Mr. Wills, please listen — '

'You — were seen!' he shouted, glaring at her from beneath his bristling eyebrows. 'Scandalous behaviour! I won't stand it! Carrying on with him — a mere boy! The son of the Senior Partner! Scandalous!'

He stopped, breathless and panting. He remembered suddenly that it was very bad for him to get excited — the doctor had said so. He had not intended to get excited like this. He had not intended to mention young Copping. There was no need to mention the young cub! He had merely intended to dismiss the girl and to say that he was replacing her with a Thoroughly Experienced Man. That was all. But the girl annoyed him — she had always annoyed him — he could not stand the sight of her! So he had got himself all worked up and said more than he had meant.

'That will do, Miss Lamington,' he said, waving her away.

'But — but I must explain — ' began Bel desperately.

'I'm busy. I've no time to listen to explanations. Two weeks' salary,' he added, pushing the bulging envelope across the table towards her.

He was beginning to get worked up again. He

159

felt queer and giddy. He felt — extremely unwell. Why couldn't the wretched girl go away and leave him to recover in peace?

'Take the money and go!' he shouted in fury.

Bel was terrified.

Afterwards she thought of all the things she should have said but at the time she was dumb. He looked so queer! He looked — he looked like a madman!

She turned and fled from the room.

2

Bel went into the cloak-room and put on her coat and hat; she went down the stairs and out into the street. She felt dazed. She felt rather sick. Her knees were shaking. For a minute or two she stood there holding on to the railing, her heart hammering madly against her side. Presently the fresh air revived her a little and she began to walk slowly down the street towards the bus.

Bel did not know how she managed to catch the bus and get home; she managed it somehow, and somehow she managed to toil up the stairs. Her hand was trembling so that she had difficulty in fitting the key into the lock and opening the door of her flat. She went in and shut the door and lay down on her bed.

She found herself trembling all over, shaking uncontrollably, her teeth chattering in her head. She lay there for quite a long time — not thinking at all, scarcely knowing where she was or why she felt so shattered.

After a while the trembling ceased and she was able to get up and make herself some tea. She drank it and ate some biscuits. She felt better — more like herself — not so dazed and stupid. She began to think about what had happened. Her thoughts came and went in a muddled sort of way.

She had been sacked — dismissed without notice. What did he mean about Mr. James? 'Meeting him in a clandestine manner'? She had met him for lunch. She had gone to the Zoo with him. Was that clandestine? It was Helen Goudge, thought Bel. She must have seen them . . . and she must have told Mr. Wills about the flowers . . . and Helen Goudge had complained that she was impertinent! That was nonsense. Bel had endured all the insults that she had received without a word — she had taken them lying down!

What would happen in the office, wondered Bel. How could anyone, however experienced, take over the work without being told about it? Everything would be in a muddle. But it was none of her business any more — she had been sacked. She had no job. She had no reference. Mr. Wills was mad. He had looked mad — quite mad. His red face and glaring eyes! The way his eyebrows had bristled; the way he had shouted and thumped on the table! Mad!

What would Mr. Brownlee think? She had promised him to stay on and do her best to keep things straight — but she couldn't stay on because she had been sacked. What would happen to Mr. James? Would he get into trouble? No, surely they wouldn't dare! Even Mr. Wills wouldn't dare to bully the son of the Senior Partner. But what would happen when Mr. James called at the office and found she had been dismissed? Would he be angry? She had a feeling he would be very angry indeed. Would he speak to his father about it? Perhaps he would walk into Mr. Wills's room and ask for an explanation. She could imagine him doing just that — asking for an explanation and keeping on asking until he got it — and she could imagine the frightful scene. She could imagine Mr. Wills shouting and thumping the table with his clenched fist!

What would happen about the estimates for the repairs to Copping Wharf? Mr. Nelson was waiting for Bel to ring him up about them — he had said the matter was urgent — she should have dealt with that before she left. But she had been sacked — told to go — told to take her money and go!

Oh heavens, I can't bear it! thought Bel, holding her aching head in her hands. I'm going crazy! I'm all in a muddle! I must talk to somebody about it — somebody sensible — like Doctor Armstrong!

If the Armstrongs had been at Coombe House she could have rung them up and talked to them; she might even have gone to them for the weekend; but the Armstrongs were miles away — hundreds of miles away — at Drumburly. Bel had had a letter from Louise that very morning telling her about their journey and what

162

comfortable rooms they had in the hotel. Telling her about the fishing, which was particularly good, and describing the river and the hills. It was all too beautiful for words. 'If only you were here it would be perfect,' Louise had written.

Then suddenly Bel thought: Why not? Was there any reason why she should not be at Drumburly with Louise? There was no reason at all — absolutely none!

Bel felt quite breathless. She took out Louise's letter and read it again. She had read it this morning of course but not very carefully for to tell the truth she had felt just a trifle vexed. What was the good of Louise enthusing about Drumburly and saying she wished Bel were there? Bel could not be there — and that was that. Now, however, Bel read the letter very carefully indeed for she had to make sure if Louise really and truly wanted her.

Louise had the gift of putting herself into a letter so that when you read it you could almost see her before your eyes, you could hear her talking to you and telling you things. (Some people have this gift and others not). When Bel had read the letter carefully there was no doubt left in her mind: Louise wanted her.

It was a loving letter and it made Bel feel quite different. She did not feel so frightened; she did not feel so alone. Somebody really cared. She sat down and took a sheet of writing-paper and wrote a hasty reply:

Darling Louise
    If you really want me I can come. I can

Part Three

15

When one has heard a great deal about a place and it has been described as an earthly paradise it is often slightly disappointing and, as the Thames-Clyde Express steamed into Dumfries, Bel Lamington reminded herself of this and tried to still her excitement. The telegram had said she would be met at Dumfries Station; it had given detailed instructions for her journey and, incidentally, it must have cost a small fortune.

Bel had followed the instructions and, lo and behold, here she was at Dumfries! It seemed a big place — much bigger than she had expected — and, what was even more surprising, the people seemed to be conversing with each other in a foreign language. There was no sign of the Armstrongs and when she had got out of the train and assembled her luggage the excitement seeped out of her and she began to feel a little frightened. It really was rather alarming to arrive like this in a strange place. She remembered suddenly that she had only a few shillings in her pocket — the fare had cost far more than she had thought — and, just supposing something had happened to prevent the Armstrongs from coming to meet her, what was she to do?

Then suddenly Louise was there, rushing at her, hugging her, and nearly knocking her hat off.

'Darling!' cried Louise. 'I thought you hadn't

come — couldn't see you anywhere! Oh Bel, how marvellous! It seems too good to be true. I just couldn't believe it when I got your letter. In fact I didn't believe you were *really* coming until this moment — this very moment when I saw you standing on the platform 'all forlorn' like the maiden who milked the cow with the crumpled horn.'

'You really wanted me?' asked Bel — quite unnecessarily one would think.

'Wanted you!' cried Louise, hugging her again with renewed ardour. 'Well, of course I wanted you! What a donkey you are! We're going to have a simply gorgeous time together. I've been making plans about all the lovely things we're going to do. I would have wanted you even if the weather hadn't been perfect for fishing.'

'Perfect for fishing?' asked Bel in surprise.

'Absolutely perfect,' declared Louise. 'It's been like that ever since we came — a nice breeze and not too bright and no thunder — and the water has been just right. It scarcely ever is,' said Louise earnestly. 'Scarcely ever! There's nearly always something wrong. And another thing,' Louise continued as they followed the porter down the platform. 'Mrs. Simpson's cousin fell off a rock when he was walking over the hills to Crossraggle and twisted his ankle and lay there all night until he was found by the shepherd in the morning — so you see how much I've been wanting you!'

Bel did not see the connection — perhaps it was stupid of her — but what did it matter? She

168

saw that Louise was really and truly delighted that she had come.

The car was waiting in the Station Yard. The luggage was loaded and the two girls got in.

'I'm afraid you'll have to share my room,' said Louise as she started the car. 'The hotel is full because of the fishing so Mrs. Simpson couldn't do anything about it. It's a very nice room with a lovely view over the river and there are two beds of course. I do hope you don't mind awfully.'

'Of course I don't mind.'

'There's a man leaving in a day or two and when he goes you can have a room to yourself. Mrs. Simpson was very sorry about it but she couldn't help it. The hotel is full.'

'It will be fun,' declared Bel . . . and she meant it. The prospect of sharing a room with Louise was delightful.

'I suppose Mr. Brownlee has come back? Of course I want to hear all about everything, but don't start telling me till we're out of the town. I want all my wits about me. The streets are so narrow and twisty and they've made a whole lot of one-way streets.' Louise giggled and continued, 'When I was coming to meet you I suddenly found myself careering gaily along a street with all the traffic coming in the other direction and everybody started waving their arms and shouting at me. Of course I didn't know what was the matter; I thought they had all gone mad . . . Oh heavens, I've done it again!'

She had done it again. The traffic was all coming in the other direction and everybody was waving their arms and shouting.

Louise drew in to the kerb and immediately an extremely large Police-constable appeared and looked in at the window.

'You've got yourself into serious trrrouble,' he said sternly.

The rolling Rs made the admonition sound very alarming indeed, but Louise was not alarmed.

'I know,' she admitted contritely. 'I'm terribly sorry. Isn't it silly of me?'

'Could you not rread the notice?'

'I didn't see it. You've made all these funny rules since the last time I was here.'

'You'll be a strrranger?'

'Oh, not a stranger exactly. We always come here for our holidays; it's so lovely, isn't it?'

'H'mm!' he remarked doubtfully.

'My father likes fishing, you see.'

'Fishing?' asked the constable, his eyes lighting up with interest. 'Would it be the Annan?'

'No, we're staying at Drumburly.'

'The Burly is a grand wee river. He'll be getting good baskets, no doubt?'

By this time the traffic was piling up and one impatient motorist started to blow his horn.

'Oh dear!' exclaimed Louise. 'I shall have to move, shan't I? What would you like me to do?' she added with a helpless air.

'You'll need to rrevairrse.'

'I suppose so. You'll help me, won't you?'

The constable agreed. He walked along beside the car until they had come to a crossing and were out of danger. He was rewarded for his trouble with an enchanting smile.

'How kind of you!' said Louise. 'I'll try to be good in future.'

He grinned and said, 'You'd better.'

Soon they were bowling briskly along another street and Bel was relieved to see that here the traffic was moving in the same direction as themselves.

'Wasn't he a lamb?' said Louise. 'And so good-looking! I do think the uniform is becoming, don't you?'

When they were out of the town, but not before, Bel broke the news that she had lost her job. She had expected Louise to be appalled at this news but Louise took it in her stride.

'Oh darling, how horrid for you!' Louise exclaimed. 'That Wills man must be crazy — but you're here, that's the main thing. I mean if you hadn't lost your job you wouldn't be here, would you? It's so lovely to have you here.'

'Yes, but you see — ' began Bel.

'You don't need to worry,' declared Louise. 'Daddy will find you a much nicer job. You must tell Daddy all about it. He'll know what to do. You aren't worrying, are you?'

Curiously enough Bel discovered that she was not worrying — or at least not worrying very much. She was here, with Louise, and it was all delightful: the fresh air, the rolling country, the purple hills in the distance, the blue sky above! Bel cast care aside and gave herself up to enjoyment.

16

Drumburly is a small town — scarcely more than a good-sized village — a cluster of grey stone houses in a little valley with rolling hills all round. The Shaw Arms Hotel stands near the bridge on the right bank of the river which laps against its thick stone wall. Long ago it had been a change-house and there had been ample stable accommodation behind the Inn, but the stalls and loose-boxes have now been made into garages for the convenience of the residents. The big arched gateway still stands, leading into a spacious cobbled yard.

The house itself is interesting and unusual; parts of it are very old; but it has been built onto from time to time so there are passages and steps in unexpected places. Some of the rooms are large and others small. The lounge is very large and comfortably furnished in an old-fashioned style with big easy chairs and Victorian book-cases and a big round table in the window with papers and magazines displayed upon it — and there is nearly always a splendid fire of logs burning merrily in the old-fashioned grate. Drumburly stands high and there are very few evenings, even in summer, when a fire is unwelcome — and in Mrs. Simpson's opinion there is an inhospitable look about a fireplace with no fire.

Mrs. Simpson was well aware that her hostelry

was not up-to-date but she refused to alter it. Her clientèle consisted chiefly of 'gentlemen for the fishing' and they appreciated the comfort of big chairs and thick Turkey carpets and solid furniture.

Upstairs there was solid furniture too (large mahogany cupboards and chests of drawers) but Mrs. Simpson had installed several extra bathrooms, and basins with hot and cold water in all the bedrooms. She had seen to it that the basins were the right size and shape for a gentleman to shave with comfort and that the electric light was in the correct position. Last but not least all the beds were fitted with interior-spring mattresses.

All this had cost money but Mrs. Simpson was reaping the benefit of her outlay. The gentlemen returned to The Shaw Arms year after year and sometimes brought their wives. Quite often they mentioned the place to their friends, and their friends came and discovered that it was every bit as comfortable as they had been led to believe . . . and came again.

The cooking at The Shaw Arms was good and plain. It was the sort of food that appealed to gentlemen who had been out in the fresh air all day long. Mrs. Simpson was very particular about the cooking. She saw to it herself.

The staff of The Shaw Arms consisted almost entirely of young girls from the surrounding country-side, big buxom lassies with rosy cheeks and bright eyes who endeavoured to make up for their lack of experience by cheerful, willing service. Mrs. Simpson found them a little too cheerful and willing for they were inclined to sing loudly whilst cleaning the stairs and they were only too ready to abandon their proper duties to help each other. Quite often the kitchen-maid was discovered helping to make the beds instead of peeling the potatoes; the chambermaid scrubbed the scullery; the cook, thrilled at seeing a car draw up to the door, would rush out to receive the arriving guests and to carry up their luggage.

This was very nice in some ways, it showed a Christian spirit, but Mrs. Simpson would have preferred a well-trained staff. However, as this was impossible to get — or keep — in an isolated place like Drumburly, she made do with what she had. She trained the girls as best she could and kept them in tolerably good order.

As a matter of fact Mrs. Simpson was famed far and wide for her ability to train young girls in the arts of domestic service. She spent her days making silk purses out of sows' ears. It was very hard work but she would not have minded if she could have kept the silk purses when they were made. This was never possible; the girls came to learn and no sooner had they learnt than they departed. Either they married or else found a more exciting post in Edinburgh or Glasgow where there were bright lights and fascinating shops and picture houses. Then Mrs. Simpson had to start all over again with another rosy-cheeked lassie who had not the faintest idea how to lay a table, hand a dish of vegetables or tidy a room.

These troubles might have soured some

women and made them thin and irritable and dyspeptic, but Mrs. Simpson was not like that at all. She was large and comfortably padded with solid flesh; her cheeks were pink, her eyes were bright and kind and she had a ready smile. The fact was she enjoyed running The Shaw Arms, she liked making her guests comfortable, she loved chatting to them. If ever there was a round peg in a round hole it was Mrs. Simpson — and the best of it was she knew she was happy; she would not have changed places with the Queen.

When Mrs. Simpson went into the lounge and saw her guests sitting on her comfortable chairs warming themselves at her cheerful fire and reading the nice glossy magazines which she had provided for them her heart turned over in her bosom and she loved them. Yes, she loved every one of them — even the troublesome ones who threw their towels on the floor and flooded the bathroom and complained about their food — she loved them like an indulgent nannie.

But even an indulgent nannie has favourites and Mrs. Simpson's favourites were naturally those who returned year after year to enjoy the amenities of The Shaw Arms . . . and the chief of Mrs. Simpson's favourites was Dr. Armstrong. In Mrs. Simpson's eyes Dr. Armstrong was absolutely perfect. She loved Miss Armstrong too — everybody loved Louise.

Unfortunately Louise Armstrong was not enjoying her holiday as much as usual. Mrs. Simpson knew this and was sorry. The doctor fished all day, which was right and proper, but Miss Armstrong was not fond of fishing. On previous occasions when the Armstrongs had stayed at The Shaw Arms Miss Armstrong had taken sandwiches in her pocket and had been out all day, walking over the hills and watching the birds and had returned in time for dinner with a glowing face and sparkling eyes and an exceedingly good appetite for Mrs. Simpson's wholesome fare. Dr. Armstrong had been slightly worried about these expeditions but had given in to his daughter's persuasions and allowed her to have her way. This year, however, it had been different and Dr. Armstrong had absolutely forbidden his daughter to go far afield.

Mrs. Simpson was all the more unhappy about this because she felt it was her fault. It was unreasonable to feel guilty about it, for of course she could not help it, but it was her cousin George who had had that nasty accident when he was on his way to Crossraggle Farm. George had missed his footing and given his ankle a bad twist and had lain in the heather all night. It was a fine dry night and the experience had done George no harm — his ankle had recovered and he was now as fit as a fiddle — but Dr. Armstrong had taken fright when he heard about George for the accident had shown what could happen — and happen very easily — on the rolling solitary hills. Supposing the same thing happened to Louise! The idea was too dreadful to contemplate. So Dr. Armstrong had put his foot down very firmly indeed and Louise was obliged to confine her ramblings to more frequented ways.

Mrs. Simpson liked people to be happy, so she

was delighted when she heard that Miss Armstrong was having a friend to stay. The two girls could go off together and walk over the hills to their hearts' content and Dr. Armstrong could enjoy his fishing in peace. It was most unlikely that two girls could both fall down and twist their ankles at the same moment; if one of them were incapacitated, like the unfortunate George, the other could go for help. It was for this reason that Mrs. Simpson was looking forward so eagerly to the arrival of her new guest.

Mrs. Simpson was on the steps of the hotel when the two girls arrived and her welcome to Miss Lamington was very cordial indeed. Miss Lamington was astonished at the warmth of her welcome. She had been told that Mrs. Simpson was very kind but this exceeded her expectations. It was quite extraordinary. She had a feeling that Mrs. Simpson was about to envelope her in a loving embrace! Mrs. Simpson did not do so, of course (she managed to refrain) but she enquired with the greatest solicitude what sort of a journey Miss Lamington had had and whether she were tired and suggested that Miss Lamington might like to go straight to her bed and have a bit of supper on a tray.

'Oh no, I'm not a bit tired. The air is so lovely,' said Bel. 'Nobody could feel tired here.'

At this Mrs. Simpson was even more delighted with her new guest, for the invigorating air was one of the amenities which she was proud to offer. She could not have been more proud of it if she had provided it herself at great cost — as she had provided the new bathrooms and the mattresses with their hidden springs.

'We're late I'm afraid,' said Louise. 'But I expect you've kept something for us, Mrs. Simpson. Perhaps we could have it in the little dining-room at the back.'

'That's just what I thought,' replied Mrs. Simpson nodding. 'Your dinners will be ready in ten minutes — that will give you time to get tidied. The doctor's not back yet from the fishing, but he'll not be long and you can all have your dinners together at the wee table in the window. Will that do?'

Louise said it would be perfect and, taking her friend's arm, led her upstairs to wash off the dirt of her journey.

2

When Dr. Armstrong returned from fishing he found his daughter and her friend finishing dinner. It was dark by this time but the curtains had not been drawn. The table stood near the window and was lighted by a shaded lamp which threw its light upon the two heads: the one dark and curly, the other brown with big smooth waves. The two heads were close together and their owners were talking hard. This did not surprise the doctor in the least.

'Hullo!' exclaimed the doctor, advancing and laying his hands firmly upon their two shoulders. 'How are you, Bel? You can't imagine how pleased we were when we heard you could come after all.'

'It's lovely,' declared Bel, looking up and smiling at him.

'Lou met you all right?' he asked. 'Everything went according to schedule?'

'Oh yes, it was all quite easy.'

'Except Dumfries,' said Louise giggling. 'I kept on rushing along one-way streets but there was a perfect lamb of a policeman who rescued us and put us right.'

'Did the lamb book you by any chance?' enquired Dr. Armstrong somewhat anxiously as he sat down and unfolded his table-napkin.

'Goodness, no! He was far too nice and kind, and far too interested in fishing.'

'Interested in fishing, was he?'

'Yes, frightfully. He wanted to know if you fished the Annan.'

'Really?' asked Dr. Armstrong. He was a little surprised that an unknown police constable should take such an interest in his doings.

'Yes, really,' declared Louise. 'And, talking of fishing, did you have a good day?'

'Not bad at all. Six nice trout.'

Louise nodded. 'Good, we'll have trout for breakfast — but what a pity that big one got away.'

'Yes,' agreed the doctor. 'Yes, it was very annoying. He was all of two pounds . . . but how on earth did you know?'

Louise could not reply. She was giggling.

'Oh, you wretch!' exclaimed Dr. Armstrong. 'Oh, you wicked little monkey to tease your poor old father like that! Isn't she naughty, Bel?'

Bel smiled. She could not see anything very

179

funny in the fact that poor Dr. Armstrong had not been able to catch the big fish, but her two companions were laughing, so she supposed it must be a joke. Having been brought up by a maiden aunt Bel knew nothing about fishing. The gentle art of angling was a closed book as far as she was concerned. Of course she had seen pictures of gentlemen in waders standing in rivers with rods in their hands — but that was all. Fortunately she was aware of her ignorance and had decided to go warily until she saw what was what. It was obvious that fishing was serious and important to Dr. Armstrong, and Louise seemed to know all about it. Say nothing and smile, thought Bel. That's the best way.

They went on talking about fishing for several minutes. Dr. Armstrong explained how he had hooked a good one on his tail-fly, a Bloody Butcher, in the pool just below Mureth House; how it had gone down and lurked beneath a stone so that he thought he had lost it, and how it had appeared again and leaped and run up the river like an arrow from a bow and how he had played it carefully and gradually enticed it towards the bank and finally waded in and netted it.

Louise listened and made the appropriate comments. Bel listened and nodded and smiled.

When the saga was over, but not before, Louise said, 'Listen, Daddy. Bel is awfully worried because she's lost her job.'

'Oh, I'm sorry about that!' exclaimed Dr. Armstrong in consternation. 'No wonder Bel is worried. What happened exactly?'

'There was a frightful row,' said Louise. 'A horrible man called Wills told her to go away then and there. It was all because he was jealous, you see. He was terribly jealous because Bel took Mr. Copping's son to the Zoo.'

'Oh Louise! I didn't say that!' exclaimed Bel.

'I know,' agreed Louise. 'You didn't tell me that, but I've been thinking about it and that's what it was. There's no other possible explanation. Jealousy is a dreadful thing,' said Louise earnestly. 'I was reading an article about it in the papers just the other day and it said that nearly all the wickedness and misery and nastiness in the world is caused by jealousy.'

'Yes,' agreed Dr. Armstrong. 'I think that's true, but I still don't see — '

'That horrid old Wills is jealous,' Louise explained. 'He's as jealous as anything because Mr. Copping's father and grandfather were in the firm and his son is going to be in the firm — and horrid old Wills never had a father or a grandfather and he hasn't got a son. So of course when Miss Goudge told him that Bel had taken the Copping boy to the Zoo he perspired all over with rage and sacked her.'

'Oh Louise, it wasn't that at all!' cried Bel in dismay.

'I don't see it,' declared Dr. Armstrong with a puzzled frown. 'I suppose the gentleman you refer to as 'horrid old Wills' is one of the partners of the firm but I simply can't understand why he should have minded Bel taking the little Copping boy to the Zoo.'

'He isn't 'little', he's enormous,' said Louise. 'But that isn't the point. The point is Wills was jealous. That's clear enough, isn't it?'

'Not clear to me.'

'Well, never mind,' said Louise. 'We don't need to bother about that. All we need to bother about is to find Bel another job — a much nicer job. I told Bel you would.'

'Yes,' agreed the doctor. 'We must see about that. But I think it would be a good plan if you were to allow Bel to tell me exactly what happened. At the moment I'm completely at sea.'

'But I've told you, Daddy!' exclaimed Louise in surprise. 'I told you about that man being so horrid to poor Bel and telling her to go. Bel was terribly upset about it. Anybody would have been upset.'

'Yes, it must have been very unpleasant,' said the doctor. 'I'm sorry about it — very sorry indeed. I must say I should like to hear the whole story, so if Bel would like to tell me — '

'Of course Bel will tell you!'

'Well, give her a chance to tell me,' said Dr. Armstrong smiling at his daughter very kindly.

3

By this time they had finished their meal and the table had been cleared. It was peaceful and quiet in the small dining-room so they decided that instead of moving to the lounge, which would be full of fishermen, retailing long stories about their day's sport, they would stay where they were and continue their conversation in private.

Dr. Armstrong lighted his pipe and prepared himself to listen.

The story took a long time to tell for Bel wanted to explain the whole miserable business from beginning to end. She wanted the doctor's advice and reassurance and she realised that unless she told him everything it was useless to ask for his help. At first she found it difficult, but Dr. Armstrong was so kind and listened with so much interest and understanding that it all came pouring out . . . all about her talk with Mr. Copping and the rudeness of Miss Goudge and the sudden unexpected appearance of Mr. James; all about the translation of the letters and the bouquet of sweetpeas and the visit to the Zoo; all about the appointment of Mr. Anderson and Mr. Nelson's telephone message and finally about the frightful interview with Mr. Wills.

'Well, that's all,' said Bel at last. 'I think I've told you everything. It's very good of you to have listened.'

'It's almost incredible!' exclaimed Dr. Armstrong. 'A man in his position to behave like that! To dismiss you at a moment's notice without any proper explanations! My dear girl, you shouldn't have taken it lying down!'

'I was frightened,' said Bel in a very small voice. 'I know I'm silly — but — but I get frightened rather easily.'

'I've a good mind to write to him and — '

'Oh no, you mustn't!' cried Bel. 'It would be

no good. Besides, what could you say? It's terribly complicated. You couldn't possibly explain.'

'I could explain the reason for your kindness to young Copping.'

'But it wouldn't be any good,' said Bel desperately. 'Mr. Wills doesn't listen to reason — and anyhow it was all mixed up. He began with complaints about my work; it was only afterwards when he was angry that he got on to the subject of Mr. James.'

'Had he the right to dismiss you?'

'The right?' asked Bel in surprise.

'Yes, you were Brownlee's secretary, weren't you? Had Wills any right to dismiss you?'

'I don't know,' said Bel miserably. 'Perhaps he had. He's in charge while Mr. Brownlee is away. He said that. He said 'I'm in full charge of the affairs of the firm'. So I suppose it's true. Anyhow, what could I do? I couldn't stay when he dismissed me. Could I?'

'Of course you couldn't,' declared Louise in a comforting tone of voice. 'Obviously the man is mad — mad as a hatter. You're much better out of it. Don't worry, darling Bel, you'll get a much nicer job quite easily — and meanwhile we're going to have a very happy time together. It's all for the best.'

'But I don't like it,' said Dr. Armstrong frowning. 'I don't like it at all. The man insulted Bel and sacked her at a moment's notice without giving her the chance to explain. He oughtn't to be allowed to get away with that sort of behaviour. How would it do if I were to write to

Mr. Copping, himself? He's the head of the firm and — '

'Oh no! Please! You mustn't do that! Mr. Copping is ill — it would never do to worry him — besides, he might think . . . '

'What would he think?'

'I don't know,' said Bel blushing. 'He might think there was some truth . . . I mean he might be angry with Mr. James.'

'Is there nobody in the firm with any sense at all?' asked Dr. Armstrong with pardonable irritation.

Bel did not answer that. It was difficult to answer. Instead she said incoherently, 'Oh goodness! When I think of all the talk! When I think of all the muddle! If only I knew what was happening!'

'Don't think about it,' said Louise. 'It's no good worrying. Just forget about it and enjoy your holiday. When Mr. Brownlee comes back he's sure to write to you, isn't he?'

Bel was silent. She didn't know whether Mr. Brownlee would write or not. He had not written to her all the time he had been away, in spite of his promise to let her know how things were going, so why should he write when he got back? They would talk about her to him . . . they would tell him . . . he would think . . . perhaps he would be angry!

It was only afterwards that Bel realised that Mr. Brownlee could not write to her when he got back — even if he wanted to — for the simple reason that she had not left her address. She had been so stunned, and so hurried in her preparations for departure, that she had never thought of leaving her address. She had not even filled up a form at the Post-Office for her letters to be forwarded. Of course she could do that now. There was nothing to prevent her from getting a form here, at Drumburly, and sending it to London. But what was the use? thought Bel. There would be no letters — or at least none that she wanted to receive. She didn't want to hear from anyone, not even from Mr. Brownlee. She just wanted to be away from it all and to forget about what had happened. All the talk and suspicions and nastiness had made her — had made her feel — dirty. Yes, dirty, thought Bel. Here it was clean — beautifully clean and fresh — so perhaps when she had been here for a bit she would not feel dirty any more.

Louise had said, 'Just forget about it and enjoy your holiday'. Louise was right. That was the thing to do.

17

The following morning was Tuesday. Louise had made an arrangement to go to Mureth House to a coffee-party at eleven o'clock. She had intended to take Bel and introduce her to the Johnstones, but Bel, having had her breakfast in bed, was feeling somewhat lazy. She was never at her best with strangers and the idea of getting up and going out to a party did not appeal to her at all. She explained that she was looking forward to meeting Louise's relations — but not now.

'Not now?' asked Louise in surprise.

'Some other day,' said Bel vaguely. 'You see I've just arrived. I haven't got properly settled yet. I'll just have an easy morning and get up later and go for a little walk and look about. You must go to Mureth House, of course. I shall be perfectly happy by myself.'

'Well, if you're sure — ' said Louise doubtfully. 'They'll be very disappointed because I told them I would bring you . . . but you're tired after the journey.'

'Yes, I am rather tired,' agreed Bel.

The fatigue from which she was suffering was not really physical. She was spiritually exhausted by all she had been through. She felt dazed; it had all happened so suddenly. This day last week she had been doing her work at the office with absolutely no idea that anything would ever change her usual routine — and now here she

187

was at Drumburly! No wonder she felt dazed.

'All right — if you're sure,' said Louise. 'I'll be back to lunch.'

Bel stayed in bed for a bit, reading the papers, and then got up and went out. It was delightful to be able to take her time and to do exactly what she wanted: no rushing off madly to the office; no bus to catch; no hurry at all. She wandered slowly down the steps of the hotel and into the street, enjoying every moment.

There was only one street in Drumburly; it sloped gently up from the bridge and on either side there were shops. They were quite good shops. The butcher's was hung with carcases of beef and mutton and venison; the marble slab in the window of the fishmonger displayed piles of appetising fish. There were several grocers' shops — all well-stocked — and quite a number of bakers! Bel saw a sweet shop which advertised Drumburly Rock and decided to buy a box of it as a small present for Louise. She had just completed her purchase and was waiting for her change when she heard her name.

'Miss Lamington?'

She turned quickly and found herself face to face with one of the most beautiful young women she had ever seen. The ravishing creature was a good deal taller than herself, with bright blue eyes and a cream and rose complexion and gorgeous golden hair.

'I'm sure you're Miss Lamington,' declared the young woman with a friendly smile. 'There's nothing very mysterious about it. You see I've lived here for years and years and I know

188

everybody, so when I saw somebody I didn't know I knew it must be you. Louise told us all about you and that helped. Of course you don't know me from Adam.'

'You're Mrs. Dering Johnstone!'

'Goodness! How did you guess?'

Bel had not guessed. She had known quite definitely the moment she saw Mrs. Dering Johnstone that this was Louise's cousin's wife, for Louise had said that James's wife, Rhoda, was perfectly beautiful — just like an angel — with wonderful golden hair. There could not be two people in Drumburly to fit this description, so obviously this was she.

Of course Bel was much too shy to explain, so she blushed and said, 'Oh well, I just thought — '

'But why aren't you at Mamie's party?' asked Mrs. Dering Johnstone. 'I ought to be there myself but Flockie isn't well. Miss Flockhart is our cook, she's been with us for years and years — ever since we were married — she looks after us and does everything, she's quite marvellous, so when Flockie isn't well I'm lost. Of course the poor darling wanted to get up and carry on as usual — I almost had to tie her down to her bed with ropes!'

'How awful for you!' said Bel a little breathlessly. As a matter of fact Rhoda Dering Johnstone quite often had this effect upon people — the effect of taking their breath away. It was not only her beauty, it was her personality. She was full of vitality; she radiated friendliness.

'So I'm doing the shopping you see,' added

Mrs. Dering Johnstone.

'Yes, I see,' said Bel.

'I tell you what,' said Mrs. Dering Johnstone. 'You and Louise must come to tea at Tassieknowe, but we'll wait till Flockie's better because she makes the most delicious scones. They melt in your mouth. I don't know how she does it. As a matter of fact I've watched her dozens of times and I've tried to make them myself. I've made them exactly the same — most carefully — but they turn out completely different. Flockie's scones are as light as feathers and mine are as tough and leathery as old boots. Can you explain it?'

'No,' said Bel laughing.

'Neither can I,' declared Mrs. Dering Johnstone.

They came out into the street together. The sun shone down upon Mrs. Dering Johnstone's hair; the gold of it was almost blinding.

'What do you think of Drumburly?' asked Mrs. Dering Johnstone. 'I remember the first time I saw it I thought it looked foreign, and I thought the people were talking to each other in a foreign language, but now I'm quite used to it of course. Have you been down to the bridge? It's beautiful. You really ought to see it — and go to the middle of the bridge and lean over and watch the river swirling through the arches. There's something fascinating about watching a river. Some people do it all day long.'

'All day long?' repeated Bel in surprise.

'Mostly old men who haven't got anything else to do,' Mrs. Dering Johnstone explained.

'They're a sort of decoration to the bridge — if you know what I mean.'

Bel was not at all sure what she meant so she smiled and said nothing. As a matter of fact she was aware that her contribution to the conversation had been meagre in the extreme but fortunately Mrs. Dering Johnstone did not seem to mind.

'I must fly,' declared Mrs. Dering Johnstone. 'I've got two boys at home and they're probably doing something frightfully naughty. Flockie is the only person who can manage them and she's in bed. I'm awfully glad we've met,' she added with a warm friendly smile.

'So am I,' said Bel with enthusiasm.

'Goodbye. I'll ring up about tea when Flockie's better. Anyhow I'm sure to see you again soon,' said Mrs. Dering Johnstone. She sprang into her car, waved from the window and was off like a flash of lightning.

Of course Bel did exactly as she had been told. She walked down to the bridge and admired the graceful spans, and she went to the middle of the bridge and leaned over the parapet and watched the river swirling beneath her. There certainly was something very fascinating about the way the water plunged between the arches of the bridge; Mrs. Dering Johnstone had been perfectly right. She had been right about the old men as well, for there were several old men upon the bridge, leaning over the parapet and watching the river. They were in a mesmerised condition. They were there when Bel arrived and they were still there when she left, so it was easy to believe that they remained there, watching the river, all day long.

2

Dr. Armstrong returned to The Shaw Arms for lunch. This was contrary to his usual practice but Bel gathered that the day was too fine and sunny. Louise also returned. She had enjoyed the coffee-party and had met several old friends.

'But you didn't meet Mrs. Dering Johnstone,' said Bel.

'How do you know?' enquired Louise in surprise.

'Because I met her,' replied Bel laughing. 'I met her in the sweet shop and I knew her at once from your description — beautiful as an angel.' She proceeded to give an account of the meeting and to ask questions about her new acquaintance.

'Oh yes, she has two boys, Harry and Nicky,' said Louise. 'Rhoda says they're terribly naughty but I think they're rather amusing. They run about the farm and learn some very queer language but they can speak quite nicely when they like. I told you they live at Tassieknowe, didn't I? It's farther up the river from Mureth — frightfully isolated. Sometimes in the winter they're snowed up for days on end.'

'Tassieknowe is an interesting place,' said Dr. Armstrong. 'It stands on the site of an old Roman Fort. The name originates from the Roman General Tacitus — or so it is said.' He added 'I wonder if Bel would like to try a cast or two this afternoon.'

'You mean fishing?' asked Bel. 'Oh yes, I should love to — if it isn't a bother.'

'You won't catch anything, except yourself,' declared Louise.

The warning was unregarded and presently all three of them went down to a large pool below the bridge which Dr. Armstrong had chosen as a suitable spot for Bel's lesson. Louise had brought a book and settled herself comfortably with her back against a rock; she had watched fishing so often that she was bored with the whole affair. Bel, on the other hand, was intensely interested in the elaborate preparations. She watched while her instructor fitted the sections of the rod together, fixed on the reel and threaded the line through the loops. She watched the cast being knotted to the line and suitable flies chosen. The fly-book was fascinating — each fly so small, so beautifully made, so colourful. It seemed very strange to Bel that fish should be deceived into thinking that these were ordinary flies; even more strange that fish should like to eat them.

When all was ready Dr. Armstrong showed Bel how to cast the line across the pool. The line flew out and the cast fell gently upon the water. It looked easy but it was not as easy as it looked. When Bel took the rod it felt heavy and cumbersome, the line tangled, the cast splashed in the water like a bomb.

'Try again,' said Dr. Armstrong encouragingly.

This time the line twirled round her and one

of the hooks caught in the back of her jumper.

'I said you would catch yourself,' remarked Louise.

'Leave her alone,' said the doctor as he released his pupil. 'We'll make a fisherwoman of her before we're done.'

'You won't,' declared Louise. 'Anyhow she won't catch any fish this afternoon. It's far too bright — and you know it.'

'There might be some clouds later,' said the doctor hopefully.

'If there are clouds there's less chance than ever of Bel catching a fish because you'll take the rod yourself, Daddy.'

'Am I so selfish!' exclaimed Dr. Armstrong.

'Yes, every bit,' replied Louise giggling.

There were no clouds — there was not a cloud in the sky — so the lesson continued for about half-an-hour by which time Bel's arms were aching and the doctor was tired of disentangling the line. Bel had caught herself three times and the doctor twice but she had not caught a fish. She had not even seen the glint of a fish in the pool. Secretly she was convinced that there was not a fish in the river.

'It's no good. I shall never learn,' said Bel at last.

'I expect you're tired,' said Dr. Armstrong. 'We could have another lesson some time.' He hesitated and then added, 'I think I'll take the rod and go up the river a bit; there might be a chance in the broken water above the bridge.'

18

In the days that followed Bel came to realise that the river was of paramount importance. The river was — so to speak — the theme song of Drumburly. Bel heard it at night, gliding past beneath the windows of the room she was sharing with Louise. She listened to it lapping gently against the thick stone wall of the house. Sometimes if she woke in the night she would rise and look out of the window and see it, silvery in the moonlight or dark as indigo beneath a clouded sky. She saw it in the morning prancing along with the sun shining down upon it making the wavelets glitter and sparkle. In some places the river moved slowly and powerfully; in other places it streamed along in its rocky bed chattering gaily as it went, swirling round stones, hesitating in pools, tumbling down miniature cataracts. It poured through narrow fissures and spread out fanwise over stretches of clean yellow gravel. Smooth black rocks shouldered the green water into great curves like polished glass.

The river was the reason for the existence of Drumburly. The little town would not have been there at all if the bridge had not been built. The bridge had been the first thing, then the change-house where coaches halted for fresh horses, then the little town had gradually grown up with its houses and shops and the church upon the hill.

The river was the reason for The Shaw Arms and it was the reason for Mrs. Simpson's prosperity. All the people staying in the hotel were here because of the river. The river was the subject of conversation: it had risen so many inches in the night; the water was clear — or drumly; the fish were taking — or not taking. People talked incessantly of the different pools where the big trout lay waiting to be caught.

Quite soon Bel got to know the people staying in the hotel. There were Mr. Drummond and his sister — both of them keen anglers — both of them tall and slender with dark hair and eyes like peaty pools. Mr. Drummond was much better-looking than his sister and a great deal more agreeable. The Drummonds had been staying at The Shaw Arms when the Armstrongs arrived so they were friends already. Alec Drummond and Louise Armstrong were calling each other by their Christian names.

There were Mr. and Mrs. Plack. He was a retired banker, rather plump, with a rosy face and iron-grey hair. In spite of advancing years Mr. Plack was a skilful fisherman; he was as keen as mustard and went out in all weathers to stalk the wily trout. Mrs. Plack was small and wispy. She took no interest in sport but spent her days writing letters or knitting or reading books from Mrs. Simpson's well-stocked library. Sometimes she could be seen wandering vaguely about the town buying sweets and stamps and wool, or soap-powder with which to wash her nylon stockings and her husband's socks. Bel felt sorry for Mrs. Plack — it must have been a dull sort of holiday for her — but Mrs. Plack seemed quite contented, at least she did not complain.

There were other people besides these in the hotel; some of them were staying indefinitely, others came and went. Two young men arrived in a large Bentley; one of them extremely tall and thin, the other of more normal proportions — Mr. Thornton and Captain Wentworth Brown — but they were not accepted into the inner circle of The Shaw Arms for, instead of spending all their days fishing the river, they piled all their fishing gear into the car and went off at speed to fish in some other place — nobody knew where. Mr. Plack was of the opinion that they indulged in loch-fishing for which he had the greatest contempt.

'Sitting all day in a boat!' said Mr. Plack.

'I like it for a change,' declared Alec Drummond. 'The doctor and I had a very good day on the loch on Saturday.'

'No fun,' said Mr. Plack. 'Sitting all day in a boat!'

People talked to each other at meals. Each party had its own table but this did not prevent a certain amount of conversation from taking place. People talked to each other in the lounge. They talked all the time about the fish they had caught — or had not been able to catch — or sometimes about the weather.

Bel found to her surprise that they liked talking to her. She knew nothing about fishing but that did not seem to worry them. All that they wanted was somebody who would listen — and Bel was a good listener. As a matter of fact Bel enjoyed listening to the fishing stories; she might have got bored if she had had to listen for too long, but it was all new to her — it was like looking out of a window at a strange prospect — everything was completely different from what she had seen before.

It soon became evident to Bel that Alec Drummond had another interest in his life — besides fishing. It was Louise. There was nothing strange about this for Louise was exceedingly attractive. Indeed it would have been strange if a young man, thrown into the company of Louise, had not looked upon her with delight. He looked upon her constantly (Bel noticed). He would stop in the middle of a fishing story when Louise came into the room. Sometimes he would sit quite silent and gaze at her in adoration.

Bel was interested of course (she was tremendously interested in everything to do with Louise) but for some days she was merely an onlooker; she had no idea what Louise was thinking. Although she and Louise talked incessantly in their usual uninhibited manner Alec Drummond's name was never mentioned. What did this mean, wondered Bel. It seemed impossible that Louise was unaware of the havoc she was causing. Her manner to the young man was perfectly natural and friendly — but Louise was friendly to everybody in the place!

Bel was aware that a good many young men had fallen in love with Louise but none of them

198

had touched her heart; none of them was to be compared with Dr. Armstrong. Louise had told Bel this when Bel was staying with the Armstrongs at Coombe House. Bel wondered if Alec Drummond was just another unfortunate young man or whether he was to be the fortunate one.

Alec Drummond was exceedingly nice — Bel liked him immensely — there was something solid about him, he was modest and unassuming, he was kind. It was obvious that Dr. Armstrong liked him for they often went fishing together and they were good companions, chatting and sharing jokes.

Naturally Bel thought about it a great deal and wondered. She wondered what the young man did for his living. She had heard Miss Drummond say to Mrs. Plack that she and her brother were staying at The Shaw Arms indefinitely and when they got tired of it they would probably go on somewhere else.

'For fishing, I suppose,' suggested Mrs. Plack.

'Yes of course,' replied Miss Drummond.

Was it possible that Alec Drummond had no business to attend to? What did he do when he wasn't fishing, wondered Bel.

2

One evening when Bel had gone upstairs to fetch a book she encountered Alec Drummond lurking on the landing. She smiled at him and was about to pass on but he stopped her.

'Miss Lamington,' he said. 'I've been waiting for you — I hope you don't mind — it's about Louise. You're her friend and I just wondered — if you knew — anything.'

'Knew anything?'

'Perhaps I shouldn't talk to you like this but I'm really desperate,' he declared. 'Absolutely desperate. Of course you don't know what I'm talking about, but — but the fact is I'm terribly in love with Louise.'

Obviously Alec Drummond expected his hearer to be astonished at this news. She was not astonished, but she was considerably taken aback to find herself being made the recipient of his confidence. She did not know what to say. She did not know what he expected her to say. She looked at him in silence.

'No wonder you're surprised,' he continued, taking out a large handkerchief and wiping his forehead. 'I'm surprised myself. I'm thirty-seven, you see, and I've never fallen in love before. It's quite — quite devastating. She's wonderful, isn't she?'

Fortunately that was easily answered. 'Yes, she is.'

'She's the most wonderful girl I've ever seen. I never knew there could be anybody so wonderful — so beautiful and good and sweet. Louise! It's a beautiful name; Louise! She couldn't be called anything else!'

Bel agreed with him. She could not imagine Louise being called anything else. The thought passed through her mind that Alec Drummond resembled Orlando; he would have liked to wander through the woods carving the name of his beloved upon trees. He couldn't, of course, because he was much too civilised. It was a pity, because it might have done him good. She felt very sorry for him.

'I didn't mean to talk to you like this,' said the unhappy young man. 'I meant to be quite sensible and just ask you if — if you had — any idea — any idea whether there was any hope. I mean you're her friend, aren't you? I wondered whether she had ever said anything . . . ' He paused and looked at Bel like a spaniel asking for a biscuit.

'No, nothing,' said Bel regretfully.

'You'll tell me if she does, won't you?'

'Oh no!' exclaimed Bel. 'I couldn't possibly promise that!'

'No,' he said sadly. 'No, of course you couldn't. Silly of me to ask. It's just — I don't know what to do. If there was any hope I'd stay on and — and go on trying. I'd go on trying for months if there was any hope! But if not I'd better go away. I can't go on like this. Of course I know I'm not nearly good enough for Louise but — but I'd do my best to make her happy. I'd do anything for her — anything. Do you think there's any hope?'

'Why don't you ask her,' suggested Bel.

'Oh, I've tried. I've tried twice — leading up to it, you know. It isn't the sort of thing you can blurt out all of a sudden. But — well — I don't seem to be very good at it. Somehow I don't seem to be able to — to get there — if you know what I mean. She sort of rides me off and the next minute we seem to be talking about something else.'

'Fishing?' suggested Bel.

'Yes.' He wiped the palms of his hands and put away his handkerchief. 'Oh goodness!' he exclaimed. 'I don't know what to do. What do you think I ought to do?'

Bel had no idea what he ought to do.

'I can't go on like this,' he declared. 'It's making me quite ill. I think about it all the time. Even when I'm fishing I keep on thinking about Louise. If I were certain that there was absolutely no hope I'd leave here tomorrow. Jean would be annoyed but that can't be helped. Jean could stay on here by herself if she wanted to.' He heaved a sigh and added, 'If there's no hope I've a good mind to leave here and go to Loch Leven.'

'Loch Leven?'

'Yes. That ought to take my mind off — if anything could.'

Bel was surprised. She was so abysmally ignorant that she associated Loch Leven with Mary Stuart; that unfortunate queen had been imprisoned upon an island in the middle of Loch Leven and had escaped in a small boat under cover of darkness. It was very romantic, of course, but Bel failed to see how it could help in the recovery of Orlando.

'Do you think you could possibly help me?' asked Orlando. 'I've no right to ask you, I know,' he added hastily. 'No right at all. I just thought if you could possibly — I mean if you could sort of — sound her about it. If you could put in a word

202

for me and — and — '

'I don't think so,' said Bel reluctantly. 'I'm sorry, but honestly I wouldn't like to interfere.'

'It wouldn't be interfering.'

'It would, really — and it might do harm. Louise is the sort of person who likes to manage her own affairs.'

Bel might have added that Louise liked to manage other people's affairs as well — it would have been true — but it might have given quite a wrong idea of her character, for although Louise certainly managed people, and liked doing it, she was not what is usually described as 'a managing person'.

The conversation seemed to have come to an end. They were both silent. It was rather an embarrassing silence so Bel was not sorry when Mrs. Simpson came up the stairs. Mrs. Simpson was on her way to see if the new girl had put in the hot-water-bottles and turned down the beds in the correct manner. The girl had been shown exactly how to do it, and she seemed fairly intelligent, but Mrs. Simpson wanted to make quite sure.

'The glass is falling,' said Mrs. Simpson cheerfully. 'There's going to be rain. It'll be a grand day for the fishing tomorrow, Mr. Drummond.'

'Oh, good,' said Mr. Drummond with a surprising lack of enthusiasm.

19

The river was particularly interesting to Bel, because she had never known a river before. She had seen rivers of course — she had had a nodding acquaintance with them so to speak — but she was getting to know the Burly as if it were a friend. It had a definite personality. All the same it was pleasant to get away from it occasionally; Bel and Louise had several delightful walks over the hills, taking their lunch — sandwiches of brown bread and ham, little rolls filled with tomato-puree or salad, and scones with honey in them. Mrs. Simpson made a speciality of delicious lunches.

One day the girls walked over to Crossraggle. Another day they crossed the bridge and walked along a very hilly road to Boscath Farm. It was a perfectly lovely morning with bright golden sunshine and blue skies; not the sort of weather to suit fishermen, but delightful for a walk. The road was little more than a cart track; it wound hither and thither amongst the rolling hills where there were patches of boggy ground and outcrops of rocks and heather. The heather was now at its best, the hills were covered with purple blossoms; they smelt of honey, sweet and tangy; the pollen was thick and yellow. Thousands of wild bees were at work, their small brown bodies burrowing avidly amongst the tiny flowers. There was a curious toughness about the heather with its thick springy brown stems coiling about the rocks and stones, straggling across the path. It was a plant of the hills, hardy and strong. Here and there small silver burns ran down amidst tiny valleys of bright green grass. It was here that the sheep liked to gather; the smooth sheep-bitten turf was soft as velvet.

A grey misty cloud with rainbows in it came up quickly from behind the hills and in a moment the sun went out like a blown candle and the girls were enveloped in a sharp stinging shower of rain. They sheltered for a few minutes behind a giant boulder and then quite suddenly the sun was shining again and the rain-cloud fled across the valley trailing its shadow on the ground, leaving behind it diamonds upon the heather, diamonds glittering amongst the grasses, diamonds glistening upon a spider's web.

'How lovely it is!' said Bel with a sigh of delight.

'Yes, lovely,' Louise agreed. 'We'll have our lunch here, shall we? I'm going to have a drink from this little burn.'

They sat and had lunch and drank the clear water and were very happy and peaceful.

2

Bel was enjoying every moment of her holiday; she enjoyed the walks, she enjoyed the good plain meals, she enjoyed shopping in the little town. By no means the least delightful moments were those which were spent getting ready for bed; undressing in a leisurely manner while she chatted to Louise about the events of the day. Neither of them had ever known what it was to have a sister so this was an entirely new experience. It took them a long time to get ready for bed but that did not matter for time was not important at Drumburly. Bel had said it would be fun to share a room with Louise, and so it was. They liked it so much that when a room fell vacant and Mrs. Simpson offered to move Bel they decided to remain as they were.

'I like Alec Drummond,' said Bel one night when they were getting ready for bed.

Bel had not intended to say it — she had told Orlando quite definitely that she wouldn't interfere — but she was so distressed at his love-lorn condition that she had changed her mind. It could do no harm to mention his name to Louise.

'Oh yes,' said Louise. 'Alec is a perfect dear.'

'He thinks you're a perfect dear.'

'I know,' agreed Louise. She sighed and added, 'It's taking me all my time not to fall in love with Alec.'

Bel was silent.

'Daddy likes him too,' Louise continued. 'That's important, of course. Daddy is very wise. I go a lot by what he thinks of people. He sums them up, you know, it's part of his job. Daddy has made friends with Alec.'

'Yes, I noticed that.'

There was another little silence and then Louise said, 'Sometimes I think it would be delightful to fall in love with Alec — but it wouldn't work.'

'Wouldn't it?'

'No,' said Louise, shaking her head. 'No, it wouldn't.'

'Why?'

'Look at Mrs. Plack!'

'Mrs. Plack?' echoed Bel in astonishment. 'What has Mrs. Plack got to do with it?'

'Everything,' replied Louise. 'When I begin to think too much about Alec I've only got to look at Mrs. Plack. That pulls me up with a jerk.'

'But why — '

'Look at her!' exclaimed Louise vehemently. 'Just look at her! The woman who marries Alec Drummond will be just another Mrs. Plack; sitting in hotels all day long and knitting shapeless jumpers, trailing round the shops and buying all sorts of things she doesn't really want — just to put off time. That's what Mrs. Plack does every day and all day long: she-puts-off-time! What sort of life is that? It isn't a life at all. It's an existence. I'd rather be the wife of a ploughman and cook and scrub and wash his clothes! I'd be more use in the world, wouldn't I?'

'Oh — yes,' said Bel, somewhat startled at this outburst. 'Yes, I see what you mean, but I don't think Alec . . . I mean he's very devoted to you, and — '

'I know,' agreed Louise. 'It would be quite all right at first — everything would be *couleur de rose* — but when the rapture wore off a bit Alec would return to his old love and his wife would

207

be Mrs. Plack. Fishing is an incurable disease,' added Louise. She sat down at the dressing-table, seized her hair-brush and began to brush her hair with unusual vigour.

'But I wonder whether — ' began Bel.

'Oh yes,' declared Louise. 'Oh yes, I know what I'm talking about. I've been through it with Daddy. Of course Daddy only gets three weeks' holiday in the year. I can bear it for three weeks. In fact I can bear it quite easily because I like the dear old darling to enjoy himself. He deserves it. He works so frightfully hard the rest of the time. You know that, don't you?'

'Yes, indeed!'

'When a person works frightfully hard for forty-nine weeks he's entitled to three weeks' holiday. That's what I think.'

Bel thought so too.

'It would be quite different with Alec,' Louise continued. 'Alec has got pots of money and doesn't need to bother about his business.'

'What is his business?'

'Oh, something in Edinburgh,' said Louise vaguely. 'At any rate — whatever it is — it seems to be able to carry on quite comfortably without Alec.'

Bel hesitated for a few moments and then she said, 'I think you should tell him.'

'Tell him what? Oh, you mean tell him I won't be Mrs. Plack? But I can't refuse the man till he's asked me, can I?'

'He's tried to ask you several times.'

'You seem to know a lot about it!'

'Yes,' said Bel. She went over to the

208

dressing-table and put her arms round Louise's neck. They looked at each other in the mirror. Bel was very serious. Louise was smiling.

'Well, go on,' she said. 'What did he tell you?'

'Quite a lot,' said Bel, putting her cheek against Louise's curls. 'He loves you quite desperately. He asked me if I thought there was any hope.'

'What did you say?'

'I said I didn't know — he had better ask you himself — so then he said he had tried but you wouldn't let him. He said you 'rode him off'.'

'Yes, I did,' admitted Louise. 'As a matter of fact it wasn't very difficult. Go on, Bel.'

'Well, then he said would I sound you.'

'And you said yes.'

'I said no. I said I wouldn't interfere.'

'But you are interfering, aren't you?'

'I suppose I am, really. I didn't mean to but I'm awfully sorry for him. He really is quite desperate. He said if there was no hope he would go to Loch Leven.'

'Loch Leven!' exclaimed Louise, beginning to laugh. 'Oh Bel, that's the funniest thing I've heard for ages! If there's no hope he's going to Loch Leven!' She was laughing uncontrollably now. She put her head down on the dressing-table and laughed and laughed. Perhaps there was something a little hysterical about her laughter but for all that it was infectious.

Bel was obliged to smile. She said, 'I wish you'd tell me the joke. What's so funny about Loch Leven?'

'Nothing — f-funny,' declared Louise, still

laughing helplessly. 'Nothing — f-funny — except that it's — t-teeming with f-fish.'

'Oh, I see,' said Bel. As a matter of fact she saw a good deal. She saw that she should not have interfered. It certainly would have been better for Alec if she had kept her mouth shut — but how was she to know? Anyhow it couldn't be helped. Things that have been said can never be unsaid. What an alarming thought!

When Louise had recovered from her paroxysms she sat up and wiped her eyes. 'Well, that settles it,' she declared. 'I was swithering a bit — as Mrs. Simpson would say — but that absolutely settles it. Alec can go to Loch Leven.'

'Oh Louise, are you sure?'

'I won't be Mrs. Plack,' declared Louise with determination. 'I've made up my mind quite definitely, so you needn't try to persuade me.'

'I wasn't going to,' said Bel. She went across the room and got into bed.

Presently Louise came and kissed her. 'Goodnight, darling Bel,' said Louise. 'You were quite right. I was being rather a beast. It was just that I couldn't quite make up my mind. You understand, don't you?'

'Yes, of course.'

'I was swithering, but I'm not swithering any more. I shall tell Alec to go to Loch Leven and I hope he'll catch lots and lots of fish.'

'Oh Louise, are you sure?'

'Quite, quite certain,' said Louise.

20

It was a very wet morning. The rain was falling gently but inexorably; it looked as if it could go on falling like that for days on end without stopping for a moment. The anglers did not mind, of course, they all went off quite cheerfully, swathed in waterproof from head to foot. The only people left in the lounge were Bel and Louise, sitting by the fire, and Mrs. Plack writing her interminable letters.

After a while Mrs. Plack got up. '1 think I'll go out,' she said. 'I shall put on my mackintosh and take my umbrella. Is there anything I can do for you in the town.'

'No, thank you,' said Bel.

'Not stamps or anything?' asked Mrs. Plack in surprise. 'I find I get through such a lot of stamps. I never seem to have enough.'

'No, thank you,' said Louise. 'It's very kind of you, but there's nothing we want in the town. Is there, Bel?'

'No, nothing,' said Bel.

'Perhaps I had better get some darning wool,' said Mrs. Plack, hovering indecisively. 'And I might go and have a cup of coffee at the tea-shop. That would help to pass the time.' She drifted out of the door and shut it behind her.

'Poor soul!' said Louise with a sigh. 'She would be so much happier if she had married a ploughman.'

Bel was inclined to agree.

'I've told Alec,' continued Louise, leaning forward and lowering her voice to a confidential whisper. 'I got hold of him this morning before he went out. He's going to Loch Leven.'

There was a little silence. The flames in the fire leapt up in a cheerful manner and licked round the logs.

'Nice fire!' said Louise at last. 'I shall order some logs when I get home. It would be fun to have a log fire in the winter evenings. What a happy time we've had, haven't we, Bel?'

It was the way Louise spoke — more than the actual words — which gave Bel a qualm of dismay. Louise had spoken as if the holiday at Drumburly were nearly over! Bel suddenly remembered that the Armstrongs had been here more than a week before she had come and, as the doctor only got three weeks' holiday, they were due to return south on Thursday. How silly she had been! How absolutely crazy to have spent her time enjoying herself without thinking about the future! What on earth was she going to do when this blissful interlude came to an end?

'Bel, you're not listening,' said Louise. 'You must listen because it's important. We've got to make plans. I've been talking it over with Daddy. You must come back with us to Coombe House until you get another job. That's fixed. Daddy will be able to find another job for you. He'll see about it when he gets home. It will be quite easy.'

'Not without a reference,' said Bel in a queer, strained sort of voice.

'A reference?' asked Louise in surprise.

'I haven't got a reference. I was dismissed at a moment's notice. I told you that.'

Evidently this was a new idea to Louise. 'Will that matter?' she asked in a doubtful voice.

'No firm will engage me without a reference.'

There was silence for a few moments and then Louise said firmly, 'They must give you one, that's all. Daddy will make them give you a reference. It was all a mistake, wasn't it? The only thing to do is to get the whole thing cleared up.'

'Oh no!' Bel exclaimed. 'No, you don't understand!'

'But, Bel — '

'No!' cried Bel. 'No! It's all finished and done with. I don't want to think about it any more. I've been trying terribly hard not to think about it. You've no idea how dreadful it was — all the jealousy and the tale-bearing and Mr. Wills so angry! I hate rows and shouting and disagree-ableness — it makes me feel quite ill!'

'But, Bel, it ought to be cleared up — really,' said Louise in a reasoning tone of voice. 'Daddy would go and see Mr. Wills and explain — '

'No, no!' cried Bel frantically. 'No, he mustn't! There would be a frightful row — and anyhow it wouldn't be any good. It can't be explained. I've told you that before. It's all mixed up — lies and truth together! It's true that I had lunch with Mr. James; it's true that he came and worked with me; it's true that he brought me flowers.'

'But there was no harm in it, was there?'

'All that is true,' cried Bel, taking no notice of the interruption. 'All that is true — so it can't be explained away. And by this time everybody in the office has been talking about it and making the worst of it. They all hated me because I was promoted to be Mr. Brownlee's secretary — with more pay and everything — so of course they'll be terribly pleased. I can't bear to think about it. I just want to wash out the whole thing. It's like a nightmare!'

Bel had been trying so terribly hard to wash out the whole thing and to a certain extent she had succeeded. Her holiday at Drumburly had been so full of pleasures and so absolutely different from anything she had experienced before that she had had very little time to brood. Every now and then the nightmare had descended upon her but she had banished it as quickly as she could.

It would have been easier to banish the nightmare if she had not been so interested in the firm. For months and months her only real interest in life had been the affairs of Copping, Wills and Brownlee. She felt bound up with them — as if she belonged. She knew all their business inside out; knew all the names of the firms they dealt with in the different ports all over the world; knew all the ships which came to Copping Wharf with their cargoes of 'ivory, apes and peacocks'. She knew about the warehouses, when they had been built and their storage capacity. Bel had been proud to work for the firm, proud of its traditions and of the men who had built it up to be a power in the world of merchandise. When she had said to Mr. Copping, 'Four generations of Coppings!' she had said it with pride.

It was all over now. It was all spoilt. She could never go back. Even if they wanted her she couldn't go back — and of course they wouldn't want her. Wash it out! Begin again! Take a job somewhere else! But would any reputable firm engage her without a reference? (Bel imagined herself being interviewed: 'Where have you been working since you left the training school? Oh, Copping, Wills and Brownlee. They'll give you a reference, of course.')

'Bel, darling! Don't look like that!' exclaimed Louise in alarm.

'Look like what?'

'As if — as if something terrible had happened.'

'It's my face,' said Bel in a shaky voice. 'I can't help my face. Besides it is — rather — terrible. What's going to happen to me?'

'It will be all right,' declared Louise, leaning forward and taking Bel's hand in a firm clasp. 'It will be all right — honestly, darling. You can stay with us as long as you like. You mustn't worry. Daddy will find you a job. I'll explain to Daddy that you don't want him to go near those horrible people. Horrible, horrible people to treat you like that! Look, darling, we won't talk about it any more. We'll forget about it. We'll pretend that there isn't such a firm as Copping, Wills and Brownlee.'

'Yes, that's the — best way,' said Bel with a little catch in her breath.

21

There were still several days before the Armstrongs and Bel had to leave Drumburly. On Monday Louise and Bel went for another expedition on the hills, on Tuesday they had been asked to tea at Mureth House. Unfortunately Bel was unable to enjoy these days whole-heartedly. There was a cloud upon her spirits. She had agreed with Louise that the best thing to do was to forget all her troubles: but it is one thing to know what is the best thing to do and quite another thing to be able to do it.

Bel was not looking forward to the tea-party. Louise had been to Mureth twice, but both times Bel had managed to find an excuse. Bel was not sociably inclined; she shrank from the idea of meeting a lot of strangers and being expected to take part in their conversation. She would far rather stay at home. This time however it was impossible to find an excuse, for Louise would have been disappointed. Louise was so anxious for Bel to meet her relations — and it was the last chance.

'You'll like them,' said Louise as they set off together in the car. 'They're perfect darlings; especially Aunt Mamie. Uncle Jock is nice too. You won't feel a bit shy. Nobody could feel shy of them, they're so natural and friendly. Rhoda will probably be there too. You liked Rhoda, didn't you?'

'Yes,' said Bel. As a matter of fact Bel had been thinking quite a lot about Rhoda Dering Johnstone since their unexpected meeting in Drumburly. Once you had met Rhoda and had felt the impact of her personality it would have been difficult to forget her. Bel had hoped to see her again but apparently 'Flockie' was still in bed — tied down with ropes — and Rhoda was too busy to take part in social occasions.

The road from Drumburly to Mureth was like a switch-back — or perhaps more like a scenic railway — it went up and down and the scenery was perfectly beautiful. There were heathery hills on one side and glimpses of the river on the other. Bel wished the drive would go on and on but after five miles of it they arrived at Mureth House, turned in through the big stone gateway and drew up at the door.

'We don't ring,' said Louise. 'We just walk in. That's one of the things about Mureth, they never lock the door, night or day. It's because once, long ago, Dr. Forrester got lost in the snow and staggered into the hall and collapsed on the floor. If the door had been locked he would probably have died. So ever since then Uncle Jock and Aunt Mamie have never allowed the door to be locked.'

Bel was naturally interested in this saga, and despite her shyness she was interested in Mureth House. The hall was wide and spacious; there was a blue carpet on the floor; at one side there was a dark oak table, beautifully polished, on the other side was a curving flight of stairs.

It was dim in the hall but when Louise threw

open the door into the drawing-room there was a sudden flood of light, for the sun was shining in through the bay windows. It was a big room, slightly shabby but comfortable — with cretonne-covered chairs and solid furniture. Bel received the impression that this was a room which was lived in constantly, not kept for special occasions. She had no time to receive any further impressions because its owners were there.

Mamie Johnstone leapt up from the sofa where she had been sitting and kissed Louise fondly. 'How lovely to see you!' she exclaimed. 'And you've brought your friend this time!' She turned to Bel and added, 'Louise has told us such a lot about you, Miss Lamington.'

Jock Johnstone rose more slowly from his chair near the fire. He was a big man — big in every way, thought Bel, as her hand disappeared into his grasp. She looked up at him and saw that he was smiling at her very kindly.

'Well now, where are you going to sit?' he asked. 'Where are they to sit, Mamie?'

'Near the table,' she replied. 'We'll start tea at once.'

Tea was laid on a big round table with a silver tray and teapot and willow-pattern cups and saucers. There were plates of scones and buns and biscuits and a big fruit-cake on a silver stand, and there was jam and honey and a huge slab of yellow farm-butter.

'Isn't Rhoda coming, Aunt Mamie?' asked Louise as they settled themselves comfortably round the table.

'We're hoping she's coming,' Mamie replied. 'It all depends upon whether she can get somebody to look after the boys.'

'Could she not have brought the boys with her?' asked Jock.

'I asked her,' said Mamie as she lifted the big silver teapot and began to pour out the tea. 'I asked her to bring the boys but she said they were better at home. They're sometimes rather naughty.'

'Och, they're not too bad,' declared Jock smiling. 'They're just a wee bit boisterous, that's all.'

'I think Rhoda's boys are rather amusing,' said Louise.

At this moment the door opened and Rhoda appeared. 'Hullo!' she exclaimed. 'Hullo, Louise. You wouldn't think Rhoda's boys were so amusing if you had to look after them all day long!'

'Oh Rhoda!' exclaimed Mamie. 'We were so afraid you weren't coming.'

'It's grand to see you, Rhoda!' declared Jock.

They were all saying the same thing in different words; they were all talking at once; they were all delighted that she had come.

Bel, also, was delighted for she had been looking forward to seeing Mrs. Dering Johnstone. Bel had thought she was beautiful — and so she was — but somehow she did not seem so full of life today, not quite so effervescent. She looked tired and there were blue shadows beneath her sea-blue eyes.

'I very nearly didn't come,' said Rhoda when

she had replied to all the greetings. 'I've had an awful day. Poor Flockie has got to have an operation. They came and fetched her in an ambulance and there was a frightful scene because she didn't want to go. She clung to me like a limpet and the boys both howled. You've no idea how ghastly it was. I'd have gone with her in the ambulance if I could — but of course I couldn't. I mean there would have been nobody to look after James and the boys.'

'You couldn't possibly,' agreed Mamie. 'Oh Rhoda, how dreadful!'

'Sit down and have your tea,' said Jock, pulling in a chair for her. 'You'll feel better when you've had your tea.'

'Tell us about poor Flockie,' said Mamie.

Unfortunately Rhoda was unable to tell them much about poor Flockie except that the doctor had come to see her that morning and had decided that she had better be taken to hospital at once. Rhoda had been too distraught to listen carefully to the doctor's diagnosis. Louise suggested it might be appendicitis but Rhoda thought not. Unlike Louise, Rhoda knew very little about the ills that the flesh is heir to.

'Something wrong with her inside,' said Rhoda vaguely. 'She's got to have something taken out. She'll be in hospital for at least a month — probably more. Poor darling Flockie, I'm terribly sorry for her.'

'You'll need somebody to help you,' suggested Jock. 'Maybe you could get a woman from one of the cottages.'

'Oh, I've got Effie, of course. She's the

cow-man's daughter. She's frightfully decent and willing but she doesn't know a thing. I have to be after her all the time telling her this and that. She can't wash up a few dishes without smashing something — and it's usually something particularly nice. Yesterday she seized the cut-glass decanter which the Forresters gave us as a wedding present and plunged it into boiling water — you can imagine the result!' Rhoda sighed and added, 'Of course I always knew Flockie did a lot but I never realised just how much — until now. It wouldn't be so bad if I could cook but I don't seem to be able to. Isn't it silly of me?'

'You can paint beautiful pictures,' said Mamie in a comforting tone.

Rhoda laughed, not very mirthfully. 'Poor James can't eat pictures,' she said. 'I tell you what, Mamie; I'd take a murderess if she could cook. Of course Flockie will come back when she's better but it may be weeks and weeks — by which time James will be as thin as a skeleton and I'll be dead.'

This tragic announcement put an end to the subject and the others began to talk of something else. Bel, who happened to be sitting next to Rhoda, leant forward and said, 'Mrs. Dering Johnstone, I wonder — '

'Goodness!' exclaimed Rhoda. 'Don't call me that. It's far too long and clumsy. It would be ever so much easier for you to call me Rhoda, wouldn't it? — or wouldn't it?'

Bel hesitated uneasily. She was not quite sure whether it would.

'Do try,' said Rhoda. 'You could practise it, couldn't you? Try saying 'Rhoda, Rhoda, Rhoda' twelve times out loud.'

It was so ridiculous and Rhoda looked so serious that Bel began to laugh.

Rhoda laughed too. She said, 'I quite see the others might be a bit surprised, so perhaps you'd better practise in private.'

'Here, what's the joke?' asked Jock.

'Not very funny, really,' said Rhoda.

'Then why are you laughing,' Mamie, not unnaturally enquired.

'Come on, Rhoda,' said Jock encouragingly. 'Tell us the joke. You're not usually so blate.'

'I'm not 'blate',' declared Rhoda. 'My worst enemy couldn't accuse me of being 'blate'. In fact some people think I'm a bit too forward. I'll tell you what we were laughing at if you really want to know. It was just that I asked Bel to call me Rhoda and she seemed a bit doubtful about it so I suggested she should practise it in private.'

Told like this the joke was not in the least funny. Nobody laughed.

'I told you it wasn't funny,' said Rhoda. 'As a matter of fact it seemed rather funny at the time, but it doesn't seem a bit funny now. That's the worst of jokes; they're never so funny when you repeat them.'

'Some are,' said Jock chuckling. 'I'll tell you a good one. A chap told it to me last week at the market — ha — ha! It's about a bull — ha — ha — ha!'

'Jock!' exclaimed Mamie anxiously. 'Are you sure it's quite suitable?'

Jock hesitated and looked round the table. 'Well, maybe you're right, Mamie,' he said doubtfully. 'Maybe it's not just quite the thing — but it's awfully funny — ha — ha — ha!'

'Jock, tell us at once!' exclaimed Rhoda imperatively.

'No, no,' said Jock chuckling. 'No, Mamie's right. It's not quite the thing. It's a pity — because it's awfully funny.'

'I'll get it out of you some other time,' declared Rhoda. She rose as she spoke.

'You're not going!' exclaimed Mamie in dismay. 'Rhoda! You've only just come!'

'I must,' said Rhoda regretfully. 'I've got to prepare some sort of meal for James and the boys. Eggs or something,' said Rhoda vaguely. 'How do you make an omelet, Mamie?'

Mamie began to describe the method of making an omelet but before she had got very far Louise chipped in and told her quite a different way.

'I shall boil them,' declared Rhoda. 'It's far too difficult and I can't stay a moment longer.'

When Rhoda Dering Johnstone said she could not stay a moment longer she meant it, and when she started to move she moved quickly; she did not dilly and dally over the ceremony of goodbye (besides, she really was in a tearing hurry to get home and prepare a meal for her family), so she flashed a friendly smile at everybody and waved her hand and went. She was already in the car and had started the engine when she saw Bel Lamington pursuing her down the steps.

'Mrs. Dering Johnstone!' cried Bel breathlessly. 'I mean Rhoda — please stop — just a minute — '

'Yes, what is it?' asked Rhoda. The car was actually moving but now it stopped.

'Would I do?' asked Bel, clinging to the side of the car with both hands as if she were afraid it would take flight.

'Would you do?' asked Rhoda in bewilderment.

'Would I do?' repeated Bel, still panting after her swift pursuit. 'I just suddenly thought — I mean I can cook.'

'You can cook?'

'Quite well, really. Aunt Beatrice said so and she was very particular about food.'

'I don't know what you're talking about,' declared Rhoda a trifle irritably; the girl was delaying her and she wanted to get home. It struck Rhoda that perhaps Bel Lamington was not quite all there. She had been very quiet, shy and practically monosyllabic, and now suddenly she seemed to have burst out of her shell and become like another person — all het up and talking nonsense.

'I really must go,' added Rhoda, leaning forward to let in the clutch.

'I mean I could cook for you,' explained Bel.

'You could cook for me?'

'Yes, that's what I thought. I could come and help you while Miss Flockhart is away.'

'You don't mean you want to come to Tassieknowe?'

'Yes,' said Bel nodding.

'But I don't understand!' exclaimed Rhoda incredulously. 'You're going south with the Armstrongs on Thursday. Louise told me — '

'I know,' said Bel. 'That was the idea. They're terribly kind — nobody could be kinder. They said I could go home with them and stay as long as I liked, but I must stand on my own feet. I hate people who sponge on other people, don't you?'

Rhoda did. In Rhoda's estimation people who sponged upon other people were the absolute end.

'It's been worrying me a lot,' added Bel.

'But, my dear girl, you don't sponge,' said Rhoda. 'The Armstrongs love having you. It's made a tremendous difference to Louise having you here.'

'Having me here — yes,' agreed Bel. 'But if I go home with them and can't find another job — '

'But surely you could easily find another job! You could get a secretarial post, like you had before. That's what you're used to. You aren't used to hard work.'

'I'm quite strong.'

They looked at each other for a few moments in silence. Rhoda looked at Bel with a painter's eye and liked what she saw. She liked the shape of the head, the broad forehead, the widely-spaced grey eyes; she liked the curve of the cheek and the well-set ear. It was a beautiful ear, Rhoda noticed.

'You don't really mean it,' said Rhoda at last.

'Yes I do. I could come and cook — and do

other things as well. I could help you until Miss Flockhart comes back.'

'It would be terribly dull for you at Tassieknowe.'

'I don't mind. I don't mind anything if only I could get a job.'

'But why?'

'I haven't got any money,' said Bel frankly.

'That's another thing,' said Rhoda, somewhat embarrassed. 'I couldn't afford — I mean I never thought of having anybody like you.'

'No, of course not,' agreed Bel. 'You could just pay me what you pay Miss Flockhart — or perhaps less, because I wouldn't be so efficient. I don't know anything about children, I'm afraid.'

'Neither do I,' declared Rhoda with a sigh. 'I don't know a thing about children. I'm learning on my own and I'm probably giving them all sorts of queer inhibitions and complexes. Of course by the time they're grown-up I shall know quite a lot about children but that won't be much use. I shan't be allowed to have any say in my grandchildren's upbringing, shall I? My daughters-in-law will have their own ideas.'

Bel thought they were straying rather far from the point. She said, 'You need somebody, don't you?'

'Need somebody!' exclaimed Rhoda in heart-rending accents.

'Why not try me? You said you would take a murderess if she could cook.' Bel smiled and added, 'I'm not a murderess — but I can cook. I like cooking.'

'I don't know what to say!'

'Say yes,' suggested Bel. 'You could sack me if you found I wasn't any good. Couldn't you?'

'You're far more likely to sack yourself,' declared Rhoda. She hesitated and then continued, 'Look here, Bel. You haven't thought it over properly. We had better both think it over. I shall have to ask James.' She hesitated again. Of course she knew quite well what James would say. James would say, *for goodness' sake take the girl and try her.* That was what James would say. It was James who had suggested that they should advertise in the papers for a murderess. Rhoda knew that James could not bear to see her toiling and moiling, sweeping the stairs, washing the dishes, getting up at cock-crow to prepare his breakfast . . . and James did not much care for the food she cooked though he was too decent to say so. James ate underdone chops and overdone beef and sloppy milk puddings and pretended to enjoy these disgusting viands. Poor James!

Bel had been watching Rhoda's face. She said, 'You really need somebody, don't you? Shall I come on Thursday?'

'Thursday!' echoed Rhoda with a sudden gleam in her eyes. 'Could you really come on Thursday?'

'Yes,' said Bel.

22

Tassieknowe stood upon a little hillock in a bend of the river amongst the rolling hills. The river was very much smaller here than it was at Drumburly, it was little more than a good-sized stream. The house was of grey stone and, like most of the houses in the district, it was solidly built; its roof of grey slates fitted snugly without any unnecessary ornamentation. It was a house eminently fitted to withstand the winter gales, a house with no nonsense about it.

There was no nonsense about the inside of the house either. The rooms were of a reasonable size and well-proportioned and the stairs were well designed. Ten years ago when James and Rhoda had taken up their abode in Tassieknowe the whole house had been redecorated: the woodwork painted white and the walls distempered in various soft colours. Nothing much had been done to it since then so it was a trifle shabby, but that did not seem to matter. There was a homely friendly sort of atmosphere about the place. When Bel walked in at the door she knew at once that she would be happy here.

Bel had not been able to take up her new post without a great deal of heated argument. The Armstrongs had opposed the plan strongly and had done their best to persuade her to give it up and go south with them as had been arranged. Louise especially was amazed and distressed when she heard about it and declared that it was absolutely crazy. Tassieknowe was at the back of beyond; it would be terribly dull; the work would be much too hard; Bel would be wasting herself. She would be nothing more nor less than a skivvy, cooking and scrubbing and cleaning from morning to night.

'But you said Mrs. Plack would be much happier if she had married a ploughman,' Bel pointed out. 'You said you would rather marry a ploughman and cook and scrub and wash his clothes than marry Alec Drummond. You said it would be more useful.'

'That isn't the same thing at all,' declared Louise. 'You aren't going to marry a plough-man.'

'You never know,' said Bel smiling. 'There might be an absolutely fascinating ploughman at Tassieknowe.'

'That isn't the point,' said Louise crossly.

Of course Bel knew it was not the point but there was truth in what she had said. She felt — rightly or wrongly — that she would be much more useful and a great deal happier helping Rhoda to run Tassieknowe than typing letters and adding up columns of figures in an office in the City — an unknown office where she would know nothing about the business and which would be full of unknown women who would look at her askance. There might be another Helen Goudge, thought Bel with a shudder. There might be another Mr. Wills! Besides, there was always the fear that she might not get another job in an office in the City even if she wanted it. Here was a job to hand. She had got it and she intended to do her best to keep it. She felt that it was MEANT.

Rhoda had given Bel a room at the end of the passage with a view up the river. It was not a large room but it was comfortable and pleasant. There were several pictures on the walls; one of them was of a landscape covered with snow, but instead of being white it was full of all the colours of the rainbow. Bel had been told that 'Rhoda painted beautiful pictures' and she wondered if Rhoda had painted this. She had learnt enough about pictures from Mark to recognise the professional touch. If Rhoda had painted this she was 'good'.

Bel had unpacked her clothes and was gazing at the picture when her new employer came in.

'Do you like it?' asked her new employer with interest.

'Yes,' said Bel thoughtfully. 'Yes. It gave me rather a shock at first but the more I look at it the more I like it. I like pictures that make me want to walk about inside them you see.'

'Renoir said that — or something like it.'

'Really?' asked Bel in surprise. She added, 'Is it a real place or just a fantasy.'

'It's a real place. I meant it to be a study in Chinese white and sepia and then I saw that the snow was full of colour — so it came out like that. Do you know a lot about painting?'

'Nothing,' replied Bel. 'I used to know a painter but I was always saying the wrong things. It really was very difficult indeed. He painted me but it wasn't a bit like me. It wasn't intended to

230

be like me of course.' She hesitated when she had said it, for it was strange to think of Mark. She had not thought of Mark for so long — it seemed like years. How very strange it was to remember that she had been so terribly unhappy about Mark!

'You must tell me about it,' said Rhoda, scenting a mystery. 'You must tell me why he painted you and yet didn't intend it to be like you. When I paint people I intend it to be like them — and as a matter of fact it usually is,' she added thoughtfully.

'Some time, but not now,' said Bel briskly. 'We had better go down to the kitchen and arrange about food.'

Rhoda was a little surprised to find her new employee taking charge like this, for she had been of the opinion that her new employee was an extremely gentle creature — in fact slightly 'wet' — but she agreed that this was not the right moment for a heart to heart conversation, however interesting, and led the way down to the kitchen without more ado.

2

Bel's new job was no sinecure; since Miss Flockhart had been confined to bed, everything had got into a muddle. Miss Flockhart was extremely methodical — not so Rhoda and Effie. If Rhoda had occasion to use a dish or a pot or any sort of kitchen gadget she left it lying about; and Effie, finding it, shoved it into the back of a cupboard and forgot all about it. These idiosyncrasies had turned Miss Flockhart's beautifully arranged kitchen into a higgledy-piggledy mess.

If Bel wanted anything to cook with she had to search for it and this took time. She searched high and low for the mincer — surely there must be a mincer in Tassieknowe kitchen! — and finally discovered it in the boot-cupboard. She found the large roasting-tin on the top shelf in the larder. There seemed to be no bread-knife. This came to light, quite by accident, in the drawer which Miss Flockhart kept for dusters.

For the first few days Bel had no time to do anything except cook meals and get the kitchen into order. She was considerably hampered in her tasks by Rhoda who kept popping in to the kitchen and asking if she could help. Rhoda was worried about her new employee; she worked too hard. How dreadful if she broke down under the strain!

'Let up, for goodness' sake!' exclaimed Rhoda. 'You're wearing yourself to a shadow. Please come and sit down.'

'I will when I've got the place in order,' Bel replied. 'No, you can't do anything to help. Just leave me alone. Once everything is in order it will be quite easy. The food is all right, I hope?'

The food was more than 'all right'. Bel's cooking was quite as good as Flockie's — and more imaginative. Rhoda was enjoying her meals and, even more important, James was enjoying his. It seemed to Rhoda that in three days James had already put on a little weight, his cheeks had filled out and his eyes were brighter. When he came in after a long morning on the hill he would rub his hands together and exclaim delightedly, 'Ha! Veal and ham pie! That's the stuff to give the troops!' and fall to with gusto.

Rhoda had spoken of Effie, the cow-man's daughter, in derogatory terms but Bel found her quite a useful assistant. She required supervision, of course, but when told what to do she did it to the best of her ability. Effie was sixteen, she was the eldest of a very large family and the cares of the world sat heavily upon her shoulders. She was tall — much too tall for her age — and very pale and droopy. Everything about Effie drooped. Her lank hair drooped over her forehead, the corners of her mouth drooped and her skirt drooped at the back. Bel decided that Effie was half-starved and made her drink milk. This was not easy, for Effie despised milk, in her opinion it was a beverage suitable only for very young children, so Bel was obliged to stand over her every morning at eleven o'clock and see that the half pint went down Effie's throat and was not emptied into the sink.

At first Effie tried to converse with Bel but she soon found that it was hopeless for Bel had the greatest difficulty in understanding a word she said. Fortunately Effie understood Bel without the slightest trouble. This seemed inexplicable to Bel. Why was it? If the girl could understand her so easily why couldn't she understand the girl?

'Ye talk Bibby Cee,' explained Effie.

'I talk Bibby Cee!' asked Bel in bewilderment.

'Ugha,' said Effie.

(By this time Bel had discovered that 'Ugha' meant yes. When she asked Effie to peel the potatoes Effie said 'Ugha' and peeled them forthwith).

The mystery was intriguing. Bel puzzled over it all morning and finally asked Rhoda about it.

'Effie says I talk Bibby Cee,' said Bel. 'She says that's why she can understand me.'

'Oh yes,' said Rhoda. 'They've got a wireless. They listen in every evening.'

'B.B.C.!' exclaimed Bel. 'How silly of me!'

They looked at each other and smiled. Already they understood each other and had discovered that they had a great deal in common; chiefly a sense of fun — which is quite a different thing from a sense of humour and more rare.

3

Bel had heard a good deal about 'Rhoda's boys' but she did not see much of them. She saw them at breakfast but after breakfast they went off to school in the school-bus and did not return until tea-time. After tea they rushed out to play with the cow-man's children or, if it were wet, they settled down to a game of tiddly-winks until it was time for bed.

It was one of Bel's duties to put the boys to bed. She had been looking forward to this for she had thought it would be amusing to bath them and have fun with them, but it was not in the least amusing. They took advantage of her inexperience and were uncontrollable. When they liked they could speak reasonably good English but quite often they conversed with each other in the local dialect, which they had picked up from their playmates. It annoyed Bel when she could not understand what they said and one evening when she was struggling to bath them — and to wash their ears, a process which they both disliked intensely — she remonstrated with them.

'It isn't a bit pretty,' said Bel. 'Why don't you talk like Mummie? You can talk so nicely when you like.'

'You're silly,' replied Harry. 'You're not as nice as Flockie.'

'We don't like you,' added Nicky frankly.

'We don't need to worry,' said Harry. 'She'll get the boot when Flockie comes home.'

'She'll get the boot when Flockie comes home!' chanted Nicky gleefully.

Bel found this slightly discouraging. She was not used to children.

Rhoda was not used to children either; she had said that she was 'learning on her own'; she had bought various books which described the correct method of bringing up children and studied them carefully. She had a whole shelf of little green books on the subject.

'You should never whip children,' said Rhoda. 'Sometimes I feel inclined to give them a spanking — especially Nicky, he really is so terribly annoying — but all the books say you should reason with them. We must reason with them, Bel.'

This was one evening when the boys had been

particularly uncontrollable in the bath, had absolutely refused to have their ears washed and had drenched Bel from head to foot with soapy water.

It was rather surprising that Rhoda, who was so sensible about other matters, could be so foolish about her children. If she had burnt all the books and had managed the boys according to her own good sense they would have been easier to live with. At least that was what Bel thought.

'You should never take anything away from them by force,' continued Rhoda earnestly. 'You should just ask them kindly but firmly to give it up — and of course you should never say 'don't do that'. You should take their minds off by suggesting something else. I must say I find that very difficult.'

Bel found it difficult too. In fact she found it impossible. When she saw Nicky was about to throw a wet sponge at her she found herself shouting 'Don't do that!' She found herself snatching the sponge out of his hand. When the boys came in to the kitchen whilst she was preparing breakfast and Harry made a bee-line for the stove and began to clatter the lid of the porridge-pot, Bel shouted 'Don't, Harry! You'll burn yourself!' On occasions like these there was no time to take their minds off by suggesting something else.

Curiously enough the boys were much better with Effie who had read none of the books. If Harry bothered her when she was scrubbing the larder she merely said, 'Are ye wantin' a clout on the lug, Hawrry?' and if Harry persisted in annoying her she dealt him a cuff on the side of the head which sent him staggering across the floor. This was dreadful of course — all the little green books would have turned red with horror at the bare idea — but, instead of reprimanding Effie severely, Bel went on beating up eggs and pretended she had not seen.

Effie had very little trouble with Harry after that. Of course Effie was used to children, she had innumerable brothers and sisters. There was no time to reason with them. If they were troublesome they got 'skelped' or 'clouted' so they learnt quite quickly that it was better not to annoy their elders. Bel had a feeling that Harry and Nicky would have learnt quite quickly too.

One of Nicky's most annoying habits was to burst into floods of tears. The corners of his mouth went down and enormous tears spurted from his eyes like fountains. He could turn on the waterworks whenever he liked — at any moment. He turned them on when he was sent to wash his hands or if he were denied an extra piece of chocolate. He turned them on when Harry beat him at tiddly-winks and when Bel was trying to wash his ears.

'I don't know why he cries like that,' said Rhoda anxiously. 'The books all say you should keep children happy.'

'But he must have his ears washed,' Bel pointed out.

23

Apart from her trouble with the boys Bel found her new job very much to her liking. Once order had been established in the kitchen premises the work was comparatively easy. She got up early, made the breakfast and tidied the house. She cooked the midday meal and helped Effie to wash the dishes. After that she was free to go out and do what she pleased. Occasionally she went with Rhoda to Drumburly to do the shopping and one day she went to The Shaw Arms and had tea with Mrs. Simpson in her private sitting-room.

Some people might have found Tassieknowe very dull indeed, for certainly it was 'at the back of beyond', but Bel did not find it dull. She was interested in the farm and she enjoyed exploring the country and the Dering Johnstones were so kind to her that she felt very happy in their company.

Louise wrote to her several times — her letters were always a joy — and one morning Bel received a letter from Mark Desborough which had been forwarded to her from Coombe House. She was surprised to get it for she had not expected to hear from Mark; he had vanished from her life and to tell the truth she would have been better pleased if he had vanished entirely.

Bel unfolded the letter with reluctance, noting

that it was from London — so Mark had returned!

The letter was quite long and very friendly. Mark explained that Edward had been very tiresome and selfish so he had decided to leave Florence and was now back in his old studio in Mellington Street 'painting like mad'. He had sold several pictures and had got good prices for them. He had been climbing about on the roofs and had gone down to Bel's garden but had found the flat shut. The garden was in a horrible condition, very dirty and untidy with bits of paper blowing about; most of the plants were dead and one of the window-boxes had fallen to pieces and the earth was leaking out all over the stones. Mark had peered in through the sitting-room window and everything was covered with dust.

The letter continued:

I wish you would come back. I want you to pose for me. I have got a wonderful idea for a picture. Let me know your plans as soon as possible. I rang up Louise but for some reason she would not give me your address — silly little owl! But she consented to forward a letter if I sent it to Coombe House. Dear little mouse, do come back soon. I miss you dreadfully.

Much love from

Mark

The letter disturbed Bel for several reasons; but principally because it mentioned 'plans'. She had no plans. Of course she would stay on at Tassieknowe as long as Rhoda needed her, but when Miss Flockhart came back she would have to go — and Miss Flockhart was reported to be making good progress. After that Bel did not know what she would do. Perhaps the best thing would be to return to her flat and try to get some sort of job, but not an office-job, thought Bel. Dr. Armstrong had told her that he might be able to get her a post as receptionist to a doctor — something like that. It had seemed quite a good idea at the time, but with Mark in residence in his studio — popping in to see her whenever he felt inclined — it did not seem a good idea at all. She did not want to see Mark and, quite definitely, she did not want to pose for one of his strange pictures. She would have to take a firm line with Mark — and how Bel hated taking a firm line!

Oh, what a bother! thought Bel. What a frightful nuisance Mark is! Why on earth couldn't he have stayed in Florence with Edward What's-his-name?

Mark would have been considerably surprised if he could have known of the feelings which his letter had aroused in the bosom of his dear little mouse.

2

Tassieknowe was a sheep-farm but the Dering Johnstones kept a few cows to supply the house and the cottages with milk. They did not go in

240

for a modern cow-parlour with all its hygienic appurtenances and they had no electric milker. The cows were milked by hand; they were out all day in a pasture near the river and spent their nights in an old-fashioned byre. Bel loved the byre, especially in the evening. Quite often after supper she put on her coat and went out for a stroll round the farm and she always visited the byre. Sometimes she sat there and enjoyed the peaceful feeling it gave her. It was dim and mysterious, warm with the warmth of the beasts, full of the scent of hay, silent except for soft breathing and the rustle of straw.

It was in a place like this, thought Bel, that Mary and Joseph had found refuge and Jesus had been born. There was no room at the Inn, but there was room here — in a place like this — and surely it must have been a more peaceful refuge than a hot over-crowded hostelry with people coming and going all the time, shouting and laughing and making a lot of noise. There would have been no peace at all at the Inn.

This was quite a new idea. At least it was new to Bel.

There was another place in the farm which she liked to visit and where she was always sure of a welcome. This was the shepherd's house. It stood a little apart from the other buildings, higher up the hill.

It was a delightful little house, bright and cheerful and clean as a new pin. The furniture was good solid stuff and there were a great many ornaments — some of brass and some of china — all shining and glittering as if they had been washed and polished that very day. There was a book-shelf full of books and above it a shelf of china dogs. The books belonged to Sutherland and the china dogs to his wife. The dogs were of all shapes and sizes, some were pretty and others extremely ugly but Mrs. Sutherland loved them all; she showed them to Bel, taking them down from the shelf and retailing their history. This one had belonged to her grandmother; that one had been picked up by Sutherland at a sale and given to her for their silver-wedding anniversary. The one she loved best of all was a hideous little Pekinese which had been sent to her by her son from China.

'Ian's in the Merchant Service,' explained Mrs. Sutherland. 'He's got his First Mate's Certificate,' she added proudly.

Bel was suitably impressed.

Sutherland was quite different from the other people on the farm; he was a giant of a man, big and bony with a weatherbeaten face and light blue eyes. He spoke differently too, his voice was deep and slow. There was an impressive dignity in his whole demeanour. Originally he had come from the north — from Helmsdale — but he had been in the district for more than thirty-five years.

'All the time at Tassieknowe?' Bel wanted to know.

'Most of the time,' replied Sutherland. He hesitated and then continued: 'I was here with Mister Brown and then the place was sold to a man from London, Mister Heddle his name was, but Mister Heddle was not a good man to serve.

There was no pleasure in serving a man like him.'

'We had to go,' put in Mrs. Sutherland. 'We had to leave our nice wee house that we'd been in ever since we were married. It was a heart-break, Miss Lamington. We went over the river to Hawkbrae and there we were in a miserable wee cottage, just a but and a ben — away up on the hill — with no hot water and no light!'

'Och, it was not so bad,' declared Sutherland. 'And anyway it could not be helped.'

'You were as pleased as me when Mr. Johnstone bought Tassieknowe and we came home to our own wee house,' declared Mrs. Sutherland.

'Och yes, I was pleased,' agreed her husband. 'I know the hirsel here as if it was my own back-garden and Mister Dering Johnstone is a fine man to serve. It was a good day for us when we came home to Tassieknowe.'

'Mistress Dering Johnstone is nice too,' said Mrs. Sutherland.

'A grand lady!' agreed Sutherland smiling. 'There is not a finer lady in the whole of Scotland than Mistress Dering Johnstone. Do you know this, Miss Lamington, she painted my picture and it was real good. It was sent to Edinburgh and they hung it up in yon big picture gallery at the foot of the Mound.'

'We went all the road to Edinburgh to look at it,' said Mrs. Sutherland proudly. 'And there was Sutherland, his very self, among all the other pictures. It was as like him as two peas. There was a gentleman spoke to Sutherland about it. He knew it was him in a minute. A very nice gentleman, he was, very free and friendly-like, and the end of it was he bought the picture.'

'He gave fifty pounds for it,' declared Sutherland in tones of awe. 'Fifty pounds for my picture!'

'It was Mistress Dering Johnstone's picture,' Mrs. Sutherland reminded him. 'It was because it was so well painted that the gentleman gave all that money for it.'

'That's true,' agreed Sutherland, slightly deflated.

3

Few people came within the orbit of Rhoda Dering Johnstone without being seized by the short hairs and dragged up to her studio at the top of the house. Rhoda was first and foremost a portrait painter — probably because she was intensely interested in human beings — and unfortunately there were not many human beings at Tassieknowe for her to paint. Thus it was that when the kitchen had been put in order and things had settled down a bit she decided to paint Bel.

They went up to the studio together and Bel was surprised to see that it was extremely tidy and clean. Rhoda, who had wrought havoc in the kitchen premises, was very particular indeed in her studio. It was her own proper milieu — that was the reason of course.

There were quite a number of canvases stacked against the wall. Rhoda seized one and put it on an easel.

'Oh, it's Mr. Johnstone!' exclaimed Bel in delight.

'Yes, it's Jock,' agreed the painter, putting her head on one side and surveying the portrait critically. 'I did it for Mamie's birthday — it's a secret. You mustn't tell.'

'It's wonderful,' declared Bel. 'I like the way he's leaning forward in his chair. He looks as if he were going to speak to you!'

Rhoda nodded, 'Of course he's a very good subject with that nice, kind, craggy sort of face. This is one I did of Flockie,' she continued, producing another portrait. 'I've done several of Flockie but this is the best. Of course you don't know Flockie.'

'No, but I'm sure it's like her,' said Bel.

Rhoda had painted James and the two boys and several other people on the farm. She had painted Sutherland, but his portrait had been hung in the Scottish Academy and had been sold. Rhoda explained this to Bel and was somewhat surprised to hear that Bel knew all about it already.

'Oh, they told you, did they?' said Rhoda. 'They're awfully funny about it. Between you and me and the bed-post it was rather a good picture; I wouldn't have let it go for fifty if the Hoover hadn't suddenly gone phutt.'

Bel laughed. Her new employer amused her considerably.

'Well, we had better get on with it,' said

245

Rhoda, suddenly assuming a serious business-like manner. 'I want you to sit a bit sideways because I simply must have your ear.'

Bel sat as directed; she had posed for her portrait before but this was a very different affair. Rhoda did not invite her subject to kneel upon a stone floor but settled her comfortably in a very large armchair and told her to relax. It was Rhoda's habit to chat to her sitters and encourage them to talk, for in this way she got them in their natural state; not all keyed up and rigid.

There was a good deal to do in the house so the sittings were limited and the portrait did not get on very quickly but Rhoda managed to entice her model out of her shell of shyness and learnt a great deal about her affairs. She heard about the flat in London and about the little roof-garden, which had been neglected for so long that it was little more than a rubbish heap. She heard about Bel's worries. She even heard about Mark.

'You can't possibly go back to your flat with that young rotter dropping in on you at any moment,' declared Rhoda in horrified tones. 'It isn't the right thing at all.'

'It would be a frightful nuisance.'

'A nuisance! It would be much more than a nuisance. It wouldn't be safe. Honestly, Bel,' said Rhoda earnestly. 'You simply aren't fit to be loose.'

'Not fit to be loose?'

'You need a keeper,' explained Rhoda kindly. 'You can't rely upon your Guardian Angel being always on the job — but never mind, we don't need to worry. You can stay at Tassieknowe as long as you like. James and I love having you and even when Flockie comes back she won't be fit to do a great deal. I must have somebody to help her, and that somebody had better be you.'

'But Miss Flockhart may not like me,' said Bel in doubtful tones.

24

At Tassieknowe the midday meal was the main meal of the day and when it was over Bel was free to go out. Sometimes she walked along the river and sometimes she walked over the hills. Her favourite spot was a cranny in the hills high up above Tassieknowe. She came here quite often and sat in a sheltered place amongst the rocks. There was a wonderful view from here; she could see the road winding up the valley beside the river; she could look down upon the farm. It looked very small from here — like a toy farm — and the people who moved about on their lawful occasions looked like toy-people. There was a rowan-tree growing amongst the rocks; it was twisted and gnarled by the winter winds but it was immensely strong and sturdy. To Bel this tree was a mystery for there were no other trees near. Perhaps long ago a bird had dropped a rowan-berry amongst the rocks. How else could it have come? There was a tiny rivulet near by — a baby burn that welled into a bowl of moss and overflowed, trickling down the hill.

One afternoon when Bel had been in her new job for about a fortnight she was sitting in her favourite nook. She saw a car come up the road from the direction of Drumburly and turn in at the gates of Tassieknowe and, after an interval of about ten minutes, she saw somebody come through the farm-gate and walk up the hill. It

248

was a man — she could see that — and he was walking briskly as though he had a definite purpose.

A bird soared — and Bel watched it. When she looked again the man was nearer, near enough for her to see that he was wearing grey slacks and a grey pullover. He was hatless and his thick brown hair was ruffled by the breeze. Bel watched him idly. It was unusual to see anybody on the hill, except the shepherd, and this certainly was not Sutherland.

Bel expected the man to turn and walk along the old cart-track which led to the quarry but he crossed it and came on to where she was sitting.

It was not until he was quite near that she recognised him and even then she could scarcely believe her eyes.

It was Ellis Brownlee.

Bel was so amazed, so absolutely flabbergasted to see him that she could neither move nor speak. She had thought of him as being in America attending the conference in New York . . . and here he was at Tassieknowe! She could give him no greeting; she could only gaze at him.

He came and stood and looked down at her. 'It's taken me weeks to find you,' he said.

'Weeks — to find me!'

'You vanished.' He sat down as he spoke. He was smiling at her. His skin was tanned and he was thinner, but he had the same smile; his eyes crinkled at the corners in exactly the same way.

By this time Bel had recovered a little from her astonishment. 'Did you say you had been looking for me?' she asked incredulously.

'Searching high and low. Surely you knew I would look for you?'

'Look for me?'

'Yes, of course.'

'I thought you were still in New York.'

'It's wonderful how quickly you can get about the world if you put your mind to it.'

'I don't understand,' she declared.

'You will — in time. There's no hurry now that I've found you. We can leave all the explanations until later. This is a lovely place, isn't it?' he added.

He took out his pipe and filled it and lighted it, sheltering the match with his cupped hands; he began to smoke peacefully, looking about him with pleasure.

'I've seen lots of beautiful places during my travels,' he continued, 'but nothing to beat this. You've chosen a wonderful place to hide in.'

The strange thing was that he looked in his element. Bel had seen him in London, dressed in formal clothes, and he had looked in his element there. Here, on this bare hillside, he was still himself but he did not seem out of place. Bel thought he looked exactly like the little boy in the photograph which Mrs. Brownlee had shown her; the photograph of Ellis digging on the sands.

'I'm always finding you in strange places,' continued Ellis after a short silence. 'Do you remember that day in London when I discovered you in your queer little back-water having your lunch? We talked about people being different sorts of people when they were in different places.'

'Yes, I remember.'

'Well, here we are! We're several hundred miles away from that little back-water. We're in a very different sort of place. Are we the same people or not?'

Bel was not sure. She said, 'But Mr. Brownlee, don't let's bother about that. I want to know what has happened.'

'There's an awful lot to explain,' he said with a sigh.

'Please tell me first of all why you were looking for me.'

'No, Bel, that comes at the end. I think I had better begin by telling you what brought me home in such a tearing hurry. It was a cable and it just said, '*We think you had better come back immediately*' and it was signed 'Frances Brownlee, James Copping'.'

'Those two!' exclaimed Bel in astonishment.

'Those two,' he agreed. 'Mother and Jim in cahoots! I can't think of anything that would have brought me home quicker. I chucked the conference; I chucked everything and caught the first plane I could get. I had never flown across the Atlantic before and the weather was perfect but I didn't enjoy the trip. I was worrying far too much — wondering what the dickens had happened. I couldn't think of anything to fit.'

'How do you mean — 'anything to fit'?'

'Don't you see? Mother and Jim on the warpath together! That's what puzzled me. It seemed inexplicable. This is what I thought:

supposing Mr. Copping had taken a turn for the worse the cable would have been despatched by Mrs. Copping — and possibly Jim. If Rose Hill had been burnt to the ground Mother would have got in a panic and sent for me. If something ghastly had happened at the wharf Wills would have cabled. If Wills had pegged out suddenly the cable would have come from the office. See what I mean?'

'Yes,' said Bel. She began to laugh.

Ellis Brownlee laughed too but not very heartily. 'Oh yes, it seems rather funny now, but believe me it wasn't a bit funny at the time.'

'What had happened?'

'Oh, it's quite simple when you know. Jim blew in as usual to translate the letters and of course you weren't there, so he asked Miss Goudge and she told him you had been dismissed at a moment's notice. Jim could scarcely believe his ears! When he did believe them he marched straight into Wills's room to demand the reason. You've got a doughty champion in James Copping, Bel.'

'Oh, what did he say!' exclaimed Bel in horrified tones.

'Apparently he said quite a lot. He began by telling Wills that he had no right whatever to dismiss my secretary. Wills replied that he was in full charge of the affairs of the firm and therefore had the right to dismiss anyone who was incompetent; Jim replied that you were extremely capable — he had worked with you so he knew.

'Then Wills said that Jim had no right

whatever to question his decisions and Jim said he was representing the head of the firm and went on to remind Wills that his great grandfather had founded the firm and therefore he had a moral status if not a legal one. Wills didn't like that much. I've sometimes thought that Wills is a bit jealous of the Coppings. Anyhow, according to Jim, he began to get 'a bit ratty'.'

Bel could imagine it!

'That didn't worry Jim,' continued Ellis. 'As a matter of fact 'our Mr. James' is a courageous person with no fear of man nor beast. I believe his great grandfather had the same characteristic. So the interview continued; it was a pretty stormy interview, I gather. Wills lost his temper completely. Jim says he went round the bend, gibbered like a maniac and nearly had a fit.'

'Oh, goodness!' cried Bel, looking at Ellis with eyes as round as saucers.

'Eventually,' said Ellis, continuing the tale. 'Eventually Wills told Jim to go to hell, but instead of obeying orders he took the first bus to Beckenham.'

'Beckenham?'

'Yes. Apparently you had told Jim that Mother was 'very much all there', or words to that effect, and as he had just had an interview with a maniac he decided she was the right person to see. Jim explained the whole thing to Mother and Mother caught on at once. She may not be a good business woman but she's extremely intelligent — and of course you had told her a good deal about the state of affairs at the office

253

so she wasn't really surprised.

'Mother suggested that Mr. Copping should be consulted, but Jim said no. He explained that he didn't want to bother 'the Guv'nor' but in his opinion a maniac was not a suitable person to be in full control of the firm. Mother agreed. So then they rang up Copping Wharf and got hold of Nelson and discovered that Nelson was intensely worried about the muddle at the office — no sense to be got out of them, important letters unanswered for days, and urgent messages ignored! Mother and Jim wasted no time after that. They put their heads together and concocted the cablegram which brought me tearing home.'

Bel was silent. There was so much to be thought about that she could find no words.

Ellis knocked out his pipe and put it away in his pocket. He said, 'The first thing I did, when I had heard their story, was to go straight to the office. They didn't know I was back so it gave them a bit of a shock when I walked in. Wills wasn't there — he was playing golf or something — and the new man was struggling along on his own. He's not a bad chap, really, and I think he'll be quite useful when he finds his feet — but that's by the way. I was talking to the fellow and trying to get things sorted out when Miss Snow appeared and asked to speak to me in private.'

'Miss Snow!'

'Yes, our friend the ice-berg, but she wasn't quite so 'icily regular' as usual. In fact, if you could possibly imagine Miss Snow being a trifle excited and 'put about' you can imagine what she looked like.'

Bel could not imagine it.

'We had our private chat,' Ellis continued. 'At first she was somewhat incoherent but after a little encouragement she got down to brass tacks. She explained that when Miss Goudge was off with 'flu, Mr. Wills had sent her to look for the address book which was kept in Miss Goudge's desk. Behind the address book there was a little packet of letters.'

Ellis took the little packet out of his pocket and dropped it into Bel's lap. 'There it is,' he said. 'Miss Snow was a bit worried as to what was the correct thing to do. If she had known your address she would have forwarded the letters to you, but you hadn't left your address so she decided to keep them and hand them to me. I assured her that she had done the right thing which comforted her considerably. Look at the letters, Bel.'

Bel looked at the little packet, it was secured with an elastic band. There were five letters, written upon flimsy paper; they were unopened. They had come by air-mail from America and were addressed in Ellis Brownlee's writing to Miss B. Lamington, c/o Copping, Wills and Brownlee.

'In Miss Goudge's desk!' exclaimed Bel in horror. 'Does that mean — '

'It means she intercepted them,' said Ellis grimly.

'Oh no! Oh, surely not! Oh, how dreadful!'

'Yes, it's almost incredible, isn't it.'

'Incredible!' cried Bel. 'Of course I knew she hated me, but how *could* she have done such a horrible thing! How could she have been so mean!'

'Despicable,' agreed Ellis. 'I felt like sacking the woman then and there — and then I realised it would make a frightful stink.'

'So you didn't?'

'No, I didn't. I just called her into my room and suggested quite kindly that she might like to resign her post. At first she seemed very much annoyed and then she caught sight of the little packet of letters which happened — just happened — to be lying on my table and she resigned quite gracefully.'

'Oh!' exclaimed Bel. She added, 'You are clever, aren't you?'

'Fairly crafty,' he agreed complacently.

'And you *did* write to me,' added Bel. Somehow the knowledge that he had written to her as he had promised seemed vastly more important than the despicable behaviour of Miss Goudge.

'Of course I wrote! I'm not in the habit of breaking my promises. You know that, Bel.'

'That's — what I thought,' said Bel with a little catch in her breath. 'That's why I couldn't — understand.'

Ellis stretched out his hand and laid it on her knee with a firm pressure. 'You understand now, don't you?' he said. 'And perhaps you're just beginning to understand why I had to find you.'

There was something in his voice that scared Bel. She gave the subject a slight twist and said quickly, 'How did you know I was here?'

'I didn't know where you were. You had disappeared and covered your tracks. No murderer could have covered his tracks more completely. Why did you do it, Bel? Why didn't you write to my mother and tell her what had happened? You have a warm friend there.'

'I don't know,' said Bel miserably. 'It was all so horrid. I just wanted to get away and forget about it.'

'Did you succeed in forgetting about it?'

'Not really,' said Bel.

2

Once more they were approaching dangerous ground. Bel pulled herself together. 'You haven't told me how you found me,' she pointed out.

'Oh, that's a long story,' declared Ellis Brownlee. 'I went to your flat of course and found it all shut up. None of your neighbours knew anything about you except an old chap who lived in the attic. He was frightfully lame, poor old boy. He said he had seen you occasionally on the stairs — but not lately. He said you were friendly with a young man who painted pictures.'

'Mark Desborough,' said Bel. 'Yes, I was friendly with him at one time.'

Ellis Brownlee looked at her. She had spoken casually and in the past tense which seemed to please him.

'Oh, I see,' he said cheerfully. 'Well, anyhow,

that was all the information I could get — so that was a dead end. I had to start again from scratch. Mother and Jim were anxious to find you too, so we went into a huddle and discussed ways and means. It seemed pretty hopeless until Mother suddenly remembered that you had mentioned an Inn — a very interesting old place called The Owl at Shepherdsford. She rather thought you had stayed there for a week-end, but she wasn't sure. It was all a bit vague but I decided to go and have a look at it. I went down there on Sunday — it was the only day I could go. The place was full, but I managed to get hold of the proprietor and I asked him about you. Your name wasn't in the visitors' book, so obviously you hadn't stayed there, but when I described you he remembered that you had been there to lunch one day with Miss Armstrong. Mrs. Palmer remembered you too, she suggested I should ask Miss Armstrong about you and she gave me the Armstrongs' address. So then I went over to Ernleigh and found the doctor sitting in the garden and explained the whole thing.

'The doctor told me you were at Tassieknowe — so I came to Tassieknowe — and Mrs. Dering Johnstone said you were out on the hill — so I climbed the hill. That was how I found you,' added Ellis with a triumphant air.

Bel was silent. It seemed most extraordinary that he had taken all that trouble to discover her whereabouts. He had come all the way to Drumburly! All the way to Tassieknowe! Hundreds of miles!

At last after quite a long silence she said, 'But

why did you bother. I mean I can't possibly go back to the office. You wouldn't want me, would you? Honestly, I simply couldn't bear it. There would be such a lot of talk — and anyhow I'm not an office sort of person. Really and truly I'm not. And I simply hated all the noise and bustle of London. I was a square peg in a round hole.'

'You're happier here?'

'Much happier. Of course I can't stay here indefinitely — just until Miss Flockhart is better — and I don't know what I'm going to do after that, but — but — '

'We'll find a square hole for you,' said Ellis Brownlee.

Bel glanced at him quickly. He looked peaceful and contented. He looked confident and calm. He was absolutely trustworthy; she trusted him completely. He had said he would find a square hole to fit her so there was no need for her to worry any more about the future — no need to worry.

Bel heaved a sigh of relief and leant back comfortably against the rock.

25

The explanations were now over and, as it was getting late, Bel and Ellis Brownlee walked back together to Tassieknowe. The family was just sitting down to tea so Rhoda at once asked Ellis to stay and have it with them; he accepted the invitation with alacrity.

Bel was interested to see how well he fitted in with the Dering Johnstones. In a few minutes they were all chatting together as if they had known each other for years. It was obvious that Rhoda and James liked their guest immensely. He made friends with the boys by the simple means of giving them some Brazilian coins which he happened to have in his pocket. They wanted to know where the coins had come from so Ellis was beguiled into retailing some of his adventures in South America and about his flight home across the Atlantic.

Bel did not say much, she was content to listen, it was delightful to see her friends getting on so well; and it was delightful to look at Ellis Brownlee and to know that he had not forgotten her but was still interested in her welfare. The little packet of letters was safely in the pocket of her cardigan and she looked forward to reading them when she had time.

Ellis was staying at The Shaw Arms (the Armstrongs had told him to do so) and James suggested he should come to Tassieknowe tomorrow for a day's fishing.

'I could lend you a rod,' said James; he added thoughtfully, 'I might take a day off, myself. The river is in pretty good condition at the moment.'

'You must come to lunch,' added Rhoda. 'I daresay Bel will consent to cook an extra potato for you.'

'Or we might take sandwiches,' suggested James. 'We'll wait and see what sort of a day it is.'

Bel wondered how long he intended to stay at Drumburly, she was aware that there must be a lot for him to do at the office, but Ellis did not seem to be in any special hurry to get home. He agreed to come to Tassieknowe tomorrow and stood up to take his departure.

'Oh, but you mustn't go!' exclaimed Rhoda. 'I want to show you my painting of Bel. It isn't finished, but I'd like you to see it.' She added, 'We don't often have unexpected visitors at Tassieknowe — it's so far from everywhere — so when we do have anybody we hang onto them as long as possible.'

'Couldn't he play tiddly-winks with us?' asked Harry. 'It would be much more fun for him than looking at a silly old picture.'

'We want him to play tiddly-winks!' cried Nicky.

'Don't be silly,' said James. 'Mr. Brownlee doesn't want to play that ridiculous game.'

'It's not a dickiless game!' wailed Nicky; his mouth went down at the corners and two large tears spurted out of his eyes.

'Perhaps I could do both,' suggested Ellis

hastily. 'We could have a game of tiddly-winks — I used to be rather a dab at it — and then I could see the picture. How would that do?'

'Wouldn't it bore you frightfully?' asked Rhoda. 'It really is very naughty of Nicky to behave like that. We oughtn't to give in to him.'

'We certainly shouldn't give in to him,' declared James — 'What Nicky wants is a good spanking.'

'Oh no!' exclaimed Rhoda in horrified tones. 'It's quite the wrong thing to spank children. All the books say so.'

The children were listening to this discussion with the greatest interest. They were quite old enough to understand all that was being said. Bel thought it a pity that the little green books had omitted to mention that the treatment of children should never be discussed in their presence. Of course it was not her business, so she said nothing. It was her business to clear the table and this she did.

When the table had been cleared Harry fetched the box of counters and they began to play the game. Bel had played with the boys several times but it had not been a success for they quarrelled incessantly; Harry sometimes cheated and Nicky wept copiously when he was beaten. This evening it was all quite different for Ellis took a firm line from the very beginning, he insisted on fair play, staunched Nicky's tears with a large white-linen handkerchief, and won the game without the slightest difficulty.

'You aren't very good at it, are you?' he said as he rose from the table. 'Tiddly-winks needs a good deal of practice. You'll soon learn if you practise it a bit.'

Considering that they played tiddly-winks nearly every evening this advice was somewhat damping — and actually the boys were damped. They said nothing in reply, and when Rhoda suggested it was time for bed they went off with Bel obediently without the usual fuss.

2

Rhoda had mentioned her painting of Bel and Ellis Brownlee was anxious to see it, so she took him up to the studio and showed it to him. She had said it was not finished, but it was finished except for the hands and some details of the background.

The painter was pleased with her work. She had managed to catch her sitter's characteristic expression . . . the look of a good child, a wondering sort of look, innocent and serious.

It was humility, thought Rhoda. That was the key-note of Bel's character. Rhoda had never prized this virtue — she had thought it overrated — but now she realised that she had been mistaken. Humility was not just an absence of pride, it was not a negative virtue, it was a definite 'fruit of the spirit'. False humility was horrible of course (*vide* Uriah Heep) but real humility, growing from within, was beautiful.

Ellis Brownlee stood and looked at the portrait in silence; he was astonished beyond measure at its excellence. Obviously Rhoda Dering

Johnstone was a very good painter indeed. Here was the real Bel! He had seen her look exactly like that, times without number. Here was Bel with her bright brown hair, her pretty little ear, the delicate curve of her cheek and the slope of her shoulder. Ellis had a sudden curious idea that Bel would look absolutely right in an old-fashioned sort of dress, like the portrait of his grandmother which hung above the chimney-piece in the drawing-room at Rose Hill. Bel was not really like his grandmother — for one thing her colouring was different — but she was of the same ilk. Her face had the same serious sweetness of expression.

'You don't need me to tell you it's good,' said Ellis at last.

'It *is* rather successful, isn't it?' Rhoda agreed. 'I've caught her mood. It wasn't terribly easy because she's shy.'

'Did you ever think of painting her in an old-fashioned dress?'

'Yes, of course! She would look marvellous in one of those nineteenth century frocks with bare shoulders and a tiny waist, but she would have to have ringlets — little curls like sausages hanging down on each side of her face.'

Ellis nodded. He remembered now that his grandmother had little curls like sausages.

'I'm glad you like it,' Rhoda said.

'Like it isn't the word! It's quite marvellous. Why haven't we heard about you, Mrs. Dering Johnstone?'

'Oh well, I'm busy you know,' she replied with a little smile. 'I'm a farmer's wife — first and foremost. I thought at one time that I would make painting my career and then I decided to marry James instead. I've never regretted it for a moment. I do have things in the Academy sometimes but I'm interested chiefly in portraits and there aren't many subjects at Tassieknowe.'

Ellis had a feeling that there was a good deal behind this short statement of fact. He would have liked to hear more. He had been astonished to find this extraordinarily beautiful woman in such an isolated place and it was even more astonishing to discover that she was an accomplished portrait-painter. Perhaps the most astonishing thing of all was the fact that she was completely happy in her chosen rôle of a sheep-farmer's wife. She was happy — there was no doubt of that.

'Are you staying at Drumburly for some time?' asked Rhoda.

'I don't know,' Ellis replied. He hesitated for a moment and then added, 'It all depends on Bel. I ought to be in London attending to my business — it needs my attention badly — but there are some things that are even more important than business.'

'Come over to Tassieknowe whenever you like,' said Rhoda.

There was no time to say more (Bel came in to tell Rhoda that the boys were in bed) but fortunately there was no need to say more. Rhoda Dering Johnstone and Ellis Brownlee understood each other perfectly.

26

The following morning was fine and dry but there were clouds about, so it was not too bright for fishing, and there was a slight breeze in exactly the right direction. Ellis Brownlee arrived at ten o'clock as had been arranged and found his host busily engaged in getting out the rods and tackle for the day's sport. Presently, when all was ready, they walked down to the river together.

The two men had led entirely different lives: the one as a sheep-farmer in the Border Country; the other as a businessman in the City of London. But in spite of this they found a great deal to say to each other. Curiously enough both of them were surprised. Ellis was surprised to discover a sheep-farmer at the back of beyond who was intelligent and well-read and interesting to talk to; James was surprised that a London business-man could be human and companionable.

They began to exchange information about their affairs and this was surprising too. Ellis began to realise that sheep-farming required brains and skill and quite a lot of scientific knowledge. He enquired about the breeding of sheep and learnt the importance of improving the strain by choosing the best type of rams. He learnt also that since the elimination of rabbits the sheep had improved enormously; their fleeces were thicker and heavier, their health better and the incidence of twin lambs had increased.

'Why is that?' asked Ellis with interest.

'The ewes are stronger and fitter because they get better food. And they've got much better milk when the lambs are born — that makes a tremendous difference.'

'You'll have to keep the rabbits down.'

'You bet,' agreed James. 'We don't want any more of that ghastly disease — it really was disgusting — but I mean to keep them down by trapping and shooting. That's the thing to do.'

It was now James's turn to seek information. He began by saying rather enviously, 'I suppose you can take a holiday whenever you like?'

'Good heavens, no!' exclaimed Ellis. 'Just between you and me I do most of the business of the firm. One of my partners is a delicate man and he's just recovering from a serious illness, and I heard this morning that my other partner has been wafted away to a Mental Hospital.'

'That's bad!'

'Well, I'm not really surprised. He's been a bit queer for some time . . . more than a bit queer,' added Ellis thoughtfully. 'I doubt if he will ever be fit to come back.'

'You won't be sorry,' suggested James who had deduced this from his companion's manner rather than his words.

Ellis smiled and said, 'Not very. We'll take young Copping into the firm. He's very young but he's got his head screwed on all right. It will be Copping, Brownlee and Copping — not quite so euphonious and a bit difficult to say but otherwise satisfactory.'

'Good,' said James nodding. 'Let's hope the man will recover sufficiently to enjoy life but not sufficiently to return to work.' He hesitated and then asked, 'Does that mean you'll have to rush back to London?'

'It means I certainly ought to rush back to London. It means I ought to be rushing back to London at this very minute instead of fishing for trout at Tassieknowe.'

'But you're not going to?'

'I'll wait a day or two,' said Ellis with an odd sort of look. 'A day or two won't make much difference. Fortunately we've got a very capable chap as manager of the wharf.'

'Tell me about the wharf,' said James. 'That's your principal concern, isn't it? Just as the hirsel of Tassieknowe is mine. What happens at the wharf?'

'Now you're asking!'

'Yes, I'm asking. I'm abysmally ignorant about business matters. I want to know what goes on. Don't tell me if you'd rather not,' he added hastily.

'Of course I'll tell you,' declared Ellis.

As a matter of fact Ellis was delighted to talk about his business affairs to James. He told James about Copping Wharf, its history and its traditions and about the ships that came to the Pool of London from Greece and Turkey, from India and Ceylon, from Italy and Spain and a dozen other countries. He explained how the goods were unloaded and stored in the huge warehouses and later distributed in a fleet of vans to different towns all over the United Kingdom.

'For instance,' said Ellis. 'Those little cakes we had yesterday at tea were full of sultanas.'

'You mean they may have come by way of Copping Wharf and your warehouses?'

'Quite likely.'

'By Jove, that's interesting!' exclaimed James. 'I always thought business was stodgy!'

'I used to think sheep-farmers were a bit dim,' retorted Ellis.

They laughed and decided that you were never too old to learn.

There was another thing that Ellis had learnt during this conversation. He had learnt why Rhoda Dering Johnstone was perfectly happy living at the back of beyond.

2

Bel had been making her bed. She looked out of her window and saw the two men walking up the bank of the river side by side. They were talking earnestly, she noticed, but suddenly they stopped and looked at each other and roared with laughter. Then they walked on again. She wondered what they were talking about and what had made them laugh.

Last night she had opened the little packet and read the letters. She had waited until she was in her room, preparing for bed. The letters were very friendly and interesting, full of information about what the writer was doing and all the things he had seen. Of course Bel had typed hundreds of letters for Ellis Brownlee (letters about business affairs) but these were not business-letters and they were written in a very different style. Bel liked them immensely, she read them several times. She decided that they were exactly like the writer; she could almost hear him talking. There was one thing about the letters which distressed her considerably. The first letter said, *Be sure to write to me;* and gave the address of the Bank at Buenos Aires to which letters were to be addressed. Subsequent letters said, *Why haven't you written?* — or words to that effect. The last one of the sequence said plaintively, *I do wish you would write. I hope you aren't ill or anything. Please let me know.*

It was all the fault of that horrible woman! That despicable woman! Of course Bel would have written if she had received the first letter and had known the address!

3

Bel was still watching the two men walking up the river when Rhoda came into her room.

'Oh, there you are!' exclaimed Rhoda. 'I've been looking for you everywhere. I want a sitting.'

'Oh no! Not this morning! I can't, really! I've got an awful lot to do,' declared Bel in consternation.

'I want your hands.'

'But, Rhoda, honestly — '

'I want your hands,' repeated Rhoda. 'Hands are troublesome and I feel in the mood. Effie can carry on without you.'

Bel was aware that when Rhoda was feeling 'in the mood' it was useless to protest so she gave in with as good a grace as possible and followed her employer to the studio.

'There's no need to bother about lunch,' said Rhoda as she settled Bel in the big chair and arranged her hands in a suitable position. 'James said all they wanted was sandwiches and coffee. We can give them a good solid meal in the evening when they come back. It's nice for James to have a day's fishing — he enjoys it — and he doesn't take a holiday very often.'

'No, he doesn't,' Bel agreed.

'They won't have gone very far,' added Rhoda. 'We can make the sandwiches later and you can take them to the river in the picnic-basket. That will be the best plan.'

'Yes,' said Bel meekly. She had intended to make a steak and kidney pie for the midday meal but it would do just as well in the evening when the anglers would return, hungry as hunters after their day in the open air. Bel was thinking about the steak and kidney pie with its rich brown gravy and its delicious covering of puff pastry when suddenly she was startled out of her gastronomic dream.

'Are you going to marry Ellis Brownlee?' asked Rhoda in a conversational tone of voice.

'What!'

'You heard,' said Rhoda smiling. She had

taken up her palette and was busy mixing paint.

'Rhoda! What do you mean?'

'Just what I said. Are you going to marry the man? I think you should. Oh, of course I've no right to butt in — you can tell me to mind my own business — but when I'm fond of people I feel they are my business. As a matter of fact I'm famed far and wide for rushing in where angels fear to tread, but I can't stand aside and watch people wrecking their lives.'

'Wrecking their lives!'

'Yes,' said Rhoda nodding. 'You wouldn't stand aside and see a ship drifting onto the rocks without doing something about it, would you? You'd shout or throw them a life-belt or something — well, I'm shouting at you.'

'Shouting at me?'

'Bel,' said Rhoda earnestly. 'Ellis Brownlee is a dear.'

'Yes I know, but — '

'He's a bit older than you are but that's all to the good. You need somebody safe and solid, Bel. He's the right man for you.'

'But Rhoda, he — hasn't asked me! I'm sure he hasn't ever thought — '

'Hasn't asked you; hasn't ever thought!' exclaimed Rhoda. 'What do you imagine the man has come for? Do you think he's come all the way from London to catch a few trout in the Burly or play tiddly-winks with the boys?'

'I don't know,' said Bel in a whisper.

'I do,' declared Rhoda. She added fretfully, 'You've moved your hand, Bel. I wish you wouldn't. Hands are so troublesome to paint.'

She came and re-arranged the troublesome hands. 'There, like that,' she said. 'You've got very pretty hands and I want to get them right. I wish to goodness you'd wear gloves when you're preparing the vegetables and washing up the dishes. Why don't you?'

Bel was not thinking about hands. She said, 'Rhoda, listen — '

'No, you listen to me,' said Rhoda. 'Ellis Brownlee loves you. He'd ask you to marry him if you gave him a chance, but you'll have to meet him half way. He's not the sort of man to sweep a girl off her feet; he's the sort that needs — well, he needs just a little encouragement, see?'

'I don't — l-love him.'

'Are you sure?' asked Rhoda. 'You know, Bel, there are different ways of falling in love. There's love at first sight — at least I suppose there is, though to tell you the truth I've never met it and I wouldn't give an awful lot for it if I did. Pretty risky,' said Rhoda thoughtfully.

'Risky?'

'It's better to know what you're in for,' Rhoda explained. 'The best kind of love — the kind that lasts — begins with friendship. It begins with knowing each other well. At least that's how it was with James and me. We were children together — almost like brother and sister. Then he was away in Malaya. When he came back — well — he was just the same — only it was different.'

Bel was relieved that the subject had shifted from her own affairs. 'So you fell in love and were married,' she suggested.

'It wasn't quite like that,' replied Rhoda, stepping back and surveying her canvas with screwed-up eyes. 'I was terribly keen on painting and I wanted to make it my career, so I swithered. When James asked me to marry him I couldn't make up my mind and my swithering was almost fatal. I very nearly lost James. He very nearly married somebody else. It was only when I discovered that Holly Douglas was after him that I knew I couldn't do without him. It sounds awfully dog-in-the-mangerish, but that's how it was.'

Bel was silent. She was aware that the marriage of James and Rhoda Dering Johnstone was as nearly perfect as any marriage could be, so it was quite alarming to think that it had almost not come off.

'Don't swither, Bel,' said Rhoda. 'For goodness' sake don't swither.'

'But — but I don't love him! At least — not like that.'

'Not like what?'

'Not to — to marry him.'

'I see,' said Rhoda understandingly. 'Then it's no good, of course. You wouldn't mind a bit if he married somebody else.'

'Oh!' exclaimed Bel. It was an explosive sound — as if someone had hit her violently in the middle of her chest and knocked all the breath out of her body.

'Well, there you are!' said Rhoda. 'It's a good test — the very best test I know. If you'd be quite happy to go to church and listen to 'The Voice that Breathed O'er Eden' and watch him being

274

married to another woman then you don't love him 'like that'. You've moved your hand again,' she added.

As a matter of fact Bel had moved both her hands and was twisting them together in distress.

Rhoda put down her brush and came over and seized the twisting hands in a firm clasp. 'It's all right,' she said earnestly. 'It's absolutely all right — nothing to worry about. Just make up your mind and don't swither. I'm sorry I gave you such a fright but I had to. You understand, don't you? I had to give you a fright to bring you to your senses.'

27

It was all very well for Rhoda to talk, thought Bel, as she walked up the bank of the river with the basket of sandwiches on her arm. It was all very well for Rhoda to say that she must encourage him and meet him half way. Rhoda was brave — she was absolutely fearless — and Bel was not. So far Bel had not even been able to call him Ellis; he had been 'Mr. Brownlee' for so long. She had noticed that he was calling her 'Bel' quite naturally; he had addressed her as 'My dear Bel' in his letters.

I ought to try, thought Bel. I really must try. I'm not going to be his secretary any more, so there's no reason why I shouldn't call him Ellis.

She remembered Rhoda telling her to practise saying, 'Rhoda, Rhoda, Rhoda', twelve times out loud; it had made her laugh at the time but all the same there was something in it. Even Rhoda's most extravagant flights of fancy contained a good deal of common-sense.

Bel walked along saying, 'Ellis, Ellis, Ellis', and laughing at herself. When she had said it twelve times it was coming fairly easily and quite loudly.

'Hullo, Bel! Here I am!' shouted Ellis Brownlee.

She had expected him to be fishing of course; she had been looking up and down the river for two men wading with rods in their hands; but Ellis had been sitting in the shelter of a rock. He

276

got up and came towards her smiling.

'Oh, Mr. Brownlee!' exclaimed Bel in dismay.
'I like 'Ellis' much better.'

'Oh — yes, it's a nice name,' said Bel in a
fluttery voice. 'It was your mother's name before
she was married. She told me about it the day I
went to see her at Rose Hill.' Bel was aware, even
as she spoke, that Rhoda would not have
approved of this at all.

'I thought you would be fishing,' Bel added. 'Is
it too bright or something?'

'No, I don't think so,' replied Ellis vaguely. 'We
fished for a bit and then the shepherd came — a
fine-looking old chap! He made me think of
Elisha or one of those other characters in the
Bible.'

'Sutherland,' said Bel, recognising the description.

'Oh, Sutherland is his name! Well, anyhow, he
wanted Dering Johnstone to go and look at a sick
sheep. So they went away together and after a bit
I decided to knock off.'

'Did you catch anything?'

'Two,' he replied. 'Come and see.'

The two trout were lying in the shadow of the
rock, covered with rushes. Ellis displayed them.
One was a reasonable size, probably about half a
pound, the other was no larger than Bel's finger.

'I think you ought to have put it back,' she
suggested a trifle diffidently.

'Oh, I know,' agreed Ellis. 'I meant to, but by
the time I had got the hook out it was pretty far
through, poor little brute. As a matter of fact
that's what sickened me off. I'm not really a

proper fisherman,' he added apologetically.

It was obvious that he was not. Bel smiled; she said, 'You know I think we ought to bury it. I do, really. I mean — '

'Yes, I know what you mean,' said Ellis looking at it doubtfully. 'Perhaps you're right. We had better get rid of the body.'

Together they scraped a hole in the gravel and covered all trace of the murder. It was rather a pleasant little task and it made them feel more companionable.

'Well, that's that,' said Ellis, wiping his hands on his large white-linen handkerchief. 'Nobody will know — unless you give me away of course.'

'I can't,' she told him. 'I'm an accomplice after the fact. Isn't that what it's called?'

They looked at each other and smiled.

'Tell me,' said Ellis. 'Do you think I ought to go on fishing or doesn't it matter?'

'It doesn't matter. They won't mind a bit.'

'Good,' he said. 'Let's sit down and talk. I didn't come here to fish. You know what I came for, don't you?'

'To — to talk,' suggested Bel in her fluttery voice.

'To find you and ask you a question. You know what it is, don't you? Darling little Bel, please say yes.'

'How can I when — when you haven't — asked me?'

'Are you going to marry me, Bel?'

She hesitated. She was frightened — not brave like Rhoda — but Rhoda had said . . .

'Bel, darling,' said Ellis earnestly. 'I know I'm

not asking you properly, but I can't do without you. I simply can't do without you — really and truly I can't. You're going to marry me, aren't you?'

'I think so,' said Bel in a very small voice. 'I mean if you really want me. I mean I simply couldn't bear it if you — if you wanted to — to marry anybody else.'

Ellis smiled. He found the answer completely satisfactory.

2

The arrangement was that Bel should take lunch to the two fishermen and return to Tassieknowe and have her meal with Rhoda — bread and cheese and salad was sufficient for their needs. Rhoda waited for Bel; she waited and waited but there was no sign of Bel. She had just decided to forage for herself when she heard steps on the gravel outside the back door. A moment later the door opened and James came into the kitchen.

'Is there anything to eat?' asked James.

'James!' exclaimed Rhoda. 'I sent your lunch down to the river. Didn't you see Bel?'

'Oh yes, I saw her all right, but she didn't see me. Neither of them saw me; they were much too busy.'

'What were they doing?'

'This,' said James. He came over to the table, put his arms round his wife and kissed her. James was rather good at kissing his wife; he enjoyed it and took his time over it.

'M'h'm,' said Rhoda blissfully. 'Like that, was it?'

'Not quite like that,' replied James. 'He hasn't had so much practice, but it wasn't too bad for a first attempt.'

'Good,' said Rhoda, nodding.

'You don't seem surprised.'

'Not very.'

'I suppose you arranged the whole thing?

'Not the whole thing, exactly.'

'Rhoda, do you realise what you've done? Do you realise that we'll be left, stranded, without anybody to cook our food?'

'I know,' agreed Rhoda. 'It is a bit sickening, but we mustn't be selfish, James. They're just right for each other. They're both such dears, aren't they?'

'That's all very well but — '

'Perhaps they'll stay on for a time — both of them. He could come to Tassieknowe, couldn't he?'

'No, he couldn't,' James declared. 'He's got to go back to London. His partner has gone off his nut.'

'Mr. Wills? Oh good!' exclaimed Rhoda, her eyes lighting up with interest. 'That's splendid news. Did he tell you about it this morning?'

'Yes, he did — and I see nothing splendid about it — and I'm frightfully hungry,' grumbled James. 'I've had nothing to eat since breakfast and it's nearly two o'clock.'

'Oh James! Poor darling! We made a lovely picnic lunch for you — '

'I daresay you did.'

'Sausage rolls and scones with honey and tomato sandwiches — and it will all be wasted!'

'They'll eat it.'

'I don't think so.'

'No, perhaps you're right,' agreed James.

Rhoda was now rooting about in the cupboard; she produced a crusty loaf, a Cheddar cheese, a large slab of golden butter and a bowl of salad.

'That'll do me fine,' declared James, sitting down at the kitchen-table and beginning his meal. 'Bread and cheese — and beer, of course. What more does a man want?'

Rhoda thought a man wanted a good deal more but she refrained from saying so. She drew a tankard of beer from the cask in the larder and put it beside James.

'Mrs. Simpson might help,' she said thoughtfully. 'She might be able to spare one of her girls now that the season is nearly over.'

'A silk purse or a sow's ear?' asked James somewhat anxiously.

'Oh, a silk purse — of course! I tell you what,' added Rhoda as she sat down at the table opposite her husband, prepared to share his repast. 'I tell you what, James. I'll get Mamie to ask her. Mrs. Simpson would do anything for Mamie.'

'Hush!' said James in a conspiratorial whisper.

Rhoda hushed obediently and listened. There were steps on the gravel and a murmur of voices.

'Yes, there they are!' whispered Rhoda. She giggled mischievously and added, 'Don't say a word, James. It will be fun to see what excuses they'll make for their extraordinary behaviour.'

We do hope that you have enjoyed reading this large print book.

Did you know that all of our titles are available for purchase?

We publish a wide range of high quality large print books including:
Romances, Mysteries, Classics
General Fiction
Non Fiction and Westerns

Special interest titles available in large print are:
The Little Oxford Dictionary
Music Book
Song Book
Hymn Book
Service Book

Also available from us courtesy of Oxford University Press:
Young Readers' Dictionary
(large print edition)
Young Readers' Thesaurus
(large print edition)

For further information or a free brochure, please contact us at:
Ulverscroft Large Print Books Ltd.,
The Green, Bradgate Road, Anstey,
Leicester, LE7 7FU, England.
Tel: (00 44) 0116 236 4325
Fax: (00 44) 0116 234 0205